Rachel Lynch grew up in Cumbria and the lakes and fells are never far away from her. London pulled her away to teach History and marry an Army Officer, whom she followed around the globe for thirteen years. A change of career after children led to personal training and sports therapy, but writing was always the overwhelming force driving the future. The human capacity for compassion as well as its descent into the brutal and murky world of crime are fundamental to her work.

Also by Rachel Lynch

Detective Kelly Porter

Helen Scott Royal Military Police Thrillers

THE
LINE

RACHEL LYNCH

First published in the United Kingdom in 2022 by

Canelo
Unit 9, 5th Floor
Cargo Works, 1-2 Hatfields
London, SE1 9PG
United Kingdom

A CIP catalogue record for this book is available from the British Library.

Print ISBN 978 1 80032 726 9
Ebook ISBN 978 1 80032 107 6

Look for more great books at www.canelo.co

Printed and bound in Great Britain by Clays Ltd, Elcograf S.p.A.

Chapter 1

The wind streaming into the jeep from the open window cooled Paul's skin as he turned the music up. A day off work spent diving was something he'd anticipated all week. A break from the job wasn't the only thing on his mind as he manoeuvred the quiet single road from RAF Akrotiri to his destination in Larnaca. It was a short journey and the local Cypriot radio station played all the current hits from Europe. His Military Police façade was well and truly stripped back on days like these.

Captain Paul Thomas checked his mirror for local police. They tended to leave the military well alone, even if one was speeding way above the limit: not willing to fill in the paperwork generated by a cursory telling-off, or even a fine, but the roads were clear. The sun was peeping above the horizon in a shimmer of blues and oranges, and the water was flat calm. It was a perfect day for a dive on the wreck of the *Zenobia*.

On her maiden voyage, in 1980, on her way to Syria, the ship had carried over one hundred lorries, full to the brim with £200 million worth of cargo, ranging from marble to frozen fish, and had sunk due to ballast problems in the bay of Larnaca, with no loss of life. However, since then, several divers had perished there, but that statistic didn't bother Paul, an advanced open-water diver with ten years' experience. The site was considered amongst the ten best in the world and lay in relatively shallow water, and was a magnet for scuba divers.

Resting on her port side, the deck could be accessed by beginners, whilst the dingy depths of the engine rooms and cargo decks offered exclusive insights for the more experienced. The lorries had never been salvaged, and so divers could sit inside a cabin and strap in for a photo opportunity. The more adventurous tried their hand at finding some of the Italian marble destined for the Middle East. Other visitors, more interested in the flora and fauna feeding on the remnants of the ship, were drawn to the super barracuda, tuna, turtle and triggerfish.

Paul's kit rattled in the back seat. He'd pick up tanks from the dive school run by an old army pal who'd settled here years ago after leaving the fold of Her Majesty's service. Everything else was his own: the buoyancy jacket, the demand valve (DV), mask, fins and watch. He carried a knife and a waterproof writing board with pen, as well as his dive log, which was almost full. He kept his kit clean and up to date, making sure nothing went wrong under water. Not that he didn't trust Eric's kit, it was just he felt more comfortable in his own. He'd make sure he got superior line from Eric, because they were going inside the engine room this morning. A frisson of excitement travelled through his body as a catchy tune from the UK chart made his body move and his foot tap, when it wasn't on the clutch.

The bars and restaurants of the Larnaca strip were closed and weary-looking from the night before: serving tourists and locals alike, with bins overflowing and chairs strewn from the night's wind. It was a scene worthy of any good night out, and the detritus spoke of sore heads and happy hedonists. Cyprus attracted its fair share of party animals, but this morning, Paul wasn't one of them. Diving hung-over was a really bad idea. Pure blood pumping around the body was vital for a good dive experience. Alcohol residue caused equalisation problems and nausea, and besides, off-gassing bubbles in the blood after any dive was a serious process, and Paul put safety first. He had plenty of other opportunities to get hammered on booze and pick up girls.

He saw Eric and waved out of the jeep window at his diving instructor. Eric was as fired up as he was. Diving inside the engine room was always a good adrenalin rush for anyone. Usually it was the preserve of men. Women tended to prefer the pretty fish in shallower water. He'd taken many a novice down there, to study the ugly grouper and watch them hunting in the deep blue. But for his own leisure time, he preferred to buddy up with somebody just as experienced as he was, like Eric, and get down to serious business.

He parked up and began unloading. Eric approached him, smiling.

'Perfect day. I reckon the water is twenty degrees, even now. It'll be twenty-three by the time we get in.'

Paul had brought a short wetsuit, tailor-made out here in Cyprus, at Cessac Beach, for a few quid.

'Visibility is about thirty metres,' Eric added.

Paul nodded. 'Perfect, mate.'

'We've got company, mate, hope you don't mind,' Eric said.

Paul held his jeep door open and looked towards the dive shop, where three big blokes looked around.

'Sightseeing? They up to it?' Paul asked.

'Yep. BSAC, mate. Don't worry, they're good, they come with good qualifications, all three of them, they're on leave from some naval ship docked in Kyrenia.'

British Sub-Aqua Club training was considered the best in the world.

'Right,' Paul said. He couldn't remember a naval ship docking anywhere near Kyrenia, in Northern Cyprus, as it was in Turkish waters, but it could be a covert British training exercise. The three men looked naval; that was for sure, judging by their physiques. They were introduced by Eric, who explained that he'd be buddied by one of them. Paul was a little disappointed because he knew Eric's style well, but if he trusted these fellas, then so did Paul.

They chatted about various dives they'd completed round the world and it soon became clear that the three men were pros. They were also good company. They swapped stories of difficult dives in Scapa Flow and one told a tale of shark diving off the coast of Cape Town, having had a close call with a bad-tempered ragged-tooth shark. They all laughed. They spoke with Queen's English accents, almost forced, and Paul knew they must be officers, hence the lack of tattoos.

'No sharks out there,' Eric said.

'Shame,' one said. Paul agreed, it was a travesty that the Med was so empty of decent-looking fish, but at least the *Zenobia* attracted some agreeably appealing marine life. But they were only interested in metal and rubber today.

The rib was ready and Eric had already manoeuvred it into position off the small jetty. They heaved their kit in and checked it over, having done so once inside the shop. They checked their air, the lines and their DVs. They each had a good 200 BAR of air pressure, and they were satisfied that none of them were panic breathers and so should be fine for a dive of an hour at least, if they kept calm.

The rib set off on its short journey of just under a mile. Only buoys awaited them: they were the first dive school out. By the afternoon, the surface above the wreck got crazy busy with ribs and snorkellers and Paul wasn't keen on the crowds. He much preferred getting out there early.

As the rib sped out towards the buoys, they made sure to hold on. The salt water splashed Paul and it felt good. On land, they sweated uncomfortably in their kit, but once on the water, they each realised why they were there. It would only get better once they pushed off the back of the rib and felt the work of their weight belts, so they could slowly descend into the cool depths, to a world of secrecy and wonder.

When they reached the site, Eric turned off the engine and they bobbed up and down on the wake as he anchored the rib to the buoy. Eric was buddied with the other two, and Paul nodded to him when it was his turn. Paul and the third man would go off first. Placing his DV in his mouth and clearing his mask, Paul held on to his lines and mask and slipped off backwards into the water. It felt wonderful and he shivered momentarily as the water filled the cavity between his body and the neoprene, warming up with his body heat to keep him comfortable during the duration of the dive. He looked around him and beneath: spotting the wreck instantly. It sat serenely beckoning him as if she'd been waiting all night. His buddy came off the rib and they equalised and signalled that they were ready. Eric and the others would follow.

They'd gone through a detailed dive plan and Paul had noted it, step by step, in his log. He'd finish it off with a summary when they were back on land. The descent was smooth and Paul looked around him, at the bright blue expanse. Having descended in stages to the side of the ship, they made their way to the rear, where the propellers lay eerily in the murk, like great mixing machines, ready to burst into life, even though they'd been lazily dormant for four decades. From there, they made their way through the lower car deck, past lorries still chained to the deck, and rusting into colours merging into the greens and blues of the ocean. Moving farther down, they swam through the mess deck, noting the checked carpet, preserved like bright jams, to their left. The pattern of orange and red squares looked out of place down here.

The entrance to the engine room was a tangle of metal, and this is where the dive got technical. They hooked their lines onto hoops fastened onto the side of the ship for just that purpose. This was where the majority of people who'd lost their lives had come unstuck: either losing their way or running out of air. It was amateur really.

Paul went first. He used a torch, but it was still difficult to navigate. He'd performed the dive three times before and knew his way, but attempting it without hooking up was unthinkable. He turned to check his buddy occasionally and the guy was turning out to be a professional and competent partner. They ceased all signals, except for 'okay' and continued. His mission today was to explore the mass of pistons and piping hidden under the ship's ten thousand ton might. Hatches and pressure valves emerged in the dark, like ghouls, respite only coming from a few windows, but even then, giving off no light.

He was aware of a torch going out behind him and assumed his buddy had taken a wrong turn. It was common. He turned to see that the chap was no longer there. He checked his BAR and he had enough left to go further and make it back to the rib, but if he had to turn back to find his buddy now, it'd be tight. Frustration piqued him and his heart rate elevated, sucking more air from the tanks on his back.

Panic gripped him as he saw that his line was no longer attached and he turned around in the dark green gloom, searching for his buddy. He saw old spent glow sticks that divers had attached to metal and counted them backwards, realising that he didn't, after all, remember the way. After five minutes or more, he floated in the dark, surrounded by rusted manufacture and tried to clear his thoughts. A ladder emerged and he went for it, hoping it led to a way out.

It didn't.

Paul checked his air again: 30 BAR. It wasn't enough. He had to leave now, otherwise he wouldn't have time to off-gas and avoid the bends. Decompression started with a slow rise and he was running out of time. He turned around and recognised the way he'd come, but a sudden gulp of nothingness engulfed him. Confusion was quick. He couldn't reach his air gauge to check, but it was too late. He couldn't breathe.

The weight of the great ship bore down on him and he turned this way and that, seeing his buddy at the last minute. He held out his arms towards him, but the diver appeared not to see him. The last thing he remembered, before he blacked out, was the man swimming towards him making the 'okay' sign, worry in his grimace, frantically checking Paul's equipment.

Blackness engulfed him and his bursting lungs gave way to a serenely calm emptiness, without the life-giving air he so craved, but he was strangely at peace.

Hands grasped at him and he was dragged out into the open water, where Eric's face was a picture of pure terror. Paul closed his eyes and sucked no more.

Chapter 2

Downtown Aleppo looked like a Hollywood movie set of Armageddon. To be fair, it depended on where you were as to whether all the buildings, or just some of them, were totalled. Some structures stood, and others fell. Piles of rubble were arranged along the streets, to make way for those vehicles that still functioned. Dust swirled everywhere, and mixed with heat and sweat, to produce some kind of cloying furnace, which stuck to every item, including the flowers on sale on street corners, in between destroyed houses. People went about their business, in between air strikes, as best they could. The days of the week were irrelevant in war.

Market sellers pushed carts through the alleyways which were once streets, hoping for mobile transactions, when once they'd sold at the squares across the city. Across the districts, civilian targets had been demolished by Russian heavy artillery and rockets, as they told the rest of the world that they were hitting only strategic military objectives. Meanwhile the people of Aleppo felt hunted and maimed, as the lines between collateral damage and war crimes were smudged. One way to bring a civilisation to its knees was to bomb the shit out of its infrastructure, fuel, food and water supply and sewage works and dress it up as incidental ruin, as it was played out across the world's media outlets as tragic and unfortunate, but, in reality, it was planned, with the purpose of either exterminating and obliterating the enemy, or bringing the combatants to the negotiating table.

In fact, it had the opposite effect. Populations rallied, neighbourhoods came together, human resourcefulness overcame, and the streets of Aleppo showed it. Electrical cables were strewn across roads and buildings (the ones still standing), food was airdropped or driven in by charities, and as far as waste was concerned, people did what they could. Raw sewage was worst by the roads, where gullies created natural valleys for debris to travel. It stank.

Children played marbles, tag and hide and seek, as well as collecting anything they could, to either sell or at least talk about with their friends. Schools were abandoned, and surviving parents became home tutors. Hospitals were bombed, and neighbours became medics; law and order ran unchecked, and local militia became God. Resilience was relative.

A black limousine cut along the dusty road, like a sleek shark hunting for prey beside a reef. The windows were darkened, and children stopped playing, and stared, wondering if they could get the wheel trims off, or at least beg for some cash. Adults turned away, ushering their kids off, guessing that whoever was inside was rich, and therefore important. No one thrived in war, except those who controlled it. The car was clean and shiny, and whoever sat behind the darkened windows, was proud. Behind it, followed two Ford Rangers, laden with armed men carrying automatic weapons and a mounted machine gun, which pointed at buildings as they drove by. Doors slammed shut, the children ran away; only the brave ones daring to run alongside; and a gloomy silence befell the neighbourhood. The few owners of shops still trading, in between wrecked garages and businesses, froze as they weighed goods for their customers, who stared at the spectacle.

Inside the limousine, Labib Hassan was on the phone. Despite the chaos, downtown Aleppo was the safest place for him to live. He could have escaped to neighbouring friendly nations, but then he'd have no way of controlling movement on the ground, plus, somebody would hand him over to the

US for a few thousand dollars. He was worth a lot more. He'd been on the West's most wanted list for a decade. But he didn't much care. It meant nothing to him. Their arrogance was what would one day make them implode, and he'd be there to watch it.

He spoke to his father, who was planning a feast for fifty soldiers. Labib didn't really have the time or the inclination to get involved in such trivia, but he respected his father, like he expected the same from his own boys. He'd lost three so far, to the war; he had six others.

'Papa, just give the chickens to mother,' he said to his father. Then hung up.

His parents currently lived on the family farm, to the north of the city, but Labib didn't go there often, and the Americans knew it. Their spy planes, listening to their conversations, abusing their human rights, as a nation, as a people, were commonplace, and no one ever knew what they heard. Labib and his men used burner phones, codes, donkeys, kids and rocks to keep communication secret, but still the Americans knew everything. Well, not quite everything. They didn't have the courage to send in ground troops; it was the biggest victory of the war so far. The West didn't have the stomach for it. Withdrawing troops from Afghanistan gave renewed vigour to freedom fighters everywhere. The West had finally run out of money, and the courage, to carry on.

The new Syria, carved from the rubble after ten years of civil war, would be stronger and more independent than ever. And Labib would play a grander part than any of his forefathers ever dreamed of. The new meritocracy, who'd taken their opportunities as neighbourhoods were blown to smithereens, was in ascendance, and he was being escorted to a secret meeting along with other senior Ba'athists. The party would prevail in the end and President Assad knew it. It was a waiting game and they had the stamina for a long one. They had the upper hand. And it was called cash.

Labib had it, and Assad wanted it. Him drip-feeding the regime secured his future, when they finally won the war. The whole region was ripe for settlement, now Russia and China backed the new Afghan republic of the Taliban. The West was on the run. He'd backed the right horse, and it was time to celebrate. But they weren't out of danger yet. Only two weeks ago, he'd been tipped off about an assassination attempt. Labib had loyal spies everywhere, including London. They dug metaphorical tunnels from there to Syria, via Russia and back again. He looked at the burner phone in his hand. He'd heard nothing yet.

The sound of cash in the bank was louder than any smart bomb that America could send from the skies. *Money makes the world go around.* He hummed his favourite *Cabaret* tune, sung by Liza Minnelli and Joel Grey. Of course, western musicals were no longer shown in theatres across Syria, because nothing was. Entertainment was a relative pastime. Songs, dances, celebrations were family-based and imports had stopped, but Labib owned ancient cinema reels and watched old cowboy movies too, with Clint Eastwood and Randolph Scott. The Wild West wasn't too far removed from his war now. The Americans fancied themselves beyond terror and guerrilla warfare, but they had it in their blood. As did the British. Bully politics, and turf wars were invented by conquerors, then banned by civilisers.

His car slowed as it approached a checkpoint, but it was waved straight through when the local guards were made aware of who was inside. He controlled this area of the city, like a tribal god. The mounted machine gun helped. In some countries, currency was the stuff of paper and computer printouts, here it was bullets, metal and hard, clean currency. And that was Labib's business.

The meeting was on the outskirts of the city. He turned off all communications equipment, including iPads and the phone he'd used to speak to his father, as they approached the only highway still in use out of the city. All except his burner phone.

He sat back and poured himself a fine whisky from the bureau in the rear cabin. He sipped from a crystal glass and felt at peace. He wondered what it must feel like for those foreign rulers whose security relied upon paid hirelings, rather than his own, which was based upon generations of mutual toil and familial respect. No one would ever betray him. Except perhaps some of the men he was about to meet.

Equals were the most dangerous of adversaries, but then Labib had something that they wanted, and he had the ear of Assad. It wasn't just food networks, access to communications sites, or even hard cash itself; it was a steady flow of superb weapons and ammunition from Russia. It had taken decades for Labib to build up his connections, and they'd come to fruition just at the right time. A perfect storm, if you like; a tempest of munitions and heavy artillery, ready and waiting for the highest bidder, who happened to be a neighbour of his.

The list included chemical weapons. He traded in anything that was in demand and the virtue signalling from western media about their horrors was irrelevant to Labib. His commodities were there to sell, and debates over ethics and morality were unwelcome and crass. Of course they attracted commentary from those who lived in peace and prosperity thousands of miles away, but war was messy and unclean, and righteous liberals would do better to keep their noses out. He'd seen the effects of sarin and ricin: he'd witnessed skin hanging off children, and the elderly coughing up their lung linings in the rubble. He admired leaders like Putin who got the job done, regardless of how many civilians were annihilated.

Collateral damage.

An oasis appeared in the desert sands and they sped towards a gilded farmstead. Ostensibly a wheat, cotton and olive producer, the sprawling estate welcomed them as prospective buyers. The huge gates swung open, and Labib was invited to get out of the car. As he did so, the phone in his hand buzzed and he froze. The message was clear. He placed his glass in a cup holder.

He waved at the driver to back up. He'd explain later, should the tip emerge as a false one. The driver did as he was bid and the doors were slammed closed. The men hanging out of the two Ford Rangers swapped grunts and looks of bewilderment, but they were paid to change plans last minute.

The message turned out to be a solid one. As they retraced their steps down the dusty track, the walls of the huge castle-like mansion exploded in a booming cloud of raging grey dust, with fiery orange at the centre. Labib didn't flinch, but the men on the vehicles did.

Another explosion came closer to them, and the driver sped up. Labib looked behind him and he became aware that he was sweating. He wiped his brow with the hand that held the phone. A few people ran from the carnage, and he saw them stumble and be still. There must have been two dozen people inside and he figured there was no way any of them would survive the hit.

He pressed his window control and it slid down, allowing him to peer up at the sky. He marvelled at the technology of the USA and flicked his middle finger up to the clouds.

'Not today, fuckers!' he shouted. 'You missed!'

He sat back and began to laugh so hard that it brought on a coughing fit. As they sped away, he looked at the burner phone in his hand and kissed it.

Chapter 3

Helen's walk along The Embankment was a pleasant one, though not without concern. She was naturally vigilant, however no one would suspect that she was a senior officer in the Royal Military Police.

Summer tourists wandered along the banks of the Thames, taking photographs of monuments and sitting in the shade. Europe was in the grip of a heatwave, and global warming was hot news again. People fanned themselves with whatever was in their bag, children sucked on ice lollies and the young, fit rickshaw cabbies sweated under the fierce sun, touting for business.

Helen's blouse was loose-fitting and she was allowed to wear tailored shorts to work in this weather. Anyone working in the Ministry of Defence's main building in London had opted to wear civilian clothes since the wave of terrorist attacks, starting with the murder of soldier Lee Rigby. Combat uniform used to be worn, to mark the seriousness and character of the MOD's work in London: the nuts and bolts of policy and operations, but now, it wasn't worth the risk. Milling about amongst millions of strangers on London streets in a British army uniform wasn't something they did anymore.

Her hair fell freely and the breeze underneath it gave her relief. The office had a decent air-conditioning unit, but there was no way she was allowing herself to stay stuck in there all day. One of the pleasures of working at the MOD was the opportunity of a leisurely stroll around Whitehall, for lunch and breaks. She could mingle silently with holidaymakers and day trippers, merging into the background anonymously, like everybody else.

Her bag was the sort that fitted across the chest; she took no chances with thieves. She wore large sunglasses and functional shoes, made for running if she had to. Her skin was tanned from climbing in the French Alps, earlier in the summer, and she admired the only ring she wore, given to her by Grant, as a farewell. It wasn't a goodbye, more a *hasta luego*, my friend. Their jobs and lives were impossibly entrenched in their own agendas. What had kept them together was no longer a bond that could keep them entwined on the same path. They'd broken off and become separate, and that could never be reversed. It didn't mean she couldn't think of him though, and often. His tanned face, the deep laughter lines around his eyes, and the way he used his body to protect her when they were in the same room. Theirs was more the union of two souls with an unbreakable narrative that had already been written. It had existed, and would never be forgotten, but it was no longer alive.

The ring was a simple band of rose gold, with three gemstones set in fairly chunky circles. It looked rustic and heavy but also sat delicately on the middle finger of her right hand. The stones were sapphire, ruby and emerald. Grant had been taken in by the meaning of each stone, as told by the vendor, but Helen simply liked it. She looked at it now, glinting in the sun, and remembered their child who'd been taken away from them far too soon: the ring was a symbol of what had made Luke, and she smiled.

She walked towards Whitehall Gardens, opposite the river. Occasionally, the whiff off the muck on the banks of the muddy river wafted up and caught her by surprise. Taxis whizzed past and red double-decker buses wobbled like old men, threatening to fall over. She watched a boat travel down the river and spied people on the deck pointing and enjoying the ride. Entering the pretty enclosed space, hidden behind elaborate railings, she wondered, as she always did, at its serenity and calm. Not many tourists ventured in here, and its shade and peace was a well-kept secret.

She took a bench facing Sir Henry Bartle Frere, the British colonial giant who'd spectacularly fallen from grace thanks to his aggressive confederacy policies in South Africa, leading to the Boer War. The monument was an ignominious celebration that brought, for Helen, ironic humour to the lush and shady retreat.

Just as she was about to bite into her sandwich, her mobile buzzed, but Helen ignored it, chomping her food instead. The ringing stopped. It rang again, and this time it caught her attention enough to peek at who it might be. The caller came up on her phone as Regimental Headquarters in Fareham, Hampshire. It piqued her curiosity and she answered after wiping her mouth.

'Major Scott,' she said.

'Helen,' said a familiar voice. It was her old colonel from when she'd been promoted on the back of a tour of Afghanistan. She'd made the giant leap from captain to major when she was still relatively young. For a woman in the Royal Military Police, it was particularly outstanding. Colonel Don Murton had her back. He was also in charge of staffing at HQ, for the whole of her regiment. He had the ear of the General Staff and a nose for trouble.

'Colonel, lovely to hear from you,' she said. It never was, no matter how much she liked him. He only called her when he had a job for her to do. But pleasantries were required. She asked about his family, and if they were settled in Hampshire. Military life wasn't for everyone. Families were split and children torn from schools and friends on an alarmingly regular basis. It was just one reason she hadn't got married as a serving soldier. Only once coming close. They chatted about the heatwave, and then he got down to business.

16

'I've got a problem,' he said. He sounded grave.

'Sir?'

'There's an ongoing investigation happening at the moment – you may have heard of it – in Cyprus, over at the Ayios Nikolaos station.'

Helen had indeed heard. Ayios Nikolaos, along with Dhekelia Garrison close by, comprised British interests on the Mediterranean island since independence in 1960. The two areas were called the Eastern Sovereign Base Area, or the ESBA. It was what was left of the empire, and hugely strategic.

'Ah, yes, the potential leaking of state intelligence,' she said. In the MOD building, one heard rumours. Apparently, noises had been picked up across the Middle East to suggest that they had a weak link somewhere in the chain. The most obvious was Cyprus, and the relatively junior RMP officer on island, posted at RAF Akrotiri, had been sent to investigate. She'd thought nothing of it, apart from how envious she was of the officer being stationed in such a lovely part of the world at Her Majesty's expense. It was a lesser-ranking role, and so she was puzzled as to why he was calling her about it.

'Sadly, the chief investigating officer, Captain Thomas…' he began.

'Yes?' she asked.

'I'm afraid he was involved in a diving accident off the shore of Larnaca on Wednesday.'

'Oh no, is he all right?' she asked. Helen had herself learned to dive with the army and knew it was a dangerous sport, she wondered if the officer had suffered a case of the infamous bends. She took another bite of her sandwich.

'I'm afraid he's dead, Helen,' the colonel replied.

'What?' she said, in between mouthfuls. She couldn't quite believe what she was hearing. She was so used to being told of men and women dying in action, in the field, on operations, risking their lives for their country, that when she learned of a comrade who'd died doing a recreational summer dive, it seemed more shocking somehow.

'He got into difficulties at quite a depth, I hear. I don't know anything about diving, Helen, but they couldn't revive him, he just couldn't ascend back up safely.'

'Who's they?' she asked. 'Who was he with?' Her investigative mind stepped in without her bidding and it began flagging up questions she longed to know the answers to. She *did* know about diving and her head was full of questions. She put down her sandwich and the wind blew the box away. She cursed and chased after it, holding on to her bag. Bartle Frere stared down at her in judgement and she silently apologised for her disparaging commentary on his career. She grabbed the container and threw it into a waste bin, along with the rest of her sandwich, and went back to her bench.

'He was with a diving school, I don't know the details. My point is, the investigation is now without a senior investigating officer and here at HQ we've decided to elevate the case, and we need somebody more senior to assume the post. Special Investigation Branch is about to send out two officers, and they need a boss.'

'I know where you're going with this, Don, but I'm delivering a policy paper here in London,' she said.

'Don't worry, it's all arranged. You can submit your paper, and the senior executive committee can then peruse it whilst you're away.'

'In Cyprus?'

'In Cyprus.'

'Why me? Surely there are others already on island? RAF Akrotiri? The Dhekelia Garrison? Special Investigation Branch?'

'No senior RMP. Captain Thomas was it. And besides, Major Scott, you're the best. I trust you.'

'You didn't trust Captain Thomas?' she asked.

'That's not quite my point. I feel – we feel – here at Regimental HQ, as do others, that there's more to this investigation than what we know so far. Thomas was on to something. There's some hotshot lawyer out there defending the four serving soldiers under house arrest.'

'Others?'

'Do I have to spell it out to you, Helen?'

'No, sir.' She was well aware that if the case involved the potential passing of state secrets through a channel such as a British base in Cyprus, then MI6 would be involved. 'Are they sending in the heavies?' she asked.

'Not yet, it's your bag. You have a week. I'll let you know the details of the SIB officers who'll be joining you as soon as I know them.'

Helen closed her eyes. A lot could happen in a week. Cities fell, babies died, presidents were booted out. 'Was Captain Thomas's death an accident?' she asked.

'His body, as well as the investigation, are on ice until you get there.'

Chapter 4

The baking heat of the Cyprus summer threatened to come inside every time analyst Corporal Danny Hewitt went out for a cigarette break. The air-conditioning unit whirred and kept the inside temperature of the small room cool, but the furnace-like clouds of air that rushed in when somebody went out sat there lingering for long seconds and meant the room never went below twenty-two degrees.

The posting was a good one, as far as his wife was concerned. She got to lay by the garrison pool all day and drive off to beaches, with other wives, to spend the day cooling off in the shallows of the Mediterranean. In contrast, Danny spent nine-to-five, five days a week, inside a dark, stuffy room, monitoring mobile phone use across the vast expanse of the Middle East, including Syria, Iraq, Lebanon, Iran, Egypt, Saudi Arabia and Yemen.

Ayios Nikolaos was like a lunar landscape full of huge satellite dishes, spinning slowly around, close to the town of Larnaca. Positioned in the north-east corner of the sea that the Romans called Middle Earth, Cyprus hovered off the shore, like a winged insect harassing its neighbours on the mainland. And that was exactly the purpose of the listening station: to bug anyone within earshot, and tell the Americans. Built in 1946, it had been run by the British, together with the station at Dhekelia, since the Second World War. But Danny wasn't here for a history lesson. He was here to further his intelligence-gathering skills, to get a promotion next year, maybe. He was aware that the British presence in Cyprus wasn't to everyone's taste, and soldiers certainly weren't welcome in the centres of some towns, like Ayia Napa, due to their past drunken antics, but the civil war was a distant memory now and the island loved tourist money.

Danny retrieved his mobile phone from the locked security box near the entrance and stepped outside. He sucked on his cigarette and considered that, in the hot sun, tobacco didn't last as long, or maybe the Cypriots imported fast-burning brands? Anyhow, before he knew it, he'd sucked down to the butt and he flicked the remainder away, annoyed. He'd like it to last longer.

He looked up to the endless blue sky that never seemed to change colour, and back at his watch, noting it was only a few hours before he could finish his shift, and join his wife at the pool for a beer, after stripping off his uniform of combat trousers and jacket, sand colour to match the desert. Not that they were working in a desert, just that it was standard issue for hot dust bowls. If he'd been in Africa near a jungle, he'd be wearing green. It was Friday, and the whole weekend spread out before them, like a party invitation. There were half-decent clubs in Larnaca and it didn't much matter that soldiers were banned from certain areas, there were still good times to be had.

It took a few minutes for his eyes to adjust when he went back inside the dark room. Soldiers concentrated on their tasks and sat with headsets on, staring at screens and monitoring printouts. He took his seat and replaced his headphones. On the screen in front of him, he had several software programmes open and running. One was a map of the countries covered by their antennae. They had thirty-five simultaneous dishes operating at the base, and fifty per cent of their running costs were paid by the USA. Billions of conversations made their way through the listening station every year, and some were considered signals of interest. Any communication that was deemed a threat to national security was monitored. That meant following intelligence gathered on land, air and sea, checking it out and following through. It was a veritable tsunami of information, but it was all about the process. There were certain factors that elevated a conversation between two mobile phone users in a livestock market in Damascus, from a mere business transaction, to quite something else. Those factors were numbered in stages, until a series of necessary details had been confirmed. The next stage was to upgrade the level of concern and observe certain individuals and organisations setting patterns. Every time a mobile number on that list was used, it bounced off a mast in Cyprus where analysts, like Danny Hewitt, could log them.

One pinged now on the screen in front of him, and he noted the location coordinates, time in the correct zone, jurisdiction regards UK, US, or other and the duration of the call. The information was passed to a senior officer and Danny would hear back as to whether or not he was to intensify the signal, isolate the number and record the conversation. Within seconds of sending the data off to a central intelligence-gathering room across the site, close to the colonel's office, the message came back to do just that.

Danny's pulse quickened. It was times like this he'd trained for, and spent two years at Beaconsfield learning Arabic, with a touch of Kurdish. He tapped his keyboard and turned up the volume on his headset, as well as pressing record on various mediums. The call was between two numbers in Syria, in the city of Aleppo. He was listening for certain key words: a mixture that ranged from names, locations and known slang used for weapons, to local enemy warlords, European powers and types of missiles. For the most part, it was a standard conversation between two blokes on a Friday night about food, and the heat. Then the discussion turned more serious. Danny realised, from months studying voice patterns, tone and inference, that he was listening to the voice of one of the most prominent Syrian warlords sought by the US in recent years. Labib Hassan.

The stuff just kept coming. Danny's Arabic was good enough to decipher some key words, including an address in Aleppo and several names. It was a goldmine of intelligence. Suddenly, a rush of hot air blew in behind him and the colonel strode in. Danny didn't know whether to get up and salute, or carry on with his job. It was highly irregular. Information-gathering was supposed to be sterile, in as much as it was passed in metaphorical gloved pockets to higher powers. Colonel Seaton striding in to the hut and essentially snooping around made him nervous. Especially during the current investigation of his colleagues.

'At ease, Corporal,' said Colonel Bill Seaton. Some called him Big Willy, but now wasn't the time.

Danny remained transfixed by the conversation and translated on the computer before him for the purpose of real time. The whole transcript would be sent to communications HQ, and from there it would reach the foreign intelligence service committee, notifying the Foreign Secretary and MI6. They would be the ones who made the decision of if, and when, to inform the CIA.

'Labib Hassan?' the colonel asked, slapping him on his shoulder.

Danny knew the information was huge, and he couldn't help but share the colonel's excitement. They could do with a break around here. Their tiny signal service in the middle of the shitstorm that was the Middle East had come under fire recently with the accusation that intelligence was being passed on from this very station. It was a grave charge and the RMP had sent a junior captain to investigate. Four of Danny's colleagues were under house arrest, pending charges, and the captain was now dead. Danny had been hand-selected by the colonel to steer the ship, as it were. He didn't want to screw up.

Danny didn't understand why the corporals were under scrutiny, and perhaps the colonel was breaking protocol because he was frustrated as well. Understandably, he wanted to prove to those in Whitehall that his ship was tightly run. The intelligence-gathering process was watertight, as in the snippets of information gathered here made no sense without context. One operative, or even four, could not, under any circumstances, pass on detailed information that meant anything to the enemy, or allies for that matter. Big Willy had every right to be perturbed.

The accusations were a defilement on the cap badge of the Intelligence Corps and had rocked HQ at Catterick, in Yorkshire. This was why Danny was so keen to do a good job, to clear the names of his comrades, stitched up for somebody else's agenda. They were all convinced, at the listening station, that if information was going awry, it wasn't the Intelligence Corps that was to blame. Somebody might be on the take, but it wasn't the fellas he knew.

Suddenly the call was cut off and Danny stared at the screen. He tried to get it back, but something prevented the connection from going through. These things happened, of course: satellites went off grid for minutes at a time, weather systems caused fuck-ups and human errors lost signals, but with current events causing jitters round here, Danny was frustrated. No one wanted the finger pointed at them.

'Keep trying, Corporal, well done. Get that recording sent to the office,' Colonel Seaton said and walked out in to the raging incinerator of mercurial heat.

Danny looked around him and felt the dust from outside swirl around his chair. He did as he was told.

Chapter 5

Helen landed in Cyprus just after lunchtime on Saturday, at RAF Akrotiri, on the south coast of the island, near Limassol, on a plane chartered from a civilian company, essentially to transport soldiers and goods to and from the island. She peered outside the window and recognised the familiar sandy colour of the earth. It'd been years since she'd been posted here, and even more since she'd sat on the dusty fields, waiting to deploy to Iraq after desert acclimatisation training in the Cypriot summer. The mercury regularly hit fifty degrees in the capital, Nicosia, and she knew that the next couple of weeks would be tough for somebody who was used to the dry and civilised heat of London. She'd packed loose, light clothing appropriate for a hot acrid summer.

Once through security, she was greeted by a driver and escorted to a waiting air-conditioned car. He took her luggage and she introduced herself.

'What's your name?' she asked, looking at his rank of corporal on his epaulettes. He wore combat uniform and was well turned out and tight-lipped, which was to be expected.

'Corporal Diamond, ma'am. They call me Gem.'

'Right, Gem, thank you.' She climbed into the back seat.

The journey to Dhekelia Garrison would take about an hour and she sat back and enjoyed the scenery. The route took them along the coastal road through Limassol and on to Larnaca. The island hadn't changed much; it was still comprised of sparkling blue sea on one side and desert-coloured buildings on the other. Billboards in Greek dotted the landscape and unfinished houses sat scattered amongst the residential areas, left like that to avoid roof tax. They made up a landscape of odd-looking structures with metal rods sticking out of them at angles, and Helen smiled at the scene that made no sense to some, but was comforting to her. The half-constructed concrete monstrosities were welcomingly familiar in their untidiness. It meant that she was miles away from London, which was a wrench in some ways, because she'd only just settled there again after being in Europe; but in other ways, it was a refreshing change.

The heat in London was something that was jarring and uncomfortable; here, in Cyprus, one expected it. The light was different here too. It was yellow and glaring and she could almost smell the burning pavements through the darkened windows. The British presence on the island, since the time of Empire, had left its mark, and fish and chip shops, beach huts stocked with buckets and spades, as well as British-themed pubs, added to the home-from-home feel. As an English speaker, one could communicate anywhere on the island easily and be understood; it was lazy tourism. Driving on the left was another notch for Cyprus and no doubt contributed to the millions of British travellers who flocked there every year, bolstering the Cypriot economy. After a five-hour flight, it didn't feel as though she was on the precipice of the Middle East, with Turkey to the north, Israel to the east and Egypt to the south.

Driving through Larnaca, along the seafront, Helen could just make out the ribs bobbing up and down over the wreck of the *Zenobia* ship, where diving was premium for the Med. This is where she'd taken her BSAC sports diving course with the army, on the famous wreck, and she shuddered to think what could have happened to Captain Thomas. The report said he was in the engine room when he got into trouble, which was close to the seabed as the wreck lay on her side, but that was almost fifty metres down. What was he doing in there? Diving in the Med should be relatively safe, and she understood that Captain Thomas was indeed a qualified diver, but to what depth? She intended to interview the diving school staff and find out who Captain Thomas's dive buddy was. There were strict restrictions on the different qualifications across world diving sites and she'd already made an appointment to meet the team at the PADI school tomorrow morning. The Professional Association of Diving Instructors was disparagingly known by some in the army as Pay And Dive In, but she remained open-minded.

They turned into the gates for Dhekelia Garrison and her stomach fluttered with memories. The ESBA police security officers on the gate studied her ID and allowed her driver through, past the Garrison cinema, where she'd seen reruns of Patrick Swayze movies back in the day. She was two-thousand miles away from London, but it felt like home.

'Garrison Officers' Mess, ma'am?' Gem asked.

She agreed; she needed to freshen up and prepare herself for the afternoon ahead. The flight had taken off from RAF Brize Norton, in Oxfordshire, in the early hours and she hadn't slept on the plane, not that she would now either. But she had to draw breath and perhaps get something to eat in the officers' mess dining room before she embarked on her visits planned for today.

The body of her fellow RMP officer awaited her back at the hospital mortuary, in Akrotiri, but the autopsy wouldn't be performed until tomorrow. She'd requested to witness it and she hoped to examine his dive kit too. But first, she'd be escorted to Captain Thomas's temporary office, in Ayios Nikolaos, to examine his notes on the suspected leaking of sensitive information from the listening station. It was a grave charge, and not since the Cyprus 7 in the 1980s, had anything like this rocked the establishment quite as much. Helen was quite aware that the said trial had collapsed, resulting in all men being acquitted because of the methods of the service police bringing into question their so-called confessions, as well as sloppy investigative methods. She had this in the back of her mind as they neared the Dhekelia Garrison officers' mess building. It would be her home for as long as it took to get to the bottom of this affair, and she had a feeling it would take more than a week. They drove past the pool enclosure and Helen heard the shrieks of service spouses and their children as they enjoyed the cool water. To them, Cyprus was a premium posting: a chance to have a two-year vacation in the sun, but to serving personnel, it was just another job, albeit with great weather.

Gem stopped and got out to open her door. A wall of heat hit Helen's face and she felt as though her nostrils might burn from the inside. She swung herself out of the car and walked into the old colonial-style building. Gem brought her bags behind her and shut the door. They greeted the mess manager, who was expecting her, and signed her in and told her about meal times and suchlike, and handed her a new identification lanyard for use here on the island. Her room was located on the first floor and she told Gem to wait for her. She'd like to go and see Colonel Bill Seaton in Ayios Nikolaos and also make sure that the office assigned to Captain Thomas was untouched. She crossed her fingers that it had been left as it was. She didn't know how she'd feel sifting through somebody else's case; somebody who she knew was dead. The mess manager informed her that he was sure he could rustle up a sandwich and have it brought to her room, she smiled broadly and thanked him.

Her room was a typical one for a single officer. There was a double bed and an en-suite bathroom. The furniture was made of cheap pine laminate and the drawers were wobbly. There was a desk and the curtains were bright and gaudy, but it was clean and the air conditioning worked. When she'd been posted here before, there was none, so they'd come a long way. Even the family quarters hadn't had it installed. The advice from the families' office was to wet a sheet and set a fan to blow through it over your body at night in bed. British army air-con at its finest. Feeling slightly giddy that she had her own unit, she went to check the controls. A knock at the door interrupted her excitement and she took a plate and a bottle of water from a young soldier, who barely looked eighteen.

Unpacked, and changed into a clean loose shirt and shorts, and refreshed from the sustenance, Helen went back downstairs. Her hair was tied back and she wore soft pumps on her feet. She'd had a conversation with Colonel Don Murton before she left and he'd suggested full uniform, but she'd argued against it. If she was spending her time inside the ESBA, pursuing regular RMP work, then all well and good, but she wasn't. Her role here was likely to take her into civilian territory, as she followed Captain Thomas's work, and she'd rather stay inconspicuous. Colonel Murton had relented and she got her way. She knew she'd attract some stares of disapproval, but she really didn't give a fuck. If Captain Thomas had spent his whole time in desert combats and his red beret, then, she figured, what chance did he have of getting to the bottom of a highly sensitive intelligence scandal? Zero. She'd packed her uniforms, of course, but she hoped they wouldn't see the light of day during her trip.

Two huge carved ebony elephants sat in the doorway to the mess entrance, watching her with intent, reminding her that she was standing in the middle of a ruined empire that was once great but not anymore, and for a good reason. She almost wanted to ask if the trinkets and trophies on display could be sent back, but she knew the answer. A rhino horn sat in a glass case, next to silver awards and goblets, inscribed with glories past.

The mess manager clocked her civilian clothes but didn't remark. She smiled at him and thanked him again for the food, walking past him and the elephants, and out into the sunshine, into the cool car again.

'Ayios Nikolaos,' she instructed.

British interests on the island of Cyprus, in the ESBA, were shaped rather like a dumbbell. One weight being Dhekelia Garrison, by the beach, and the other Ayios Nikolaos, near the

Turkish border. The handle in between was comprised of the road which joined them. Either side of that was farmland, and she'd read in Captain Thomas's notes that it was strike season. The farmers often took industrial action, when campaigning for pay and conditions and the like, and the summer, when the heat made everyone crazy, was a favourite time. Sometimes it disrupted the work at the listening station, and Helen noted that this had happened rather frequently of late.

The drive took them the back way out of camp through the tiny little village of Xylotymvou and Helen remembered the excellent bakery there. Sure enough, the shop was still in business and she looked in the windows at the pastries lined up, making a mental note to come and stock up, when she had the time.

Gem slowed the car as they approached the Turkish border. Small camps had been set up along the road, with what looked like abandoned vehicles and tents dotting the roadside. They were local farmers and it appeared to her as though they'd been pitched here for quite some time. It wasn't the job of the British Army to move them on, as long as they didn't compromise the integrity of the listening base. They stared back at her as Gem drove past them and on to Ayios Nikolaos. They looked like any protesting encampment that was dug in for more than a few hours: happy and belligerent at the same time. Children played in the fields and women cooked over pots set up by the road. A few local press vans were in attendance too and a woman with a camera took a picture of their vehicle.

They arrived at the station and Helen flashed her ID. She was aware that her presence wasn't something that brought joy to the small outpost. She wanted to tell the guards on the gate that she wasn't here to cause trouble, but how did she know where her investigation might take her? Especially when everyone knew that four soldiers were under house arrest accused of very serious crimes. As expected, the guards paid her a little extra attention, not least because she wasn't in uniform and she was a senior rank. It was obvious to her that they clocked why she was here, and who she was replacing. They stood to attention and saluted her, as they had to.

Gem drove on and stopped outside a building, which had a sign saying JSSU: Joint Services Signal Unit. She thanked him and he told her where he'd be waiting for her. She got out. The constant switching between hot and cold air was making her tense. She showed her ID again to Colonel Seaton's second in command and he told her to wait as the colonel was on his way. He sat at his desk and busied himself. She remained standing and couldn't help a yawn. She'd been up at two a.m. to get the taxi to RAF Brize Norton, a two-hour journey. Then there had been security delays through the air base, as well as the long flight. It wasn't short haul or long haul, it was irritatingly in-between. Now, twelve hours later, she was ready for a break, but she had to throw herself straight into the investigation. She tried to make small talk, but Major Nick Graham wasn't interested, and he continued with his work, no doubt passing judgement on her association with the investigation, like all the others. The major would have his eyes on promotion to colonel, and not on helping a member of the RMP, and she felt it.

A tall man strode towards her and outstretched his hand. His voice boomed appropriately, as Helen expected for someone of his era and rank, and she took his hand and shook it firmly. She never let a man out-grip her, regardless of the weighty epaulettes on his shoulder. She looked him dead in the eye and he smiled but looked away, to Major Graham, to order iced tea. She wasn't asked if she liked iced tea. She said nothing, not wanting to challenge his authority further, as everybody knew why she was here.

Helen followed him into his office and sat down when told to. The interior was covered in military photos and paintings, as well as awards and medals for gallantry and service. The man was decorated, there was no doubt about that. And he was proud of it. He looked to be in his late fifties, and must be close to retirement. He was part of the old guard, on its way out because the MOD couldn't afford them anymore. She guessed that, out here, he had an inappropriately large house, staff and tax-free benefits. Overlooked colonels usually took postings like these for the perks, but she checked herself for judging him too harshly.

'So, terrible business about Captain Thomas. He was doing a great job,' Colonel Seaton bellowed. He didn't need to speak quite so loudly or commandingly, but Helen had come across his type before. She knew that their existence and validation rested upon how stridently and widely they swung their cocks. She wasn't intimidated. Just keen to do her job.

'I'm here, sir, to ascertain whether or not there has been a crime committed, and if so, to find out what crime and who is responsible. When I've done that, I'll leave.' She smiled and waited.

'You don't mess around, do you?' he said.

She got the impression that she might be invited to dinner, to calm down and take a load off, before tinkering around with press briefings and closing up the case cosily, like a dutiful woman. She raised an eyebrow.

'My wife and I would like you to join us for dinner tonight, Major,' he said.

'I'm sorry, sir, with all respect, I've got some serious catching up to do.'

'It's not a request, Major. My house, eight o'clock.'

Oh Christ. She'd forgotten how late all these colonial sorts ate when they were pushed to the perimeters of the empire. The forgotten, running their own shows, in the maddening sun, about as far away from Whitehall as one could get, figuratively of course. It wasn't geographically that far away, but this garrison, as old as the hills, might as well be a million miles away.

'Yes, sir,' she said.

Chapter 6

The office assigned to Captain Paul Thomas was a small windowless room around the back of JSSU. Helen was aware of the stares from a few uniformed personnel, as she walked between buildings. She nodded greetings and carried on, focused on the job in hand. Once she closed the door behind her, she leant against it and looked around. Box files were stacked neatly upon the desk, which was eerily tidy. The base was quiet but always manned, despite it being the weekend. Terrorism didn't take breaks, and she heard faint noises outside as people went about their business of spying on suspects thousands of miles away.

She'd visited the listening station before, years ago, and it had remained unchanged: still like a wasteland but for the slowly moving dishes, enormous in their perfection. They were pristinely kept, but around them, faded burnt grasses blew as if keeping watch towards the wire perimeter fence, and the ever-present Turkish army, monitoring their neighbour. British territory was marked out by a collection of metre-high white perimeter plinths, and strangely, every year, they moved a little. It was a combination of necky Turkish soldiers, and greedy local farmers, and every year, the British Army moved them back. It was a delicately polite dance between all sides, but the integrity of the ESBA was the sole remit of the base, along with guarding the listening station.

Helen relished the coolness of the small office and took a metal chair to sit on. The walls were blank and the carpet worn and stained from years of use. It was more of a box room and Helen guessed that's exactly what it was until the RMP investigation necessitated a space to do their work. No one wanted the RMP on their patch more than they had to be. Usually they investigated speeding on the ESBA and domestics between husbands and wives. Her presence meant that somebody, somewhere, had done something wrong, and that made her unwelcome. She turned to the files and opened them, one by one, searching for answers.

Captain Thomas was thorough, and his notes were in good order. The files were numbered and well organised. She approached his work as she would any case: with fresh eyes, looking for any anomalies and taking in every piece of information, as if she were starting from the beginning. She made notes of the soldiers and officers Paul had interviewed so far and read their statements. She also read the communications he'd had with the legal aid lawyer assigned the defence of the four corporals. Her name was Juliana Barnaby, and she was a mere twenty-five years old, no doubt shipped off by a law firm in London, to make the initial enquiries. She read that Ms Barnaby's defence was that the men were plainly innocent because they were accused of the impossible. Intelligence gathering wasn't done by single operatives, or even small groups of four, sat in a room, privy to all the dots that needed to be joined. It was much more sophisticated than that. Information gathered by lowly corporals was collated elsewhere, and it was more important people, who sat in comfy chairs in Whitehall and Washington, who made the decisions, not junior soldiers in this dust bowl. So why all the fuss?

She began with the original intelligence, which had been flagged up by a signals operator at General Communications HQ in Cheltenham, UK. A keen eye had been processing the British involvement in an air strike on Syria, three weeks ago. She read a note passed to the joint defence staff at the MOD main building in Whitehall that questioned why a target, close to the city of Aleppo, singled out for obliteration from one-hundred-thousand feet, had changed his plans at the very last minute to avoid the route, confirmed by a unit of Special Forces on the ground. The target was an arms dealer, trading out of Iran, who happened to be visiting one of his many delivery sites across Syria. The hit was supposed to disrupt the chain, and thus destroy a vital supply route overland via Mosul in Iraq. Chains such as these had spread unchecked, taking advantage of the political chaos of the region, caused by the two Gulf wars. It wasn't Helen's job to sit here and consider whose fault it was; just to work out where the intelligence had leaked. However, she despised people like Labib Hassan, who rose up like giants wherever war wreaked havoc. People like him were responsible for thousands, if not millions, of deaths worldwide. She also knew the risks the men and women on the ground took to gather intelligence on his sort, giving their lives and often not seeing their hard work pay off. As in this case. Something, somewhere, had gone wrong.

She saw that the surveillance of the whole operation had come through Ayios Nikolaos, and had done for the whole duration of the war in Syria. That meant that every word, every deal and each strategic move, had travelled through this dusty outpost in the weeks preceding the planned hit. She read the transcripts of the information in their original form, as they were sent back to the UK and, in turn, shared with allies.

Helen was afforded the highest security clearance and that meant that she was asked questions about her finances, sexual orientation and anything considered potentially embarrassing to her. Enemies looked for levers, and that was why personnel were turned by spooks. It wasn't usually for money, or personal revenge, it was almost always because they were blackmailed with something. If sensitive information had indeed been leaked, then she was looking for someone with something to hide.

She sat back and created scenarios for every bit of knowledge that had potentially led to the target in Aleppo. Each one brought her back here to Cyprus, more specifically, this base.

Captain Thomas was on to something, she was sure. She opened his file, which had travelled with her all the way from London and stared at his military profile photo. He had a handsome face, but a uniform helped any man's kerb appeal. Their paths hadn't crossed and she didn't know him personally. The RMP was a relatively small regiment, and often they shared postings in distant places, huddling together due to the hostility from other parties, but she hadn't known him, plus he was younger and Helen wondered why the MOD had assigned someone so junior when, clearly, the intelligence showed that this was a major problem. He'd been sent here alone, put in this small box room, and now he was dead.

His efforts so far had been centred on the personnel here and maybe, she thought, that was his first mistake. Had he been bullish and asked the wrong people the wrong questions? But her imagination was running away with her. She was assuming he'd met a violent end, and she'd already been told that he died during a difficult diving ascent. However, she wouldn't believe that until she'd questioned everyone involved herself, and witnessed the autopsy.

Next, she turned her attention to the target in Aleppo; Labib Hassan, the local warlord who'd done well under Assad's wrecking ball that had annihilated most of the country, with Russian help. Every way she turned, stinking politics was always rife. Vermin, like this man, who called himself a general, no less, always sought out the cracks in the earth's crust, and it just so happened that the almighty fissure that was the Middle East was the perfect canvas on which to rise to greatness. The guy was a billionaire, but no one knew where his money was. Probably inside the London laundromat, via Russia. Western banks said they no longer touched dirty money, and oligarchs now cleaned it through the penthouses of Mayfair, private jets, and yachts, anchored in Monaco. But it was still there, and it could fund whole countries, and armies. But Helen's agenda, like all soldiers', wasn't politically driven, it just pissed her off when people made money from death.

But her brief wasn't to investigate the legitimacy of Labib as a target, just to ascertain if Ayios Nikolaos Station was compromised. That was it. Don had told her as much. Find out if there is a leak, end of. It was frustrating, but that was her job. But Helen also knew that her colonel had chosen her because he could guarantee that in her quest to find answers for them, she'd be thorough, and if that exposed a wider network, then she'd find it.

Before she'd boarded the plane at RAF Brize Norton, Don had called her and told her to be careful. His words had popped into her head several times since she'd landed. The job ahead of her was like climbing a bare rock face without ropes: no one would want to help, this she knew not only from experience, but from her reception so far. He'd also informed her that another attempted hit on Labib had failed only this week. That was what was known as a pattern.

Unlike Captain Thomas, she'd go in from the top, starting with Colonel Seaton. Dinner at his tonight might be an entertaining affair after all. If she could gauge the man and ascertain how involved he was in his own mandate, and if he knew what his soldiers were up to, then she could well have somewhere to start. For, nowadays, anyone passing information to enemies of the state, in the middle of a warzone, couldn't go it alone. There were electronic trails on everyone, from a school teacher in Chiswick to the Prime Minister of the UK: no one could exist without leaving a static footprint in their wake. And this was the place to find it. But what she really wanted was a motive. If some lowly corporal was passing secrets to the enemy, she wanted to know why. Was it simply good old-fashioned cash, or something else? She needed to know their dirtiest secrets and, from there, if anyone could blackmail them.

The suspension and house arrest of the suspects was customary, while the investigation was being pursued, but why was Colonel Bill Seaton still in post? Surely as the man in charge, he should have been suspended. The idea that four signals corporals could cause such a panic across the Atlantic, from London to Washington, was questionable to her; why had no one flagged it up before? But then, perhaps sending Captain Thomas had been their canary bird; a warning probe to ascertain if there were lethal gasses circulating over the Mediterranean.

Chapter 7

Taxis left the Dhekelia Garrison Mess, full of officers dressed in chinos and blue cotton shirts, no doubt made-to-measure in one of in Nicosia's fine tailors, serving the British since the nineteenth century. Helen herself hadn't been above the perk; twenty years ago, she'd had silk dresses made in a sweat shop near Ledra Palace, over the Green Line, by a short man called Osman who was a genius with his sewing machine. The Green Line was the border between the two warring factions, mapped out by the UN as a temporary measure in 1964. It split the beautiful capital in two, like a cracked skull. The dresses had been stunning, and dirt cheap. She had no idea where they were now, probably given to charity when she'd changed shape, or put on a bit of weight here and there. Maybe she'd have time to get some more made before she left. A trip up to the cool mountains of Troodos would be nice too, but she knew that her work came first.

She smiled at a few young officers as they rushed out into the early-evening heat to get their ride.

'Where you off to?' she asked.

Word had already spread that an RMP officer was staying in the mess and everyone was keen to steer clear, though one of the officers hung back now.

'We're going in to Limassol, you're welcome to join us?'

He was in his twenties and Helen smiled. 'I'm having dinner with Colonel Seaton and his wife tonight.'

'Big Willy? Don't go anywhere near his cocktail cabinet, you'll never leave,' he said.

She smiled and said she'd remember the advice.

'He's got an excellent stock of Efes beer though, smuggled in by the Padre of course,' he added, smiling. Efes was the premium Turkish beer of the north. The Republic of Cyprus still didn't recognise the Turkish state in the north of the Island, and the trading of goods was strictly forbidden. But no one would dare search a vehicle driven by a man of the cloth.

'What's in Limassol these days? Is it a good night out?' she asked. She'd enjoyed plenty of boozy occasions in the city, which was a magnet for tourists, but it had been years and she was interested to know what it was like now.

'It's not bad, we'll probably end up back in Larnaca later. You should come out with us tomorrow night,' he suggested. 'Tom Fleet,' he said, holding his hand out for her to take.

'Helen Scott,' she replied.

His demeanour changed. 'You're the RMP?' he asked.

'I am, I'm sorry,' she said.

He smiled briefly. 'Oh, it's all right, good luck,' he said.

She nodded and watched him leave with the others in a taxi.

She'd already showered and changed into the only decent dress she'd packed, and now she asked Gem to drop her off at the garrison shop to pick up a bottle of wine to take with her. This was the difference between serving at home and abroad: someone dies in London, and the whole affair grinds to a halt. An officer dies here and you get invited to dinner. She hadn't wanted to go, but she accepted that it was a situation she couldn't get out of and so might as well use it to get to know Colonel Seaton better, if nothing else. After all, he was in charge here.

Captain Thomas's body awaited her at RAF Akrotiri, in the hospital mortuary, and that was her early-morning call tomorrow. She couldn't stop thinking about it and was disappointed to learn of the delay in the post-mortem operation, though he'd had to be formally identified first. It took time.

Even the short walk from the mess to the car caressed her in searing heat, which, she remembered, never let up until after sundown. But the colours were stunningly vibrant and glowed orange in the evening sun. A breeze from the shore kissed her skin and she gazed towards the coast, marvelling at how, with the coming night, the sea had calmed, as if preparing for sleep. She could make out lights over where the *Zenobia* was and shivered at the thought of Captain Thomas's fate down there, but she also couldn't help feel the pull of it and knew why people risked their lives for the sport.

Gem beckoned her and she climbed into the back seat.

The garrison shop was empty and about to close when they arrived. Originally called the Naafi, after the Navy, Army and Airforce institutes which ran it, on every UK base on the planet, the shop stocked everything a homesick Brit could wish for and she smiled as she passed tins of tuna, packets of cornflakes and boxes of tea. The imported wine selection wasn't bad, but she chose a local Cypriot one that was respectably expensive. As a last thought, she grabbed a potted plant from the flower aisle too. She tried to relax and submit herself to the next few hours of dull conversation, accepting that there was not a lot she could do about it. The colonel's wife might be a laugh, she thought hopefully, but chances of that were slim. She expected the chit-chat to be of the wives club, and not much else.

Gem pulled the car into a long cul-de-sac and stopped outside a grand house. Equality was slow to keep up to date in the army. Rank was everything and the house, as well as the street, reflected it. There was a double-fronted entrance and above that a wrap-around veranda, freshly painted, and Helen reckoned the view to the sea would be spectacular.

A gardener rounded the back corner of the house and tended to plants. He was a local Cypriot, and she said hello. Part of the British mandate on the island was to promise to employ a certain quota of locals, even if they didn't do much. He nodded at her. His skin was dark mahogany and deep creases framed his face. Helen placed him in his sixties. He probably came with the house and saw commanders come and go with the seasonal flowers. The garrison commandant's job was a premium posting for somebody wanting to hold on to their seniority but not quite ready for retirement. Suitable for those not quite up to the MOD and policy writing, their budget was generous but not as much as it had been. Clearly still enough to cover maintenance staff, though. She wondered if they had a cook too and a catering budget, and her question was soon answered when she was shown in by another local, this time a woman in an apron. Helen greeted her too and received the obligatory nod and pleasant smile. She felt herself in the midst of some imperial drama and it made her feel uncomfortable.

She heard soft music as she was invited to wait on the decking outside, in the back garden. She was impressed with the comfort and space, and noted the expensive additions to the walled garden. It was private and well-tended and she saw the gardener again, this time he was turning off sprinklers. A flurry of activity caught her attention and she turned to witness a woman in floral swathes of material wafting towards her.

'Helen, is it? Welcome to our home,' she said.

Helen didn't bother pointing out that the home belonged to the MOD or, more accurately, the taxpayer. She let it go, and handed over her gifts, which were, in turn, handed to a member of the household staff.

'How lovely!' the colonel's wife gushed.

The colonel soon joined his wife. He wore casual trousers and an open shirt without a tie. He looked different out of uniform, like most people did: less regal and authoritative.

'Canapés will be ready soon, do you want a tour? It's recently refurbished. I couldn't possibly have moved into the hovel it was before, we stayed in the Palm Beach Hotel for four months while it was renovated,' the wife said.

'Darling, have you introduced yourself?' the colonel asked his wife.

'Andi,' she said. 'With an "i". Come on, I'll show you round.'

The last thing Helen wanted was to be part of some perverse bragging rights on a very expensive refurb, courtesy of taxpayers' money, but she had no choice.

Andi with an i took her to the kitchen first.

'This is where it all happens,' she said. 'They tried to take the cook, but I wasn't having it.' Helen knew that 'they' were the powers back in the UK who controlled the budget, and she wondered how on earth Andi with an i had persuaded them to spend a ton of cash on a house in Cyprus when they couldn't afford tanks or aircraft carriers that worked. She let it go.

The kitchen was modern and quite beautiful, and a woman prepared food silently.

'Hi,' Helen said to the cook.

Andi looked at her strangely and Helen smiled sweetly.

'Of course, I don't spend much time in here,' Andi laughed.

Before they left, Helen noticed a large jar of the local, and highly illegal, pickled Cypriot songbirds, called *ambelopoulia*, on the side. She'd once been offered them and the name stuck with her as something disgusting. The trade was abhorrent and involved trapping the birds on lime sticks, or netting them. They were a delicacy to some, but why a colonel should be eating them was repulsive to her. It only made her opinion of Seaton and his wife diminish even further.

Next was the hall, with a new staircase. The walls were covered in framed photos of Colonel Seaton with foreign dignitaries and VIPs. They were all the same: big smiles, full glasses of booze and gong-laden uniforms.

And so it went on, until Helen had seen every new toilet flusher, doorknob and decking panel. She wanted desperately to run and find Tom Fleet and go out on the town with the lads. Anything to get away from Andi with an i.

Finally, they sat down to aperitifs and Helen asked for water.

'I've got an early start,' she said, to Andi's horror.

'Good God, have a drink so I don't feel like a total alcoholic,' she said.

43

The woman was nervous and it seemed that only the drink in her hand steadied her unease. Helen agreed to have a small gin and tonic.

They were waited on outside and brought nibbles to pick on. Helen thanked the servers every time something was put in front of her, garnering more stares from Andi, who treated her staff like minions.

'We serve sparkling mineral water in glass, not the pond water you get in the officers' mess.'

Helen smiled and hoped that Colonel Seaton would save her at some point, by at least acknowledging the death of her colleague. That would be a good start.

'I started to go through the work left by Captain Thomas, sir,' Helen prompted, when Andi was busy giving out orders for the main meal to be served inside.

'Did he get far?' the colonel asked.

'How do you mean?'

'Well, he was holed up in there all week and rarely came out. Every time I sent someone to check on him, he said he was working on classified documents.'

'I thought he did a good job of interviewing a wide range of people,' Helen said in Paul Thomas's defence.

'Really? And did he find out that we're a den of deceitful treacherous thugs?' Colonel Seaton laughed, but Helen didn't find him funny at all. God, she wished the freshly panelled floor would swallow her up.

The rest of the evening followed the same pattern as the colonel and his wife got slowly inebriated. The conversation turned to the officers' mess.

'Did you see them all leave tonight? I think they deserve a blowout every weekend, don't you? We're within pissing distance of the next war in the Middle East, and I think they need to be able to live a little,' he said.

Helen wasn't aware of an impending war in the region, and she put it down to the booze. He had to justify his position, she thought. Like many foreign postings in the forces now, their days were numbered, as money, and excuses, ran out. She looked at her watch and realised that it was gone eleven, and she felt uncomfortable having sat down in the same position, doing nothing, for hours. It reminded her of a regimental dinner when you weren't allowed to move, or take a piss, until the colonel said so. She also wasn't used to so much food, though it was delicious. The cook clearly loved her job. Memories from her time here with Grant had flooded back with every plate full. The aromas, the Middle Eastern influence, the meze style platters and the flavours all mingled in her mouth to create the most wonderful satisfaction.

She thanked her hosts profusely, having sat through enough, deciding to leave them to get drunk and do whatever they did on a Saturday night together.

'I really must go, but it has been lovely,' she said.

She stood up and Andi offered her hand unsteadily.

'I'm going to witness the autopsy on Captain Thomas tomorrow,' Helen said, purposefully injecting the atmosphere with some solemnity. She couldn't help herself. The man had hardly been mentioned. And that was the only reason she was here.

'Good God,' Andi said. 'Do you have to?'

'I requested to. I'm not convinced that someone of his experience would make mistakes on a simple dive.'

'No, I mean do you have to mention it?' Andi clarified.

Helen looked at the colonel.

His face dropped and he put his hands firmly in his pockets. Helen felt as though she'd outstayed her welcome, but she wasn't that bothered, because if she'd had a choice, she would have left hours ago. She moved towards the entrance hall. A waiter in a pressed white uniform was already there, opening the door. She could see from the house that Gem was asleep in the car. She wished she'd sent him away; she could have easily found her way back to the mess on her own. She left, thanking the colonel again, hoping never to be invited back.

Helen went to Gem's window and gently shook him.

'I'm sorry,' she whispered.

He woke with a start and sat up straight.

'Sorry, ma'am,' he muttered.

'Not at all, you didn't have to wait, I should have told you.'

'Not to worry, ma'am. Are you going to the mess?'

'Yes please,' she said, getting into the back seat.

'What time tomorrow?' he asked.

'I need to be in Akrotiri at ten.'

He nodded. 'I'll be outside the mess at nine.'

The journey in the dark was quick and Helen resolved to walk more. She didn't need to keep this poor man up all hours. He dropped her off at the entrance to the mess and she saw a few lights burning in the bar. She avoided it, going into one of the lounges instead. She wasn't the only one who thought better of joining the young subalterns for copious amounts of booze.

Chapter 8

The woman was dressed in jeans and a T-shirt, and certainly didn't fit in around here; she was far too casual. It must be the lawyer.

'Hi,' Helen said.

The young woman looked up from the work she was doing.

'Sorry to disturb you,' Helen said.

'You must be Major Helen Scott. I'm Juliana Barnaby. Delighted, I'm sure.' Juliana Barnaby was short and thickset, and she had red cheeks, no doubt from the sun and the exertions of her job.

'Likewise. Do you mind if I sit?'

'Off the record?'

'Of course.'

During RMP investigations, like any other on Civvy Street, it was customary for the prosecution and the defence to liaise unofficially, not least to strive for a deal or plea bargain.

'You an intern?' Helen asked.

'Opening with an insult? Nice touch. No, I'm fully qualified, despite my age.'

'Sorry, can we start again?' Helen sat down and Juliana took a sip from her drink. 'What are you having?' Helen asked.

'Water,' Juliana replied. 'It's over there in a jug, with ice.'

'You always work so late?'

'Yes. You?'

'Actually I was at dinner with Colonel Seaton and his wife.'

'There's a snake if ever I met one,' Juliana said.

47

'Sorry?' Helen was unfamiliar with her colleagues being branded with civilian slurs. She wasn't often in court, and she didn't rub shoulders with many lawyers. She was quickly learning that Juliana Barnaby said it like it was, and Helen liked it.

'God, don't tell me you're institutionalised like the rest of them? I'm not military and I don't intend to be. I'm here on my firm's request, to find out the truth about my clients.'

'The four servicemen? Of course. I have yet to have the pleasure.' Helen intended to re-interview the suspects tomorrow, even though she'd read Captain Thomas's notes in detail. They were all attesting their innocence, as well as their undying allegiance to their colonel. She knew that even if the men weren't charged, their military careers were effectively over.

Helen went to get a glass and filled it with water from the jug and returned to her seat.

'So, the truth?'

Juliana eyed her, woman to woman. Helen felt thoroughly examined. 'Those boys are innocent, and I'm going to prove it.'

'But there's clearly a spy ring operating out of Cyprus passing intelligence to our enemies.'

Juliana scoffed. 'And the Pope is still Catholic. Of course there bloody is, but it's not my boys who are responsible. You lot probably don't want to get to the real truth, so good luck with that, but one thing is for sure, my clients are walking free.'

Helen admired her chutzpah. 'What makes you so sure?'

'They're being accused of the impossible,' Juliana said. 'I told your colleague the same thing. May he rest in peace, poor sod. That's why I don't leave the base unless I have to and then I have an armed guard.'

'They gave you an armed guard?' Helen asked. She was suitably shocked. 'You better check if their weapons are loaded if you're serious, I can't imagine they are.'

Juliana gazed at her and a smile spread across her mouth. 'That's not the point. Everybody from the Baltic to the Black Sea knows I'm here and I'll get them off all charges. People are getting jumpy, that's why Captain Thomas is no longer with us.'

'That's a hefty charge. If you're right, then I'll find it too, and we'll be singing along the same tune.'

'Not likely. We're playing completely different symphonies, Major Scott. Watch your back, won't you?'

It was an odd sensation, being warned by somebody so young. Juliana acted way beyond her years. And with such confidence.

'I know that traditionally you legal people don't trust the Special Investigation Branch and you think their job is to cover their arses. I'm Military Police too, same as them, but I'm also a detective in search of the truth, let's not fight.'

Juliana studied her.

'Welcome to the circus. I'll finish my notes upstairs.'

Juliana gathered her things and left Helen staring after her. The glaring irony was that they were all paid for by the same master.

'Oh, have you found the Mata Hari yet?' Juliana asked, turning at the doorway.

'The what?' Helen asked.

'The lever? It's always a whore, is it not? We women are always blamed for the shit men get up to, look it up.'

Helen watched, speechless, as Juliana disappeared upstairs. She googled what she'd said, guessing the spelling, and finally she got a hit. Mata Hari was a Dutch courtesan accused of being a German spy during the First World War. Helen realised that she knew what Juliana was telling her, but she was familiar with the ruse by a more modern call sign coined in Northern Ireland in the seventies, when beautiful women lured servicemen to dark corners only to watch them be kneecapped by the IRA: the honey trap.

Chapter 9

On the main coastal strip of Larnaca, two blocks back from the sandy beach, the Blue Lantern was bursting at the seams with British officers. An unwritten rule made sure that soldiers of lower rank went elsewhere. It was just the way it was. No one wanted to mix ranks when being oneself. Occasionally it happened, and when it did, they behaved accordingly, as fitting any rank structure: badly. The soldiers had hangouts in other parts of the town, which were equally avoided by officers. Each group wanted to relax and be themselves, without being reported on for falling down drunk or sleeping with a prostitute. Though everyone acknowledged that's what they all did with their time, if one was single, and sometimes if one was not.

The lighting was dimmed and shone red and blue, alternately highlighting flesh and smiles. Some women frequented the joint; as was their proclivity, the dancing girls didn't mind: it was all work to them. Several private rooms were on hand for those feeling flush, or set up by their mates on payday.

Second Lieutenant Tom Fleet had had too much to drink. His shirt was stained with the Lebanese meal they'd had in Limassol to line their stomachs before heading to some of the best bars along the strip in Larnaca. Saturday night was the busiest of the week, and the mood was expectant. He sat in a corner, at a table with other officers sipping cocktails. The brandy sour was the island's best on offer. It was made with lemon and angostura bitters, as well as local Five Kings brandy. The glasses were adorned with straws and tiny umbrellas. The drinks cost the price of a dance, and their inflation, compared to other bars, was worth it. The music was low but enough to cause a buzz in one's brain. The tunes were chosen for their beat: like the pulse of sex, it was consistent and heavy. Girl after girl paraded along the catwalk, which was really the bar top. Silver poles shot up to the ceiling and the women held on, gyrating in front of punters. Tables like Tom's attracted their own custom: they were good spenders.

Tom looked for her through his haze. He knew he'd had too much booze because his vision was blurry. To focus properly, he had to close one eye and count to ten and remind himself to breath regularly. Secret doors were hidden behind flimsy screens and half-naked beauties emerged from them when it was their turn. A constant stream of lingerie-clad bodies issued forth from the slivers of colour, smiling and looking out for the best patrons, as well as new faces they could work on.

Then there she was.

Anastasia appeared through a smoky screen and walked slowly to the steps that led to the bar top. She graced them as tenderly as a kiss and it was as if she slid upwards, not stepping, but gliding on her long legs, which were tanned with the Cyprus summer, and dark cream. In the darkness, her body looked like perfection: small waist, pert exercised buttocks, firm stomach and large round breasts. Ani, Tom called her. He'd been given the honour after his second time with her, after he'd become hooked. He had a girlfriend back home, like most of them did, but Ani let you do things that ticked off a litany of fantasies that kept her clients going for the whole time they were posted on the island. For a price.

Her skin glowed, nutty in the golden hue, and she moved like a goddess. Tom sat mesmerised, knowing she'd get over to him eventually, having secured her with the highest price anytime he was in the Lantern. He had no choice. Should he fall foul of a better-paying customer, he couldn't bear to watch his hands on her, his woman. She, in turn, obliged to give new punters all of her expensive attention, and disappear upstairs as

Tom watched, desperately forlorn at the unfairness of it. The manager upped the price week on week, but Tom always paid and Ani told him she was thankful it was him.

'I'm sorry, baby,' she'd said in her soft foreign accent – Russian in origin – when he'd expected her to spend the night with him the third time.

He'd watched as another man had trumped him at the last moment and the manager, Theo, looked on. They'd had a quick chat after that and had secured the promise that Ani was his every Saturday, if he paid the right price, which he always did.

She looked at him now from under her heavily mascaraed lashes and he smiled knowingly, willing himself to sober up enough to manage to please her in an hour or so, or whenever she'd finished her dance. She prowled up and down the bar, and the men sat there stopped drinking. Her underwear was laced and sat on her flesh like a wrapper on an afternoon tea delicacy at the Ritz. Her hips swung around and Tom felt his heart leap. He watched her breasts move from side to side as she worked the lighting to her advantage. The curves of her body made him hold his breath and she slid her hands down her legs, bending over fully and shaking her head, as her hair fell out of its clip. It was jet black and long and luscious. Eager hopefuls leant over and stuffed notes into her tiny pants and she took their faces one by one, almost kissing them, but, at the same time, expertly tucking the money away in a hidden box behind the bar to make room for more.

It maddened him that she wasn't allowed to keep her hard earnings, but that was part of the game. These girls were here to earn their keep, not become millionaires.

He'd promised her he'd take her back with him when he left. It had been a foolish, throwaway remark, and one he regretted the following morning when he woke up in her bed and she was sat smoking at the window, speaking to him of what she might do in London, and how she would make hundreds of babies for him. But still he kept coming.

She was on her knees, crawling along the bar, stopping to stroke somebody's face and stare into their eyes, only for a moment, long enough for them to reach into their pockets. Tom was transfixed by her. The banter around him quietened a little. His mates watched too. Their table was comprised of a few junior officers like himself and a smattering of senior married majors, along for the ride, homesick and safe in the knowledge that the officer code would protect them.

'I've made sure she's with me tonight,' Vic said into his ear. He winked at Tom, who stared back in horror.

'What the fuck?'

'Mate, I'm joking.' Vic spread his hands in mock apology.

Tom didn't find it funny. Victor Cobb was another second lieutenant, and the joker among them. He was also famous for being extremely well endowed, and he'd teased Tom about taking Ani upstairs before. In fact, a few weeks before Tom had come here for the first time, Vic had paid for a private dance with Ani, and Tom didn't know if it had led further, but he rationalised it in his head: it was her job. He had to get used to it. When she was with him, it was real and it was different.

He ignored Vic's lewd remarks about Ani when he was drunk.

'I'd make her scream,' Vic said.

'Bullshit, she's a good actress,' Tom said.

'Well, you'd know,' Vic said.

Tom got up and moved to the bar, where the manager, Theo Charalambous, sat keeping an eye on his investments all night. The guy didn't move from his stool at the end, only to count money, which, Ani said, was kept in a huge safe behind the bar. The kitchen out the back was used as a counting house as well as for chopping the suspect meat that went into the shawarmas. Tom and Ani talked. It wasn't all about sex. Tom realised, and admitted to himself at least, that he was in love. The idea of telling his girlfriend, Freya, when he returned to the UK, was pushed to the back of his mind, and when he spoke to her on the phone, he put her off visiting, telling her they were training to deploy to Jordan, or Turkey, or anywhere he could think of. Freya had no idea where the British Army deployed, and he could get away with telling her they were flying to the moon and she'd believe him. Ani was different; she hung on every word about his job and what he did. She would gaze up at him, propped up on a pillow, after they'd made love, as he told her about what he'd done that week, how dull it was, and how he wished something exciting would come up, like a war.

'You want to go to war?' she'd asked him.

'No, I didn't mean it like that,' he'd told her. 'It's just that when you train to command, you want to prove yourself. It's like a brain surgeon never operating on his patients. I want to command my soldiers in the field.'

'The field?'

'Sorry, it's what we call the battlefield.'

'Oh. I don't want you to go to the field, Tom. I want you to stay here and take me to London to have babies.'

Usually, after conversations about work, she'd disappear under the covers, searching for him with her mouth and all thoughts of what the week would bring as she got to work on him, surprising him, thinking he couldn't possibly come again.

That was what Ani did.

His wait was almost over and Theo eyed him and nodded. She was his tonight. Theo was a decent enough bloke, but Tom wouldn't cross him. He looked a mean fucker, despite his apparent lack of physical prowess. His trousers fell below his arse crack and rolls of fat sat like baguettes around his waist, but Tom wasn't fooled. One thing was to play around in bars, picking up girls and flashing money around on this island, but to encourage real trouble could cost him his job, and all the officers knew it. Soldiers fighting was to be expected, and they often served the obligatory night in a cell in the garrison, having been marched off by the RMP who patrolled the bars regularly, and in uniform, which was a source of untold embarrassment if one was caught.

Tom had known the RMP officer who died on the *Zenobia*, and he was a good bloke. Historically, the RMP were hated in battalion, but really, it was all hot air: they were decent men and women. The one who had just arrived had interested him. She was a good-looking woman, and not like your usual dour investigator: all uniform and process. She didn't even appear to have a uniform with her. Everybody knew she was here to replace Captain Paul Thomas and he wished her good luck. It was a dull job in a party environment. Maybe she was good at her job, who knew. The RMP didn't frequent the Blue Lantern.

Tom sat next to Theo. The manager spilled over his stool. He chain-smoked locally made Camels and counted the chips that were used to purchase drinks and girls. He was kept in constant supply of plates of food, tapas style, from the kitchen, testing some as they went out. Tom had ventured in there one night, in search for Ani, and had been chased out again by a chef brandishing a skillet. But not before he'd seen piles of cash stacked up on a kitchen surface. From then on, Theo had asked him certain questions about himself, and that's when he'd promised Ani to him, should he pay the right price and answer the right questions. Of course, Tom agreed.

'You're in for a good night again, Sir Tom.'

No matter how many times Tom assured Theo that he wasn't a knight of the realm, the nickname stuck and he didn't argue.

'Thanks, Theo,' Tom said, offering his hand.

Theo reciprocated: a big, sweaty hug of a handshake that shook Tom to his core. Not for the first time, Tom clocked the Makarov 9 mm pistol in Theo's back pocket.

He sauntered back to the table, where Vic was telling a story, no doubt about the girl he was intending to pay to sleep with him tonight. Tom sat in the corner once more and shut out Vic's voice, concentrating on Ani's buttocks as she slipped off her knickers and stuffed them into a pint glass. Next, her top would come off and Tom would have to fight to control himself as he imagined his lips around her nipples and her moaning for him, like Vic could only dream of.

He smiled and reached for the jug of water placed on every table, pouring a large glass of it. They were allowed a few pints of the stuff, as long as they ordered cocktails and champagne all night. Tom didn't much care how much his bar share came to tonight, even if he didn't drink anymore. He wanted to perform for Ani later, and waited patiently, sipping and watching.

A smart female, who Tom never saw stripping here, approached Theo from out back. Tom had seen her before and figured maybe she was the brains behind the business and Theo was just the muscle. She took a seat next to the big man and they exchanged words. He'd heard Theo call her Katerina. She couldn't be his wife, she was too beautiful.

Not for the first time, Tom saw her pass Theo a file. It was one of those that was tied with a string, and usually contained notes of some sort. It was undoubtedly the figures for the week, or something of that nature. She slipped off the stool and straightened her suit. Whenever Tom saw her, she wore the same dark tailored ensemble, not like a working girl at all. His eyes followed her hips as she made her way to the exit, without looking back. But tonight, she did, straight at Tom. Her cheekbones were high, like Ani's, and her eyes steely. Even in the dark, Tom could tell that she was in charge.

He looked away first, and saw Theo check the file. Tom watched the woman leave, with one more glance back to his table, and then he flicked his attention back to Theo, who pulled a tiny black plastic card from the file. Tom wasn't familiar with the item, but when Theo held it in his palm, he knew that it was a tiny mobile phone. He smiled to himself and a thrill of excitement passed through his body. It was quite obvious to Tom that this place was used to sink some pretty heavy fucking deals; and the girls, the gun, the piles of cash were part of it.

Tom looked at Theo's waistline, which seemed to expand right in front of him, as he sank another pitta, and he smiled to himself.

Good for you, Theo, Tom thought. *A damn fine example of entrepreneurial spirit.*

Chapter 10

Helen woke early and forgot for a moment where she was. The window was fully open and she remembered flinging it wide, sick of the freezing air-con, and she tutted. Now it was too hot.

She got out of bed and stretched; it had been a good night's sleep, which surprised her. A breeze wafted her curtains and she peeked through them towards the Mediterranean Sea. It shone pale blue in the morning haze, and the sun spilled like molten gold on the horizon. It would be an excellent day for a dive, but she had other plans.

She intended to get to the dive school before the morning divers assembled. Sunday would be a busy day out there. She'd already made contact and spoken to the man in charge. He was in fact an ex-soldier, who'd fallen in love with the island when he was posted here twenty years ago. After his sixteen-year pensionable point, he'd retired and come back to start his own dive school, and he was living the dream. Captain Paul Thomas was his first fatality and it had hit him hard.

Eric Dukakis had distant Greek relatives and made the most of this fact when applying to set up business here. It was an attractive prospect: forgetting it all and moving abroad. Helen had been tempted many times. She was posted to some of the most intriguing and alluring places on the planet – barring the operational tours to war-torn deserts – and could have easily settled somewhere warm and foreign, the very difference of culture and climate being the pull. She envied Eric Dukakis and his carefree life but reminded herself that her own reasons for doing such a thing would have been simply to run away.

It had to be said that each time she lived somewhere different, she missed the UK. There was something about one's homeland that was comforting and familiar, despite all the things that made you want to leave it in the first place.

The weather was the biggest factor and she felt herself seduced by the heady warmth flowing through her window already, and she'd only spent one night here. There was something about heat that made one forget problems and trivia and fancy a life free of rain and drizzle, but, she knew first hand, that the difficulties would still be there, like hungry children waiting to be fed.

She'd already requested an early Sunday breakfast from the mess manager, knowing that the other residents would be fast asleep until late morning or afternoon, nursing sore heads. After showering and dressing quickly, she locked her room and went downstairs, peering at the grand portraits of old generals on the walls.

Unsurprisingly, the mess was quiet and she had the place to herself. The items for a quick breakfast were laid out on silver platters on a table covered in a crisp white tablecloth. She smelled the faint whiff of cooking and reckoned the chef would be busy preparing fry-ups on a Sunday to soak up the booze from the night before. The place was spotless and she marvelled at how those tasked with keeping accommodation blocks clean always worked tirelessly and silently behind the scenes, so you didn't notice they were there. There was a residue of tobacco smoke in the air and the windows were all thrown open. The bar area was shut up and looked dated and neglected.

Helen yawned and covered her mouth; her sleep had been full of dreams of Mata Hari, executed by firing squad by the French. Nevertheless, she felt refreshed and looked at the food on offer, taking a plate and a knife and fork. She grabbed a croissant, which was warm, and some marmalade and butter, as well as a cup of fresh tea. She ate alone and finished quickly, checking outside if Gem was there waiting – he was. She had her bag ready and went straight out into the sunshine, climbing into the back seat.

'Morning,' she said brightly.

'Morning, ma'am,' he replied.

He knew their destination and set off for the Larnaca strip, past the security guards on duty at the front gate. The sea glistened in the foreground and the temperature was already up in the high twenties. She wore sunglasses and sat in silence, peering at the large hotels gracing the seafront, after which the land changed to the odd building dotted here and there, in between waste ground and flats.

Gem indicated to turn off and stopped outside a small shop, next to a jetty on the seafront. Ribs bobbed up and down and racks of sea canoes, kayaks and windsurfs were tidied away, waiting for the day's trade. Lines of wetsuits dried in the sun and they wafted about, like washing on a line, clean and ready for intrepid adventurers.

Helen got out of the air-conditioned car and the change in temperature surprised her again. It would take some getting used to, she thought. Her sandals sank into the soft sand that was supposed to be on the beach rather than on the path, she figured, and it stuck in between her toes. A huge sign saying 'Eric's Dive School' was painted above the shop and visible from the road to attract enquiries. It was English enough to give the tourists confidence, but it jarred Helen's senses a little, it was as if a slice of home had been transported here to the beach and enshrined in local custom.

She was happy she'd come early, as there was no one waiting. The door was open and she looked inside, knocking lightly at the side panel of the door.

'We're closed,' a voice shouted. A man came out of a back office and strode towards her. He wore a short wetsuit, which was pulled down around his waist, and apart from that he was naked. His body was tanned and strong. He had a couple of tattoos on his arms, above the elbow, gracefully swirling about his shoulder, and his feet scuffed on the sandy floor. He stopped when he saw Helen.

'Major Scott?' he asked.

She nodded and held out her hand.

'Eric?' she asked.

He smiled broadly and she held his stare, their hands lingering for more than a moment. His hand was warm and Helen felt instantly reassured by the man's presence: he hid nothing, and came to her space open and honest. She liked that. Often, when one took a handshake, there were hidden messages in it that made one wary of the giver: a side glance away, a nervous laugh or body language that spoke to her. This man was stood in front of her just as he was.

'I've just made coffee, want some?' he said. He ran his hands through his shaggy grey and white hair, kissed by the sun from countless seasons of gorgeous weather.

She followed him out the back, where a stove brewed a silver pot of the dark smoky liquid and he offered her a white plastic chair. Underwater photographs covered every wall and she guessed that Eric had dived most, if not all, of the sites depicted in them: bright fish, wrecks in blue waters, cold and murky deep dives and glorious coral dives somewhere exotic. He loved his sport.

'I'm sorry I'm not here under better circumstances, I'd love to be here for a dive,' she said, putting her bag next to her feet.

'You dive?' he asked.

'I trained here with the army, but I can't say I've kept my hours up, other stuff got in the way, but I have been out there on the *Zenobia* a few times,' she said.

He went quiet and concentrated on her coffee.

'Sugar?' he asked.

'Yes, please, and milk.'

He handed her a cup.

'I dived with Paul several times, he was competent,' he said.

He was straight to the point, and she appreciated it, and liked him more.

60

'I'm sorry. You knew him well?'

'Kind of. He was a good bloke, for an officer,' he laughed, but it was cut short by the poignancy of the moment.

She gave him a minute. He sat down with his own cup and pulled his chair closer to hers. He nursed his coffee between both hands and rested his elbows on his splayed knees. She reckoned he was at least fifty, but he was probably fitter than most twenty-year-olds.

'Can you tell me what happened on Wednesday?'

He nodded. He sat back and took a deep breath, sipping his coffee, then he looked at her and appealed to her in some deep and significant way that made her believe anything he was about to tell her. He was devastated and also felt guilty, that much she could tell by his demeanour only.

'I haven't been out since. I will do, but it's not right. Not now.'

She figured his attire was his usual garb for work and let him brace himself for his story.

'Paul had a day off. He lived on the other side of the island, on the RAF base, but he'd been working here recently and he was up against it, so he said. I gave him a freebie, I liked him. That day, I'd noticed somebody had booked in three navy guys who'd docked in Kyrenia for some leave time, and I said I could accommodate them. They were all well qualified and had all the correct paperwork, which they'd emailed to the office, and I was happy they'd be easy to show around. I buddied Paul up with the most experienced, and I took the other two.'

'Do you have their emails?'

'Of course, I've got it all ready for you.'

She waited. Her head screamed at her to jump in and ask a thousand questions about the three naval officers, but she waited patiently, sipping the lovely coffee. Hot drinks might not be the first choice of someone sitting ten yards from a beach in twenty-odd degrees, soon to be above thirty, but it was refreshingly surprising how good it was.

'The dive was pedestrian. The plan was straightforward, I'd gone over the dimensions and route electronically on my computer up here with them, and they were confident. There was nothing to suggest we might get into difficulty. It was quiet when we got out there. We descended, and scooted around the upper decks for a while, then we went round the back to enter the lower cargo decks.'

Helen nodded, it was all coming back to her.

'Paul and his buddy entered the engine room first, and I held back for a few minutes. It's tight in there. You can see the torchlight out of the cracks in the rusted metal, and they went off. All was going to plan, and the guys I took in satisfied me they knew what they were doing, but when I went in to the engine room myself, I found Paul's buddy panicking. He was all over the place, and I thought he was going to rip his DV out. I mean, I've never seen a soldier react like that, civilians, yes, but not soldiers. I followed Paul's line, to call the dive off, but found that he wasn't attached. There was no line to him, and I'd given him line.' Every time he repeated the word, he berated himself, Helen could tell.

Eric put his coffee down and held his head in his hands.

'But surely he would have attached it before entering?' Helen said.

'I know. What happened after that was so quick, one of them, I think Paul's buddy, found Paul, after swimming inside. It was too late. I was too late.'

Helen allowed him space. She instinctively wanted to go to him but held back. The inappropriateness of such a move prevented her from being simply a person listening to a tragedy. But she couldn't help herself. She leant over and touched his arm.

'I'm so sorry,' she said.

She waited for a moment.

'Paul's buddy,' she said.

Eric looked up and wiped his face. 'Yeah?'

'He was disoriented and confused, but then he swam inside and calmly found Paul?'

Eric's brow creased as he thought about what she'd said.

'Do you think it was an accident?' she asked.

'It all happened so fast. He'd run out of air, I checked his tanks myself. That should never have happened. I took him to the surface, but it was too late. Are you telling me it wasn't an accident?'

'And you'd never seen him panic before?' She dodged the direct question.

'Never. He was solid as a rock.'

'And was the line found?'

'I assumed the coastguard did that,' he said.

Helen knew that the body of Captain Thomas had been delivered to the mortuary without any safety lines at all, so either they'd been lost or taken by somebody.

'What about the three naval officers? I don't have any record of them being interviewed by the local police who were first on the scene,' she said.

The RMP had been handed the case after the preliminary reports had been filled out by Cyprus police. Because Paul was a military officer, the case had been handed straight to the sovereign base.

'They were in shock. They were allowed to leave after a few words. They're staying in the Palm Beach.'

'A few words?' she asked.

'That's what I thought. And I admit I went to find them. I had so many questions. But I couldn't contact them. It was just an almighty fuck-up and I've got to face that. It was my fault, I take full responsibility. He'd only ever buddied with me in the engine room. I shouldn't have let him out of my sight.'

'What do you mean you couldn't contact them?' she asked.

'Just that. The hotel said they couldn't confirm or deny their stay because of data protection. I've never heard anything more fucking stupid in my life, this island doesn't do rules. They'd been paid to keep quiet.'

'Really? You have evidence of that?'

'No, I just know the way things work around here. They're gone. I guarantee it. Wait, you think they had something to do with Paul's death?'

'I'm not ruling anything out. If they're serving naval personnel, I can trace them, regardless of if they've panicked and gone back to their ship.'

He looked at her and Helen waited as the enormity of her questions hit home.

'You don't think there is a ship, do you?' he asked.

Chapter 11

Helen returned to the waiting car and got in.

'Let's go to Akrotiri,' she said to Gem.

She watched as a small minibus of tourists pulled up outside Eric's and he went to greet them. He turned and waved at her and she waved back.

'What was that on the radio?' Helen asked.

'Farmers planning another strike on ESBA land, between here and Ayios Nikolaos.'

'They seem to be permanently encamped there. What's it about this time?'

'Anyone's guess, ma'am.'

They fell into silence and Helen thought about what Eric had told her about the three naval divers. A quick call back to London confirmed what she already suspected, that British Naval vessels had never docked in Kyrenia, but Eric might not know that. He'd served in the army twenty years ago, after all, and Turkey could well have made a deal with NATO by now for member states to access the northern ports, especially since the Syrian crisis had escalated. It was feasible, but Helen was sure that whatever story the three erroneous officers had spun Eric, it was a load of bollocks. She'd visit the Palm Beach later, on her way back to Dhekelia, but she already knew they'd be long gone, if they'd ever stayed there. The question was, how could she prove they'd ever existed apart from Eric's word? Eric's Dive School had no CCTV, and the patron wasn't in the habit of taking passport photocopies for ID. In time she'd process their names through the MOD, but she guessed that the three officers wouldn't exist.

What she did establish from it, though, if Paul had been sabotaged, and indeed murdered, then it confirmed that whatever he was doing when he'd investigated Ayios Nikolaos, it had ruffled feathers somewhere. The key was in his immaculate files, and she vowed to find it. He'd got close to something worth dying for. Only perhaps he hadn't known it.

Her visit to Akrotiri was to witness the man's autopsy at the military hospital there, but she'd also requested access to Captain Thomas's accommodation. In her experience, staying in multiple addresses for the duration of an investigation, she took anything sensitive with her wherever she stayed. She knew that Paul Thomas had flitted between Ayios Nikolaos and Akrotiri, depending on how late he worked. He was unmarried and therefore unaccompanied, and so he lived alone. If it was her investigating, she'd keep information pertinent to any finds close to her at all times, probably in her room, or her office. She'd been told that Paul's notes, in their entirety, were kept in the box room in Ayios Nikolaos, but perhaps they weren't and there were more in his two-bedroomed allocated quarter the other end of the island.

They approached the main gate of Akrotiri Sovereign Base Area, which had been manned by the British since 1959. Tall palm trees swayed in the breeze and they drove under the RAF heraldic motto of *Acra Semper Acria*: the peninsular is always ready. With security checks out of the way, they entered the base. This is where the Americans were stationed during the Gulf Wars, and where one of the most valuable runways in the world operated. It was a vital embarkation and refuelling point for allied forces, keeping a watchful eye on the Middle East. And heavily guarded. She could make out an American U2 spy plane on the tarmac, having already flown its mission. She knew this because its wings were being propped up by the tiny wheels that were attached after landing, when they were empty of fuel.

Her first stop was the hospital and she prepared herself not only for the chill of the mortuary, but the sight of Paul Thomas's lifeless body. She was here to ascertain what killed him, and then she could move forward with confidence that he had either genuinely got into difficulties, or foul play was suspected.

Helen was used to dealing with multiple agencies and the delays and frustrations that entailed, and part of her job was unpicking what each one had brought to the party. It would seem that Eric had called the local emergency services first, who'd responded with a coast guard ambulance. Paul had been pronounced dead, and then at some point, Eric had had the sense to alert the British military, who'd taken matters from there. Meanwhile, the three naval officers had vanished, promising to be available for interview, leaving Eric their details. The responding military personnel had at least had the wherewithal to transport Paul's body, along with his kit, to Dhekelia nursing station, from where it had been brought for examination.

She was to meet the surgeon tasked with the post-mortem operation and have a quick chat about his preliminary findings on the body. Eric said he'd checked the tanks, but Helen was interested in his dive watch. An unaccompanied officer in Cyprus for two years, keen on a water sport, would have spent money on toys for it, and she was hoping that he'd had the sense to buy a watch with a built-in computer, and if he had, that it was still on his wrist.

She was greeted by the surgeon and given an overall and offered a sweet-smelling oil to spread under her nose, which she accepted.

She followed him to the lift shaft and they descended into the basement of the hospital. Families attended this facility for operations, check-ups and births, so the last thing they wanted to see was signs to the mortuary. They were always well hidden in the bowels of any hospital.

The doctor was functional and got straight to it as he led her into a sterile room full of steel, where a body lay on the slab.

There was no introduction or warning, but she was used to it. Pathologists were a certain type and expected that everybody possessed a strong stomach, but seeing Paul like that made Helen pause. The surgeon didn't notice. She steadied herself and went over to the body, which had already been taken out of its bag. Paul's face was white and set in a look of sheer horror and Helen was taken back by the sight. She'd seen dead faces before, but his was a picture of panic and, in that moment, Helen realised that Paul's death had come quickly.

'Deep water sets rigor for longer,' the doctor said. 'It's the lack of bubbles in his blood. He died at about forty metres, and was brought up too quickly, but by then his organism, and all the matter in it, literally froze in time, including his face.'

'He was terrified,' she said.

The doctor nodded. 'Wouldn't you be if you ran out of air forty metres down?'

The body was fully naked, and Helen knew that his wetsuit would have had to be cut off, lest it raise the temperature of the remains, due to its insulating properties. She looked for a dive watch, but he didn't wear one, unless that had been removed too. His body had been kept in the chiller since Wednesday, and his skin, all over his body, was blueish. The rest of his equipment lay to the side and Helen looked at his buoyancy jacket and DV. The mouthpiece of the demand valve had been bitten off and Helen guessed that Paul had panicked when he ran out of air. No watch.

'I'll keep you informed as I go along, I assume you'll require a recording of my investigation for your case?' the doctor said.

'Thank you,' Helen replied.

'I've got a copy of his medical history, which is excellent, and his diving history, which is also exemplary. He'd never suffered any malfunction of equipment before, which might be informative. If this was his first case of kit failure, it could explain panic. The water conditions, I believe, were first-class, and local dangers were minimal. I'll be taking histology and toxicology specimens to rule out substance abuse prior to the dive. I'd like to point out, for your own information, that I've completed the army's underwater medicine course, and this is my fourth diving-related death I've examined.'

'You're well qualified,' Helen said.

'Fifty to eighty per cent of diving deaths are due to drowning,' he continued.

Helen could tell that the doctor was thorough and determined to log his every action, and it was refreshing to see that at least this part of her investigation was to be handled properly, with no vagaries.

'Of course, drowning might well be the cause of death, but I'm interested in what led to it, whether it be panic, fatigue, intoxication, or, of course, nitrogen narcosis. I've read the log, they descended at the appropriate intervals. I'm also looking for signs of other causes such as heart attack – myocardial infarction – and epilepsy. Certainly, over thirty metres, the amount of nitrogen in one's blood can impair intellectual and neuromuscular function. He wasn't ascending, so something happened when he was inside the engine room. I have no taste for it myself, I don't understand why somebody would want to go snooping into black spaces at that depth, it's not natural.'

'The same reason people skydive or rock climb,' Helen said.

The surgeon ignored her. 'He's not injured as far as I can see, so I'll be looking to rule that out.'

Helen looked at Paul's body. 'Has the equipment been tested?'

'Yes, it was done on site. The valves and tanks were working perfectly. Over fifty per cent of diving deaths at this depth are because the diver runs out of air unwittingly, because of poor practice.'

'You mean not checking?' Helen asked.

'Quite.'

'That seems highly unlikely with this man. I spoke to his buddy.'

'But he wasn't buddied with him on Wednesday, was he? It's possible the change in plan threw him and elevated his air consumption, surprising him.'

It was clear that the surgeon had read his notes in detail.

'I was told that his line wasn't attached to the bolt outside the engine room, the one commonly used by all divers who go in there. That seems strange, seeing as he'd done it before,' Helen noted.

'You're thinking of the three strangers? I know you'll want a wicked explanation for their actions, but my job is to search for the facts. People make mistakes pursuing dangerous sports, that's why they're dangerous.'

His tone was matter-of-fact and could have been taken as patronising, but Helen's experience of highly seasoned doctors was that they didn't much like their theories being challenged, precisely because they knew their shit. She watched him work.

'Was he wearing a dive watch?' she asked.

'Yes, it's downloading.'

Helen closed her eyes in a silent thank you.

'He had a CT scan within eight hours of death, which showed gas in the cerebral arteries and the left and right ventricles of the heart. Like I said, he was brought to the surface quickly, and so it's difficult to ascertain if the nitrogen bubbles are from that or narcosis at the bottom of the seabed. He also had significant pulmonary oedema fluid around his nose and mouth when he arrived here. It's gone now, as it does, but it's a classic sign of drowning.'

Helen watched as a stiff foam block was placed under Paul's back, to project the sternum up and out, and the surgeon took a scalpel from a tray, in preparation for his first incision. She braced herself for the first cut.

The noise of the electric saw cutting through Paul's chest wall reminded her of a welder's yard. But it was the crack of the ribs and the doctor pulling apart the body's armour, revealing the organs underneath, that made her gag, but nothing came up and she swallowed hard. The exertion of the surgeon muffled the sound.

He syringed fluid from Paul's heart and examined the other organs in situ, speaking in jargon Helen didn't follow. The complete report would be examined by experts back home, when his funeral arrangements were finalised and his body sent back to his family. They'd never know what state he'd been in on this table, and neither should they ever have to.

The operation was laborious, it wasn't as if the life of the patient was dependent upon time constraints, and the surgeon didn't rush, recording everything into his mic. An assistant tapped on a computer keypad and Helen watched as much as she could stomach. The doctor spent much time examining the neck and head, noting the present gases inside the arteries. Then he moved onto the lungs.

'Severe bruising impressions from the ribs,' the doctor said. 'Here we go.'

As the scalpel went into the left lung first, water spilled all over the gurney and was suctioned away along the gullies to waiting tubes.

The rest of the operation went by in a haze of alien Latin terminology, squelching and removal of lumps of flesh. Helen had seen enough and studied the notes she'd brought with her for just this reason: in case she couldn't cope. It wasn't the blood and guts, it was more the matter-of-fact way the doctor approached his work. It wasn't his fault, but the lack of humanity in his procedures always took her by surprise. Of course, anyone who believed in the sanctity of the human body wouldn't become a pathologist. He was simply good at his job.

He turned to her with bloody gloves and sighed. 'I think we can safely say he drowned. I'll have to wait for the histology and toxicology, of course, and I'm afraid there's no medical test for drowning, all I can do is examine the surrounding circumstances and the state of the body. That's what will be on my report.'

'Thank you, doctor,' Helen said, thankful to be given an opportunity to leave. 'May I see the results from his dive watch?'

'Of course, I'm interested to see them myself. Why don't I clean up, my assistant can finish here, and I'll join you in my office in ten minutes?'

Helen began removing her overalls and was shown by another assistant to an adjacent office, which still smelled of cold death. She couldn't imagine having to work in this grim, dark and lifeless place.

The computer on the desk flashed with light and she couldn't help going around the desk to have a peek. She was thankful that her assumption had been correct: Paul Thomas loved expensive kit, and a Shearwater Teric stared back at her, plugged in and downloading. It was air integrated and had been paired with Paul's regulator. It would tell them exactly where Paul was when he first began to run out of air, and how rapidly that occurred, as well as his movements after.

The doctor came in and sniffed quietly at her impertinence.

'Help yourself,' he said.

'Sorry, I couldn't help it. He was a friend of a friend,' she lied.

'I'm sorry about that, I hope my examination was sensitive. I like to think of my work as allowing the dead to give us their last communication in this world.'

'Quite. I see he had a fine dive watch,' she said.

'I know, it's an impressive piece of kit, isn't it? Let's have a look.'

Helen pulled up a chair and they sat side by side, examining the data. The doctor scrolled through the information and pointed out certain parameters indicating a normal dive, until they were near the end of the read-out.

'Well, well,' he said. 'Look.' He pointed to the screen. 'He's at forty metres and his air is still at 40 BAR.'

'That's enough to ascend. But it then drops to zero,' Helen noted. 'All the lines were intact?' she asked, referring to the air feed for the tanks. He nodded.

'At least, that's what the report said. So, either his DV was knocked out of his mouth or the tank was turned off.'

Chapter 12

Ani stretched and found herself entwined between Tom's legs. She often forgot where she was; it was an occupational hazard. She looked at him and felt nothing. Her body ached from performing last night, and then the exertions in Tom's bed. He was in love with her, she knew that much.

She lifted the covers gently, so as not to wake him, and went to the bathroom. The showers in the block were loud and Neanderthal; even worse than her hideous hovel above the strip club. They dripped pathetically, giving enough water to just about wash her face, but she desperately wanted to get rid of the oil and perfume on her skin. The ancient piping system in the British residence bubbled and gurned as she ran the stream of water to get above room temperature. If anyone else was running it at the same time, she had no chance, but the men didn't care, and this was an all-male block. She'd probably had sex with sixty per cent of them, but, bless Tom, he didn't mind. Love was surely blind, as they said in English.

She was already naked and stepped into the cubicle. The day was heating up and the water purified her soul, if there was anything left of it. The promise of work on the island had lured countless women like her away from Russia. Had she had a choice? She didn't dwell on it. She wasn't without wisdom and knew deep in her heart that adverts for girls, and the pressure they felt to do as they were told, would be warning signs for those more fortunate than her. Born into wealth, a young woman could almost choose her life plan, but for Ani, she chose money over toil. She didn't get much because she handed most of it to Theo, but she had a roof over her head and she got to sink her feet into foreign sand, and it was warm here, when she turned her face to the orange sun. It wasn't much, but it was something, and, besides, her master plan involved one more move.

She closed her eyes and soaped her hair with Tom's body wash. With the pitiful water pressure, she settled in for a long session, making every effort to get the soap out of her long black tresses before Tom woke up. She made him happy. She was good at it. He was easy to please. All she had to do was be a woman in his bed and a girl on his arm. He wanted a whore and a little sister all at the same time and she could manage it with little thought. He paid well and seemed not to be fazed every time Theo asked for more money for exclusive access to his favourite at the weekend.

She smelled bacon: it was the best breakfast on the island, in the Dhekelia officers' mess. Above the Blue Lantern, where she shared a room with ten other girls, they were given rationed tins and packets that gave some of them diarrhoea. It kept the weight off, that much was true. Some men preferred curvy girls, but Theo liked them to keep trim. She was allowed to go jogging occasionally along the shoreline, on her own, and each time she did, it was an escape into her dreams. She saw families sunbathing on loungers, at the fancy hotels, safe in their innocent naivety. These westerners had no idea what it was to be afraid every single day. Democracy was a word not bandied around too much at home. There, it was derided and ridiculed, as an Achilles heel of any strong regime. Why would any nation want to hand out scraps to those who didn't work, for nothing? Where was the incentive? But Ani wasn't interested in politics, all she cared about was living in a country that had no secret police, and what seemed to be a decent amount of accountability. In the UK, everyone said they were equal, it was a curious and mysterious concept, and she was fascinated to find out if it was real, or a big lie and people actually disappeared in the middle of the night, after all.

Her life could be worse. And it could be better. She didn't grumble much, but her heart yearned for more. And she knew she could give Tom what he wanted. She could produce babies, and keep him interested in the kitchen and the bedroom. Western women fooled themselves if they thought they were men's equals. Men were simple creatures, and it was much easier to make them feel as though they were getting what they wanted, rather than fight them. That way, the woman still ruled the world, and everything in it.

She saw it with girlfriends of soldiers here on the base. They nagged incessantly about what they expected, rather than just getting on with the fucking job at hand. They were weak and mollycoddled. That's why so many of the men came to the Blue Lantern, looking for simplicity in sex: their one basal requirement. Get a man's rocks off in the right way, and he ate out of your hands forever.

Ani relaxed in the warmth of the water. It fell in a weak but steady stream, over her tired body. For now, she had to do her job. Maybe one day, if Tom kept to his promises, she'd be able to slow down and just be a wife. That's all. It wasn't much to ask, or dream of. A wife in the UK, living free.

She turned off the taps and dried herself on a tiny army-issue towel. She kept meaning to buy Tom some large fluffy ones, but every time she thought about it, she realised that she needed to save the money. She wrapped the towel round her small body and another round her hair, and went back to Tom's room, sneaking in quietly, and taking a cigarette out of his trousers. She went to sit on the small balcony to smoke. It was the size of two chairs and looked towards the sea. She popped sunglasses over her eyes and sat down and lit up, sucking in the smoke satisfyingly.

She watched a lone swimmer crossing the bay of Dhekelia. It soothed her. She wished she could stay here forever, but, in reality she could only risk one night without raising the suspicions of Theo. It was true that Sundays at the Blue Lantern were slow, after the exertions of Fridays and Saturdays, but come Monday, she'd be required to start all over again. Young men, fit from training, and full of possibility, even after a skinful of alcohol, could still last all night and get up for work the next day. She rarely had a night off. Sometimes she had a woman and it was no less taxing. They were different: kind and gentle, but just as eager and energetic, and they lasted a lot longer, so Theo charged more. The swimmer reached the other side of the bay and stretched, preparing to get in again and swim back to his things on the shoreline.

'Hey, beautiful,' a voice said behind her.

She looked round and smiled. Tom had a cigarette in his mouth and he bent over for her to light it, and he took the other chair. He was totally naked and she examined his tight muscular body. The army boys were the easiest customers because they were up to the job, mostly. It was the older fatter tourists, on holiday with their mates, keeping secrets from wives, taking their time and making her sore, that challenged her. With Tom, it wasn't really work at all.

He kissed her.

'What are you looking at?' he asked.

'Just the sea,' she said.

'You're such a dreamer, Ani. Come on, let's get some bacon and then come back to bed. Stay with me all day? Go back tomorrow?'

It was so tempting. She'd never stayed over for two nights before. She noticed that he was semi-erect.

'You'll have to clear it with Theo,' she said.

'I can do that,' he replied, grinning. She finished her cigarette and reached over to stroke him. He sat back and placed his arms behind his head, after taking a last drag of his cigarette and stubbing it out. She let her towel fall and got up to straddle him, with her legs wrapped around his hips. He pulled the towel off her hair and held it so her neck arched back.

Ani wondered if the swimmer, making his way back over Dhekelia Bay could see the couple making love on the balcony.

How exciting and romantic it must seem: young lovers in their prime.

Tom held on to her hips, and she held onto his shoulders. With every bounce, Ani thought about how she might decorate each room, when they were married and living in an army house back in the UK: the colour of the curtains she would choose, and the flowers she'd plant in the garden. Perhaps they'd have a dog? Each thrust and every groan from Tom galvanised images in her head about the life she was going to have one day soon, and it made her hips move back and forth with enthusiastic gusto, driving Tom crazy.

'Oh, my God,' he gasped.

'Shut the fuck up!' someone shouted from a balcony below.

'Fuck off, Vic!' Tom cried. 'Jesus!' he added, as he came, and Ani slowed down, coming back to the present moment, away from the little semi-detached house in green and rainy England. She'd miss the sunshine, but that was nothing compared to the prize of freedom.

Chapter 13

Captain Thomas's accommodation was far superior to the quarters in the ESBA. Helen was let in by the families' officer, who was solemn. She took the opportunity to ask him about Paul.

'Paul was a super lad.' He used the affectionate address given to all males by a large number of serving personnel. It was disarming and told Helen that Paul was a well-thought-of individual. 'He did his work, minded nobody, and was always whistling some tune.' The man smiled and Helen reciprocated.

'I guess the CBF hand-chose him for the job?' she asked. She referred to the Commander of British Forces, Cyprus, who was a general stationed here in Akrotiri.

'Well, there was no one else, was there?' he asked.

She shrugged her shoulders. He could have requested SIB officers at any time, she thought, but it would all depend on his brief from Whitehall. Helen wasn't scheduled to meet with the general, as yet. She guessed it was because she was merely replacing like for like. Perhaps if she uncovered something she wasn't supposed to, then he might become interested in her.

'What's he like?' she asked.

'The general?' He sucked his teeth. 'A general, ma'am.'

She laughed.

He excused himself and left Helen to look around. She'd yet to receive official confirmation that Paul had been murdered, but the circumstances surrounding his death stank to high heaven.

His small quarter was well tended. The kitchen was neat and tidy and the living areas clean. It looked like the house of a single man who spent very little time here. In fact, from what Eric had told her, and what she'd managed to find out so far, Paul was a quiet man who had few hobbies. Everybody seemed to like him. From his service file, she'd also learned that he was a fine operator, which begged the question of what he'd been snooping into. This time, in his otherwise quiet life, it seemed he might have offended someone enough to be considered a threat, but who? Like Juliana said, and Helen agreed, there was always an active spy ring on this island. It was the meeting point of two worlds: East and West, and they despised each other. Had Paul crossed the sacrosanct line between nations and their right to observe one another? As far as his enquiries went, he'd only just begun to interview the four corporals at Ayios Nikolaos, and in one week, how could he have become such a nuisance?

Helen poked around in some drawers and spotted a briefcase next to a desk. For an investigating officer, it was a normal part of the furniture and contained their life's work. If Paul had a day off to go diving than it made sense that his briefcase was left at home. She checked the buckle. It was unlocked. She opened it and peered inside. This was a fellow officer's private space, and she felt somewhat disrespectful. It was also sovereign base territory, a slice of UK turf, so whatever Paul wanted to keep safe, of course he'd keep it here. No foreign nation in their right minds would send operatives into military bases abroad, it would cause an explosive international incident. Better shut him up than risk that. Her mind was wandering to what Juliana had said, and she was mindful not to be led by the lawyer. However, what she saw in his briefcase made the tiny hairs on her arms stand up straight.

There were photographs and passport details of prostitutes working in the strip clubs of Cyprus's main towns, from Larnaca and Limassol to Paphos and Ayia Napa. She concentrated on the ones around Larnaca, closest to the ESBA. The Blue Lantern seemed to be on Paul's mind, because he'd made a file for it, and it was fat with information. All of the girls who worked there had work visas stamped in Larnaca, and all were logged as contract workers such as singers and dancers, from the old states of the USSR.

In another file, she came across the notes made by a psychiatrist, flown in from the UK, assessing the mental states of the four corporals under house arrest for passing secrets to the Russians. Every time she said it, if only in her head, the idea sounded ludicrous, and she anticipated meeting the men, with Juliana present, in due course. She read that all four were deemed mentally robust and had emphatically denied all involvement in illegal activity in Ayios Nikolaos. All four came from fairly conventional working-class backgrounds, nothing pathologically striking had been noted. In other words, they weren't seen to be brazenly psychopathic liars, and none of them had erred from their original stories about what work they undertook at the listening station. The psychiatrist's conclusions were that the men were of sound mind, and healthy, and had not been subject to duress or unnecessary interrogation techniques during the inquiry. Essentially, they'd got nothing of note to add to the investigation. This must have frustrated Paul.

What the notes did say, though, was that each man, at some point, had used prostitutes at strip clubs along the Larnaca seafront, and a red flag had been raised by Colonel Seaton as to how these soldiers could be trusted in their posts when they were consorting with Russian sex workers, despite all four being married and accompanied by their spouses here in Cyprus. Helen found it odd that Colonel Seaton hadn't flagged this up before, if he'd been concerned, and why he'd left it until now to insinuate that four of his men were compromised by the honey trap.

Mata Hari jumped into Helen's head again. There was a huge question mark over her guilt, or if, in fact she was used as a scapegoat by the French to be seen as doing something to tackle a bigger problem, thus hiding their real agenda from the Germans. Maybe Helen wasn't looking for a Russian prostitute to be her Mata Hari after all, perhaps the four corporals were the fall guys here.

She packed the papers back into Paul's briefcase and took it with her. She glanced around one last time and went to the front door, closing it quietly behind her, and figured that it wouldn't be long before some family from the UK moved in.

Outside, the pretty houses reminded her of a street back home, with well-tended gardens and white fences around the edges of the properties. The paradox wasn't lost on her. She was stepping into an alien world, one that she wasn't sure she could get a handle on, just yet at least, and yet she could hear families down the street crying out in joy as they sprayed one another with water hoses. Dogs barked and a platoon of soldiers ran past in formation. It was a world away from home but felt just like it too.

Chapter 14

The Palm Beach Hotel on the Larnaca strip was the area's most expensive place to holiday. Helen had been there many times for military parties and the place was well run and comfortable. The huge entrance was adorned with marble and plants and led to the bar, adjacent to which was the pool area and, beyond that, a path to the sea and private beach. It was a fabulous place to visit, if one didn't happen to be investigating a murder.

Don Murton had confirmed that two SIB officers would be arriving on the island to aid her in the next few days. She updated him but held back on her conversation with Juliana Barnaby, after all, it was off the record. The SIB officers would be here midweek. In the meantime, she'd ascertained that the naval ship that was supposedly docked in Kyrenia didn't exist, and neither did the officers. But perhaps they'd stayed here at the Palm Beach, just under different names to the ones they'd given Eric Dukakis.

She showed her ID to the man on the front desk and asked to speak to the manager. Her capacity as British Military Police was endorsed by the local authorities when conducting enquiries pertinent to an investigation, and she could ask questions to anyone she wanted, within reason, and be left alone by local police, as long as their interests didn't overlap.

The young man looked uncertain and went to get the day manager. The woman was all suit and hair, and smiled graciously, outstretching her hand. Helen took it and it was ice cold, as was her stare.

'Can we talk privately?' Helen asked.

The woman asked to see her ID again and said she'd need to make a few phone calls before she complied with her request.

That was all right by Helen, who said she'd be in the bar. She took a high stool and ordered a mocktail. Families frolicked in the pool, playing softball, and bodies bronzed on beds positioned for the best light. Helen sipped her virgin strawberry daiquiri and checked her phone for messages.

The woman came over and handed Helen back her ID, beckoning her to follow her to an office.

'Bring your drink,' she said.

Helen slipped off her stool and followed the woman to an air-conditioned office behind the reception. She was offered a chair and sat down.

'How can I be of assistance?' the woman asked.

'It's simple, really,' Helen said, placing her daiquiri on the desk. 'We're looking for information about three guests who said they stayed here last week. These are the names.' Helen passed her a piece of paper and the woman jotted down the names. She tapped into her computer and shook her head.

'No, they didn't stay here.'

'Do you have live CCTV in the foyer?' Helen had clocked three cameras in the entrance, and she had detailed descriptions of the three men from Eric. He had also checked their dive logs and taken copies of their certificates, from BSAC. They'd turned out to be fake.

'Yes, we do. I can set it up for you for the time you need and let you look at it, I need to be elsewhere, if you don't mind.'

'Not at all, that'd be most helpful.'

The woman did as she said and beckoned Helen to take her seat in front of the computer. The footage started on Wednesday morning, when Paul was diving to his death, and Helen was free to scroll through at her leisure. When she was alone, she started the footage and watched as groups and individuals came and went. The cameras were positioned well, above the reception desks, and the footage clear. Helen was relieved and satisfied that if the men had been here, she'd see them.

Sure enough, three men, fitting Eric's description of the bogus sailors appeared on Wednesday evening, around six o'clock. Helen paused the video. She called Eric's mobile number, hoping he hadn't decided to dive today. He hadn't.

'Eric, can you pop down to the Palm Beach for me?'

'Sure. I can drive there now, where are you?' he asked.

'I'll meet you in the foyer.'

She hung up and continued to watch the reel of the men appearing to check in to the hotel and then make their way to the lift area, together. They were super confident and didn't show signs of being careful not to be caught on camera. In fact, one of them looked up to the monitor occasionally. Helen noted their lack of tattoos; something Eric had commented on as unusual for navy men. She agreed. Typically, the navy had always had looser attitudes to body art, given their histories of visiting far-flung cultures, where the practice was indulged by men on long voyages, with extended leave periods on land. As long as the images weren't offensive, or on the head. These three men had none. Sure, they styled themselves as officers, but even so, their arms and legs were pristine, as Eric had said. He'd only begun remembering details since Paul's death, not looking for anything unusual before. The mind had an amazing capacity to only focus on what it deemed important in the moment, and looking for tattoos on potential dive punters wasn't on Eric's mind on Wednesday. But after Paul's death, his mind set about reminding him of all sorts of details. Like their perfect English. Too perfect, Eric called it.

Her phone buzzed, telling her that Eric was in the foyer. She went to greet him and found herself pleased to see him again, so soon after their first meeting this morning. Then, the tragedy of Paul's death sat between them, laden with sadness and waste, but now, with Helen busy trying to get some answers, Eric was buoyed and eager to help. It was distracting him, she could tell.

He gave her a broad smile and she took him to the office.

'Are these your naval officers?' she asked.

He took her seat and looked at the screen. 'Yep, that's them, the bastards.'

'Right. So they were here, but under false names. Now I need to see if any of the staff remembers them and who they checked in under.'

'I can see where you're going with this,' he said. 'Why Paul? What had he done?'

'Nothing as far as I'm aware. He was working on a case here in Dhekelia, before his death, so I have to find out what was so sensitive about it,' she said, not giving anything away. Though this man had a way about him that made her want to trust him. She was close to his body and could smell his skin: it was clean and fresh, despite him practically living in the ocean.

Eric pointed to the man in the middle of the three. 'He killed Paul, I know it. You know too, don't you?' he asked her. 'He was Paul's buddy. I'll never forgive myself,' he said.

She stared at him, not willing to answer, not just because of her job, but also not to drag him in. 'When you said their English was too good, what exactly did you mean? Did you get any hint of an underlying accent?'

'Yes, I hear it a lot on the island because of the Russians,' he said. 'I don't mean to tar anyone with bad rep, but there's a huge business interest on this island. Cyprus is one of the few places in the world that allows foreigners to buy land without citizenship, it has meant that a lot of money from Russia has been laundered here, through casinos and the like, and is untraceable.'

'So what has that to do with the divers?' she asked. 'You never said that to me this morning, I mean about their accents.'

He looked down. 'I was embarrassed. I should have caught on to it straight away. They were good at distracting me, you know, they asked loads of technical questions. Paul fell for it too. I'd say they spoke with copybook English, but then every now and again I heard the throaty undertone of Slavic.'

'Professionals. Interesting,' she said.

'Just interesting? You don't share much, do you?'

'This is a military police investigation, my hands are tied.'

'Of course they are, like Paul's were. He didn't give much away either. Although he did show interest in the Russian strip clubs around here, and I'm not disparaging the dead, it was business.'

'What do you mean?' she asked.

Eric exhaled and looked out of the window. 'Let's go grab a coffee,' he said.

She looked around the office, then back to him. He raised his eyebrows. Helen knew he was suggesting that it wasn't perhaps the best idea to discuss sensitive issues in somebody else's office.

'Let me save these images, I want to send them back to the UK.'

Eric got up out of the chair as she copied the files to a USB and he studied the art on the walls. It wasn't fine or expensive, just cheap pictures to fill the space, but whoever worked in here had an affection for European cities. He leaned over the desk and whispered into her ear.

'Does the manager know you're doing that?'

She turned her head and their faces were within touching distance. She could hear his breath.

'Let's go,' she said. She grabbed her bag and they left the office, finding the manager at the reception desk. Helen thanked her.

The woman nodded curtly, staring at Eric, who smiled. She watched them leave and Eric shook his head.

'What's funny?' Helen asked, as they walked out into the bright sunshine.

'These hotels. They think they're exclusive havens for the well turned out, as if that has anything to do with character,' he said.

She glanced at his shorts, T-shirt, leather thongs and Ray-Bans.

'They have standards to upkeep,' she said. 'Where do you suggest we go?'

'Let's take a walk. I take it that's your driver? Is he going to shadow you everywhere?'

Gem was watching them from the car.

'I should hope so.'

'And have you questioned him?'

'Should I?'

'Well, they're glorified cabbies, aren't they? They see and hear everything. Maybe he's been used for other stuff.'

'What was your role in the army?' she asked. She'd only glanced at his file.

'Infantry. I know nothing,' he said.

She put her sunglasses down over her eyes and approached Gem's window.

'I'll be a couple of hours, if you want to head off?' she said.

'Right, ma'am.'

He stayed stationary.

'Ma'am?' he asked.

'Yes?'

'I've been told to stick with you. I can't risk you going off, I have to stick to orders,' he said.

'Whose orders?' she asked.

'Colonel Seaton, ma'am.'

'Right, well we're taking a walk, so you can follow me if you like,' she said. She left him with his dilemma and wondered why it was so important to the colonel to keep an eye on her movements. This wasn't exactly the Cold War. The thought irritated her. But then she remembered what Juliana had said about an armed chaperone.

They set off walking in the direction of Larnaca town and Gem inched behind them.

'This is ridiculous,' she said to Eric.

'You're being babysat,' Eric remarked.

'So, how well did you really know Paul, then?' she asked, trying to ignore her driver.

'We shared a few pints. He was dive mad and wanted to get better all the time, he was obsessed with his log. Between him and the navy guys, I trusted him the most, and that's why I thought he could keep an eye on one of them, despite their logs saying they had countless hours of experience.'

'Didn't you suspect any of these things when you met them?'

Eric hung his head as they walked. Spray from the sea lightly kissed Helen's skin, cooling her down.

'Paul was a confident guy. It was a lapse of judgement. That's why I'm thinking of selling up.'

'What? Really? Don't do that. If this was premeditated, then you could have done nothing. They would have got to him another way.'

'I've been taken for a fool. I should have refused to take them, without getting to know them first, or at least diving with them one time.'

'Then it might have been you who ran out of air,' she said.

'So it *was* on purpose? The fucking bastards. I knew it.'

Helen let her moment of unprofessionalism go. What could it hurt? A voice inside her head told her that she was jeopardising the whole mission, but then she needed all the allies she could get. Up until now, no one was opening up to her and she was finding the investigation like slowly ploughing through peanut butter. Eric had been transparent with her and wanted to help. Having him watch her back might not be a bad thing. Screw Colonel Seaton and his arrogant wife.

'If you're toying with the idea of selling up, what can it hurt to wait a few days and see how you feel? In the meantime, you can help me,' she said.

He looked at her and towards the sea. The sun was dipping in the sky and the beaches were still packed. 'Deal,' he said. 'What are you doing for the rest of the day?'

She shrugged her shoulders. 'I need to send the images to my boss and talk to him about what I've learned today.'

'It's been a rough one and you've already dug up something that might keep you here a while,' he said.

She smiled at him.

'I know a great meze place, it's the best. We can toast Paul. After tomorrow, the shit will hit the fan, do me a favour and take a load off with me.'

She looked at him. He was right. She'd discovered a great deal already and when working hours began in earnest again tomorrow, then she'd get little respite. Perhaps it would be fitting to sit with the last man Paul had enjoyed time with and toast his memory.

Chapter 15

The Russian Embassy in Nicosia, the capital of Cyprus, dominated a whole corner of real estate at the intersection between
the streets of Ayios Prokopios and Archbishop Makarios III.
The old Greek Orthodox clergyman had been Cyprus's first
president, and it was likely that he'd turn in his holy grave
if he was aware of the escalation in friendliness between the
two states on his island. Cyprus was undeniably one of Russia's
favourite playthings, with which to wind up NATO members,
but the influx of billions of dollars' worth of investments leaving
the island, ending up in the former Soviet Union, were in
fact hidden offshore capital gains and tax evasions channelled
through the Mediterranean state. Though, if he were still alive
and had to choose, Makarios would have probably nailed his
colours to the East rather than the West.

The great white building could be seen as a concrete
monstrosity from the air, but the entrance was classic and
elegant in style. The huge metal gates surrounding it were
freshly painted and the ambassador's residence was hidden
behind the façade of might. Tucked away from street view, the
huge palace-like building sat quietly and unassuming.

A large armoured, black E-Class Mercedes-Benz saloon
approached the gates and stopped at the barrier. Its paintwork
was immaculate and gleaming. Sentries on the gates saluted and
checked the driver's papers, glancing into the back seat, letting
them through. The barriers rose up like a dancer's arms and
allowed the sleek vehicle through, which glided silently into
the forecourt. The driver knew where he was going and pulled

slowly out of sight. Behind them, the barriers lowered and the sentries went back to their positions, holding their weapons against their chests and staring, unspeaking, at some distant point.

Behind the functioning embassy, the car slowed as it pulled into a courtyard. The driver stopped the car and got out of the vehicle to open the rear door to allow his wards out. The drive from Larnaca had taken only one hour, through city traffic. The air at this time of the year was chokingly hot and the haze from the Kyrenia Mountains hovered over the city. In the foothills, the Turkish flag, the size of four football stadiums, painted onto rocks on the hillside, and visible from space, announcing Turkish dominance and victory, was deliberately provocative. It was painted by a bunch of patriots in the eighties and served to remind every Nicosia resident of the Cypriot south that the Turks were here to stay. Minarets of Islam pierced the line of sight and were a constant reminder of the war, long finished but rumbling on through the rubble of Nicosia's Green Line. Inside the car, the air conditioning kept the men cool and unfazed by the taunting. The war was long gone and no concern of Russia, but it was a cool tourist attraction.

The driver stood back as three men stepped out of the vehicle, one by one. They each peered up at the clean façade of the ambassador's residence. Their luggage would shortly follow them, arranged by the driver, but, for now, they were to meet with Secretary Dimitri Bugov, and take tea.

None of the men spoke. They were shown into an airy reception area and asked to wait. They stood and didn't look at one another. They looked around and took in the opulence of the place. A huge sweeping staircase dominated the space, and a domestic maid walked down it, surprised by the men, but keeping to herself. They were indeed a sight to behold, each the size of a competing bodybuilder. No clothes could have disguised the condition of their bodies, which rippled with muscles and bulges in places where mere mortals didn't have them. The maid blushed and scuttled away.

A man in a military uniform ushered the men into a doorway, and they filed in, one by one, because there was no other way they'd fit. The door was slammed shut. On the other side of it, Secretary Bugov leant against a grand desk. He beckoned them to sit. Three chairs had already been laid out and a silver tray had been set on the small table, on it was a teapot, sugar and cups, with a milk jug.

'Tea?' Secretary Bugov said.

The men declined.

'It's not poison.' He laughed. 'Though you have disappointed me. No matter. This afternoon, you will board a plane to Moscow from Larnaca. And from there, you'll report to the service, giving a full report as to why you chose to expose yourselves in such an amateur fashion.' He threw photos down on the floor and the men peered at them. They stared at their own images, and worked out that they were taken from inside the Palm Beach Hotel foyer. 'The British are trying to find you.'

Secretary Bugov sat down behind his desk and put his feet up on the table.

'You stand out too much anyway. We have work for you back home. Here,' he said, pushing three Russian passports towards them. 'Learn your names, don't sit together, and wear jackets.' Secretary Bugov glanced disapprovingly at the breadth of the men's shoulders.

The three men nodded and the door behind them opened once more, allowing them out into the hall, where they still dared not communicate with each other. The door closed behind them.

—

Secretary Bugov got up from his desk and walked towards the photos he'd strewn on the floor. But it was the photograph of a woman he was more taken by. Recently arrived on the island, to replace the unfortunately deceased army captain, the major was a different ballgame. They knew from their intelligence sources in London that the woman had been drafted in specially to tackle British leaks in their intelligence services, but also to investigate the death of one of their own.

He sighed. He'd have to handle this one differently. He didn't want to draw too much attention. A little was acceptable, and the captain's death had been made to look like an accident, despite the sloppiness of his operatives, but to have his replacement end up at the bottom of the ocean, without air, as well, was another matter entirely, and was too risky.

This one required some thought.

Chapter 16

'Morning,' Helen said cheerily to a fellow officer, as they queued for breakfast. Waking up by the sea, to blue sky and wafting curtains seemed to make Monday morning more palatable. It was going to be a busy week, and she decided to take full advantage of the spread on offer. During the summer heat, hours were short and the day started early.

Eric had been true to his word; the restaurant he'd taken her to last night served the best meze she'd ever eaten. It had also given her some time to think before the stack of things she had to do today and could only get done during the working week. It was one thing working all hours in London, but that didn't happen here on *Mañana* Island. She was in a good mood. Eric had told her about his days in the army and why he left, and she'd told him about her rise through the ranks. She'd ordered Gem not to follow her. She'd drunk local wine. They'd chatted about Paul, and he'd told her about the Blue Lantern. It was a favourite hang-out for officers, and Paul knew it.

Her reverie was rudely ended by the grumpy officer. He smiled unconvincingly and muttered a good morning back.

The food on offer was a standard army breakfast: everything fried and lathered with sauce. She spied a token bowl of fruit and chose a few slices of bacon and some strawberries to go with it, and poured over some maple syrup. The chef was cooking American pancakes to order and she took one, as well as a small packet of butter. She put her breakfast down at the long mahogany mess table and went to get tea and a newspaper.

The young officer, Tom Fleet, appeared and smiled at her.

'Morning,' he said breezily. He wore a light brown uniform, and it was well pressed. His shoes were immaculate, as befitting an officer of the British Army. But his eyes looked blurry.

'Good weekend?' she asked.

'Superb, thank you,' he replied.

Helen smiled to herself remembering the outrageous nights out she'd enjoyed on the island with soldiers and officers alike. Back then, she'd had the energy to drink until four a.m. and still get up and do a battle fitness test at six. She watched Tom fill up two plates and reckoned he had a woman in his bed: good on him, and why not? She'd sneaked plenty of men into accommodation blocks over the years.

'So where did you go?' she asked. 'Back in the day it was Boogeez, along the strip,' she said.

'Back in the day? You're not past it, you should come out with us next weekend,' he suggested.

Helen noted that Tom had a cheeky, charming sliver of risk in his eyes and he looked to her like a good-time boy.

'If I'm still here, I might take you up on it, if you don't mind me tagging along.'

'Sure, the strip is banging now, so any night you have free, give me a shout,' he said.

He reminded her of a younger Grant: all deep eyes and swagger. He piled extra bacon and sausages onto the plates. She thought she'd get to know him better before asking him if he frequented the Blue Lantern.

'Hungry?' she asked, glancing at the two plates.

He laughed. 'Yeah,' he said.

Another officer joined them in the line for tea and Helen smiled at him. It was the sullen one from the line she'd just been in.

'Mate, you missed an epic night,' the officer said to Tom, ignoring Helen.

Tom turned to her and introduced him as Victor. She apologised for having her hands full, and nodded hello. He turned away rudely, for the second time.

'Mrs Fleet join you, brother?' Vic said.

'Fuck off,' Tom said to Vic. 'Excuse my language,' he said to Helen.

She hung around the conversation, pretending to stir her tea.

'What? I thought you two were getting married and living happily ever after, after you get her a passport,' Vic said.

Tom blushed and put cups on his tray. Helen watched Victor titter to himself and sidle off to get more milk. She sat down and watched Tom disappear out into the hall and upstairs to whoever was in his bed on a Monday morning. It was none of her business, but it sounded to her as if Tom had got himself into a bit of a love pickle, and it was spilling over into work days. She also thought Vic was an arsehole, but even arseholes can be useful when you need to take a shit.

Breakfast was fairly leisurely and she chatted amicably to a few officers who weren't intimidated by her RMP role. She figured if you had nothing to hide, then the RMP snooping around didn't bother many, but the banter was legendary. She wasn't really a threat to anyone here, but for some reason, Victor continued to treat her with disdain.

She took her dirty pots to a rack and placed her tray inside, and left, going back to her room. She'd arranged to pay a visit to the soldiers who'd been suspended during Paul Thomas's enquiries. They had nothing else to do and were confined to their homes, guarded by sovereign base police. Her conversation with Eric yesterday stayed in her head, and she'd sent off the images of the three men who'd dived with Paul back to the UK.

It was still quite early, but the barracks was already busy, she heard lorries outside and the rumble of vehicles come and go. Men and women in various uniforms scuttled around and the business of the barracks had commenced again. Once more, she wore civilian clothes, and she wondered if that's what put off the officer called Vic: perhaps he couldn't take anyone seriously when they were out of uniform. Or maybe he was just a knobhead.

Eric was spending his time at the dive school today, trying to trace the bogus navy men's movements before their scheduled dive with him. He was going to check with all members of his staff. It was a focus for him, until he sorted his head out and decided what he was going to do. He could let the tragedy make him buckle and give up, or he could accept it wasn't his fault, that he was duped, and carry on stronger than before. It was all in people's mindset.

But Helen felt good that she had an ally; it made her task less lonely. Of course, military investigations were generally solitary pursuits, because of their nature, but having someone on her side was a good thing and she decided to make the most of it. Eric was a good guy. He was also easy company.

—

The now familiar journey to the listening station was short and bleak. The scrubland between Dhekelia and its ward was desolate and hot. As they left the base, Helen saw up ahead a long row of tractors blocking the way back. Gem tutted.

'What are they protesting about today?' she asked. It was becoming a familiar part of her day.

'Potatoes from the north being imported when theirs lay rotting,' he said.

'Fair enough,' she replied.

She put her window down and leant out, as they passed. The men on their vehicles were jovial and waved to her. They seemed more like a group of lads on a day out to get away from their wives, rather than serious protesters. Their banners read slogans in Greek and English, demanding various concessions from the Cypriot government and the British ESBA.

'How many strikes have there been along this road in the last month, Gem?' she asked.

'About four, I'd say.'

She googled the protests and read the articles in the *Cyprus Mail*; the paper that reported all the details of the disturbances.

One date caught her attention because it was the same date that the intelligence in Paul's files reported that an important target in Syria was to be taken out. It was also part of the background that Colonel Don Murton had given her. Special Forces had been working for years on the ground in Syria to track Labib Hassan, and a meeting of arms dealers loyal to Assad had been taken out by US precision bombers only three weeks ago, but Labib had escaped. Again. The man's name kept popping up; he seemed like a cat with nine lives. The most recent one was just last week and this coincided with another close escape by Hassan, according to Don. She didn't like coincidences.

Once they arrived in Ayios Nikolaos, Helen directed Gem to the address of one of the four Intelligence Corps soldiers who'd been working on the nights, and days, preceding the moment the same target in Aleppo had escaped with his life: Labib Hassan. It had been a confidential and highly sensitive mission on the ground, led by US and UK Special Forces. They'd had eyes on the arms dealer since 2011, and the outbreak of civil war there, when Assad's government forces cracked down on citizens, excited by the Arab Spring, and waged war on the president. The conflict had turned into one of proxy, with Russia propping up the government, and the UK and the West supplying the rebels, as much as they dared, for fear of kit landing in ISIS hands.

She made her way to the home of Lance Corporal Rob Trotter, one of the four soldiers accused of passing intelligence to a foreign source. In the army, with that surname, she expected his mates to call him Oink or Rodney, but the fleeting thought of banter was short-lived as she knocked on the door.

He answered promptly and invited her in. He was expecting her.

She was shown into a small lounge, where children's toys littered every available space. Juliana Barnaby was sat in an armchair. They acknowledged one another.

The soldier's wife appeared from the kitchen and offered her a drink. Helen asked for a cup of tea.

'Builder's all right?' the wife asked.

'Of course,' Helen responded.

She settled into a chair and Lance Corporal Trotter took the other one, either side of the army issued electric fire. The quarter was decorated in magnolia paint, as standard, but adorned with personal items to make it as individual as possible, such as brightly coloured cushions, ornaments and framed photos.

She could tell that he was nervous, like anyone would be when interviewed by the police, but she hoped her lack of uniform and formality would relax him a little. The presence of his lawyer should also calm his nerves.

'Do you mind if I call you Rob?' Helen asked.

He looked at her uneasily and nodded. 'Sure.'

'Sorry to barge in on you like this. I'm here, as I'm sure you're aware, to continue the investigation of Captain Thomas.'

'Terrible what happened to him.'

'I always said to Rob it was daft diving, why go all that way under when we're not fish?' Rob's wife said, coming in with tea and giving her input into Paul Thomas's demise.

'I'm a diver,' Helen said. 'Tragedies like this are thankfully rare,' she added. 'Could I speak to you alone, first, Rob? And then I'll see your wife,' she said.

Rob looked at Juliana, who nodded.

'Hold on a minute,' the wife began.

'Shannon, give us a minute, for God's sake,' Rob spat at his wife.

She shot him a look as if to say he'd be in for it later.

'Hope you choke on your tea,' she muttered as she disappeared.

Helen was about to sip from the cup but decided against it.

'Shannon!' Rob said to her back as she slammed the door.

'Don't worry, I get it all the time. Has she something against me or Captain Thomas, or just the RMP in general?' Helen asked.

'She's, erm, tired. The baby's been up all night. That's her screaming now.'

Sure enough, Helen heard a baby cry and realised that they were under much pressure, cooped up in this small house, the whole world and its auntie thinking them guilty as hell, with only a twenty-five-year-old rookie lawyer from London on their side.

'So, I'll try to keep this brief. I see you were interviewed by Captain Thomas on three occasions and I have a transcript of them with me. I'm sorry if it's old ground to you. I've been going over them and I've got a few questions. I see Shannon was interviewed only once.'

'Well, she's got nothing to do with my job,' Rob said.

'Do you talk about what you do? In my experience, partners sound off to one another, and you work long hours, it must be hard with a young family.'

'I'm not allowed to talk about what I do,' he said.

'That's not what I asked. People talk. Especially people who live together and trust one another.'

'I told Captain Thomas everything.'

'So, tell me everything. It says here that you worked for six consecutive days up to, and including, this date,' Helen said. She showed him the report, including the dates, so he could see in black and white.

'Yep.'

'And you had a total of seven-hundred-and-thirty-three incidents of elevated communications status in that time.' Helen referred to the flagging up of sensitive information that was scrutinised further, as per the terms of the listening station's operational procedures.

'I don't count,' he said.

'Out of those seven-hundred-and-thirty-three, nine were passed on by yourself, to your unit manager. You're already aware that these nine communications were sensitive and now the focus of a breach of information. How do you explain that?'

She stared at her tea, desperate for a sip, but not trusting what Shannon might have slipped in there, sure it was bodily fluids of some sort.

'Like I told Captain Thomas, I passed on the information and thought that was it. That's my job. That's the thing isn't it with investigations like this? You always go for the small fry. How do you know the information wasn't passed on at a higher level?'

She acknowledged the question but ploughed on. 'So exactly how many people did you forward the information to, and I'm only interested in the nine reports.'

'I gave my outbox details to Captain Thomas. The initial findings go to my line manager, then the colonel is alerted and makes the final decision. After that, it's down to whoever sits behind a desk in London and collates all this stuff.'

Helen was well aware that sensitive information, and recordings of conversations that fell under this title, went through dozens of eyes before it reached MI6, if it was elevated that far. But that wasn't the point. The emails used were all encrypted and top secret. If anything had been leaked from Ayios Nikolaos, it had been through verbal means, and that meant someone on the island. There were simply too many breaches, happening too consistently, and too quickly, for it to be anyone back home, whose every move was monitored electronically. The guys out here sat in offices not protected by bulletproof glass because they weren't supposed to know how to join the dots and make sense of any of it. And it had been coordinates that had been leaked, not official secrets.

'Do you have any contact with anyone not military, or not a UK national, here on the island, who you've met recently?'

'Like a spy?' Rob smiled. He became serious when Juliana coughed and he looked at her. Again she nodded.

Helen's face didn't move. She watched Rob. He fidgeted and blinked too much. He looked like he'd sell his granny for a packet of smokes, but she had to stay neutral, for now.

'Yes, like a spy,' she said. 'They come in all guises, such as shopkeepers, speedboat owners, waiters, cleaners and women selling sex.' He blushed and looked at his hands.

'Captain Thomas noted that you frequented several bars along the strip known for supplying working girls. Everybody likes a bit of fun, but any of them seem more than a little interested in your job?'

'No.' His voice had lowered to a whisper, which was confirmation in Helen's book that he'd been a naughty boy.

'Get any freebies?' Helen asked.

'No.' His neck flushed.

'So, the reports that you met and had sex with this particular prostitute on the dates logged by Captain Thomas were never used against you to put you under duress to leak intelligence from Ayios Nikolaos listening station?' She showed him a photograph of the woman in question, from Paul Thomas's file. She'd already worked out that the Blue Lantern was frequented by officers. The one in question, visited by soldiers, was the one she referred to here.

'No.'

Juliana stepped in. 'My client will give you the same answers he gave to Captain Thomas, Major Scott. And the reason I believe him is that during the run-up to the leaked information you are investigating, Corporal Trotter's work was severely interrupted by the farmers' strike. So much so, that Ayios Nikolaos was temporarily closed because of a security threat from a group of insurgents getting overexcited about potato crops. My client couldn't have been privy to the information he's accused of passing on, because the station was closed.'

'It could have easily been passed on before the event,' Helen said.

'Time wise, it's pushing it; in fact, I have several expert analysts willing to testify to the discrepancy of this. My client simply didn't know enough to join the dots and deliver reasonable intelligence in the time frame you're suggesting.'

Helen looked at her paperwork and realised that Juliana had a point.

She spent the rest of the interview getting Corporal Trotter to confirm the identity of the prostitutes he slept with, from their passport data accumulated by Paul. But something didn't fit. This man might have been compromised, as per his security screening, but the question she was here to answer was if he could have passed complete intelligence to the enemy, and Juliana's argument would be difficult to counter in any court.

'I'll see your wife now,' Helen said.

Rob stood up and couldn't wait to get to the door. She heard whispers in the hallway, before Shannon came in with a little girl on her hip; she wasn't a baby at all, maybe two years old. She was red-faced and angry, and Helen wondered if she could ever cope with having one attached to her. The girl slapped her mother's face and Shannon lost her temper, tearing into her daughter.

'Fuck's sake, you little cow!'

Helen glanced at Juliana, who looked embarrassed. Helen wanted to do something, but she had no idea what. She smiled hard at the little girl, hoping to calm her so she didn't annoy her mother further.

Shannon plopped herself down on the couch and put the girl on the floor, where she shuffled over to Helen and busied herself with Helen's bag.

'Can you make this quick?' Shannon said.

'Your husband bought you any nice gifts recently, for the child? Or for the house? I see you've got some lovely photos of Greece on the wall, did you visit?'

Helen kept an eye on the girl, who fiddled happily with the zips on her bag.

'We did. I need a holiday once a week at this rate. He's always buying stuff. He bought a fucking windsurf last week, I told him what you want a fucking windsurf for? But he did it anyway.'

'I love Greece,' Helen said. 'Is it cheaper these days? I thought the euro bumped up prices?'

'I don't know, Rob sorts it.'

'That's a nice necklace,' Helen said, admiring Shannon's décolletage.

'Thanks,' Shannon replied.

'Is it a diamond?'

'Yeah. Well, that's what Rob told me anyway.'

Juliana jumped in. 'I know where you're going with this, Major Scott, I have the Trotters' bank accounts for the last two years, all showing they saved up to buy their treats.'

Shannon looked at Juliana and back to Helen.

'Bitch,' she said. Helen took it on the chin, and Juliana smiled sweetly.

'Mama!' the girl said.

'Was it a surprise?' Helen pressed.

'What the necklace or the kid?' Shannon said.

'The necklace,' Helen replied.

'Yeah, he does that after he fucks someone.'

'That happens a lot, then,' Helen said, not expecting an answer, and not getting one. 'And do you work?'

'Are you fucking kidding? Do you think I've got time?'

'Where's that?' Helen asked, moving on, pointing to a photo of Rob laughing on a yacht somewhere off a coastline.

Shannon paused. 'Erm, it's a friend's of his, I think. He has loads of cash and splashes it around. He parked his fancy boat in Limassol harbour and took Rob out. I wasn't invited.'

Juliana looked uncomfortable. Helen realised that the lawyer noted Shannon's error: she hadn't expected the RMP's attention to detail around the family home. Silly really, Helen noticed everything.

'Who took the photo?' Helen asked.

'I have no idea,' Shannon said.

'And it didn't bother you that there's probably four girls in the background. You're more trusting than me, I guess,' Helen said.

Shannon glared at her. 'I know what you're trying to do, I'm not stupid, but you've got it so badly wrong, it's a joke. Rob works hard, he saves loads of money, we rent this place for a hundred quid a month, and we brought money with us, we don't need it from anywhere else, and we've turned it down,' she said proudly.

Juliana sighed. 'Shannon, I advise you to say no more.'

'So, where were you offered it?' Helen asked.

'Shannon, we need to talk,' Juliana said.

'What were you offered, Shannon?' Helen said.

'Fuck him,' Shannon said to Juliana, turning to Helen. 'At the Palm Beach, by some slimy Greek.'

'Shannon,' Juliana tried to stop her.

'Did you get his name?'

'Slimy Greek? I don't fucking know. Take your pick, Stavros?'

Chapter 17

The next three quarters visited by Helen, and accompanied by Juliana, played out exactly the same scenarios she'd witnessed at Rob Trotter's house. They were young men, average to lower rank, new babies, or at least very young children, tight-lipped and armed with innocent replies to simple questions, and evidence of a level of home comforts that Helen couldn't afford on her own, on a better salary. She also met their angry wives, ready to explode not just with the confinement but the fact that their husbands had been visiting prostitutes. But Helen still couldn't work out if the men were simply morally questionable or traitors. It was all so convenient.

She had no doubt that each time she left a house to visit the next one, the previous interviewee was on the phone, informing their pal what had been said. Each time, she declined tea.

She knew that their reticent behaviour could be explained away by nerves and the invasion of privacy, as well as their access to luxury holidays and treats by a higher disposable income on foreign tours. A soldier's salary was bolstered by low rent and no utility bills abroad, and that was why postings such as Germany and Cyprus were popular. They were an opportunity to save money, and spend it. A lot of young men bought tax-free cars with bigger engines than they'd be able to afford in the UK. The popularity of the Subaru Impreza was a fine example. However, until she found solid evidence to either let them go or charge them, in which case they'd be flown back to the UK for trial, they'd remain under house arrest.

When questioned about Captain Paul Thomas's enquiries, they all showed a disdain that, to her, seemed off balance. It was as if none of them accepted that the investigation by the RMP was simply a matter of course; they showed signs of being offended, more so when she mentioned Paul's death. His body had been repatriated, this morning, to his parents back home in the UK. The histology and toxicology reports, as well as those more detailed pathological findings on his organs, would take more time, but could be done with his bits sewn back into him, to make him look presentable for his mother and father. The coroner had everything he needed to follow up on Paul's organic matter. The family had been told that his death was an accident.

The four soldiers remained suspended, on full pay, until it was determined if they were to be court-martialled or not. Now, her next task was to visit the current analysts at Ayios Nikolaos and see what they were up to: what were their practices? Did Colonel Seaton run a tight ship? Or was he lackadaisical? The *mañana* attitude was common here on the sunshine island, where the heat slowed everything and the local habit of taking siestas eventually infiltrated people's moods.

After several taxing conversations, Helen fancied a walk and declined Juliana's offer to accompany her. She made her way back to the station, telling Gem he could have a break. He declined, and drove slowly behind her. It made her uncomfortable and she wondered if he reported her every move to Colonel Seaton. She pushed the thoughts away and allowed the breeze, though hot, to waft her clothes.

The closer she got to the offices of the station, the shrubs and plants were better kept, with sprinkler systems and gorgeous indigenous palms and aloe vera sprouting everywhere. It was a full-time job and she nodded greetings to gardeners, who stared at the woman being followed by a big black car.

'You want to get in yet, ma'am?'

'No, thanks, Gem. I'm good.'

She found the building that housed the analysts and looked for a door with JSSU Station Room 3 on it. It was locked, as she expected. She knocked lightly. There was a short wait until somebody finally opened it and held it for her, without asking for her ID or even who she was. She wasn't in uniform, nor was she known here. The young soldier smiled and stood aside.

'Thank you, is this where I'll find Corporal Danny Hewitt?' she asked.

'Ah, that's me. Can I help?'

'Major Scott,' she said. She showed him her ID.

His eyes widened and he saluted, straightening his body. 'Sorry, ma'am, I expected...'

'A uniform?' she asked.

He nodded.

'Don't worry, but may I point out that you should check strangers before inviting them into your workspace?' she said.

'Yes, ma'am,' he said, saluting again, clicking his boots together.

'At ease, soldier. You can drop the formality. Danny, it's good to meet you, can I have a word?'

'Yes, ma'am.' He couldn't help himself, but at least it was a refreshing change from the soldiers this morning who'd treated her like some imposter. Helen didn't insist upon the recognition of her rank, but the four men had completely ignored it. Gone were the days when wives must pay deference to senior ranks, but a lot of them still did it, out of respect. She wasn't naive enough to believe that rank pulled in esteem as a matter of course: one earned it. However, Corporal Hewitt's actions stood out in glaring technicolour compared.

'Do you want to show me where it all happens?' she asked.

He took her inside, and her eyes took a moment to adjust to the darkness. The room was spacious but still seemed cramped and it was because of the stark contrast of the sunlight outside. People sat behind screens with headphones on and focused on their jobs.

Danny showed her to his desk and explained how everything worked.

'And these are the notifications from today?'

He nodded. 'These are the signals of interest that I've logged this morning,' he said.

'Anything interesting?' she asked.

'There's been a fair amount of interesting stuff coming out of Syria.'

'Isn't there always?' she asked.

'Bang on, ma'am.'

'But something unusual today?'

'Not just today, for a few weeks now, so I'm told. I've replaced…'

'I know. I appreciate you're filling in. What do you normally do, Danny?'

'I was on a desk, processing data, it was like an analyst's job, but I wasn't logging the live signals coming in,' he said.

'So, a promotion? Exciting,' she said.

He smiled. He had a warm, engaging face. His arms were tanned up to where he'd rolled up his combat shirt: the squaddie tan. She could see tattoos poking out from under his sleeves. He stood peering over the chair at the screen and showed her what the various bleeps and dials did. She'd had a little signals training, but she was usually on the business end of intelligence: that was in the field blowing targets up, rather than in the small cocoon of the office where it all started. It fascinated her.

'Labib Hassan?'

'Yes, ma'am.'

She appreciated that Danny's ingrained habit of addressing senior ranks was part of who he was and it was actually endearing. He didn't seem to have an agenda based on his ego, and she liked that.

'So, where was Corporal Trotter's desk?'

'This is it, ma'am,' he said.

She nodded.

'Have you been told how long you'll be required?' she asked.

'No, ma'am.'

'Sit down, Danny, let's see you in action. Have you got a spare set of headphones and a chair?' she asked.

Danny was more than willing to accommodate her and seemed to enjoy taking her through the nuts and bolts of what he did. She watched him and listened. She heard languages that she recognised as originating in the ancient lands of Persia and Iraq, but she couldn't have discerned any more detail than that. He turned to her occasionally and explained what he was doing. It gave her a feel for what happened in here, and exactly how the information travelled from the mobile handsets of persons of interest, through the air waves, and ended up being monitored and put into some kind of order of importance.

'What's that?' she asked. She was listening to a heated exchange between two male voices.

'They're bartering over chickens,' Danny said. They both laughed.

'I take it it's a prerequisite here that all analysts have talents in the local languages and dialects?'

Corporal Trotter hadn't struck her as an academic, but she chided herself for judging so harshly.

Danny nodded. 'I studied Arabic and Kurdish at Beaconsfield,' he told her.

'You obviously have a gift.'

Danny smiled again.

'Wait,' he said. 'I just need to concentrate on this one.'

She watched him flick buttons and he seemed to be recording. He also wrote down coordinates and the date and time. He listened intently. She saw him attach a code to the conversation and send it somewhere. She didn't want to interrupt him mid-task and waited until he was done. He removed his headphones and explained that the conversation was recording live and would end only when one of them hung up.

'Where is it coming from?'

'A market in Raqqa. The other end is in Turkey.'

Turkey was supposed to be a British ally, but like any intelligent player at a game of poker, the Republic shared their time and effort between those who were beneficial to state interests, as was their prerogative. That's what Helen would do. If she had neighbours like Turkey had, she'd also hedge her bets. They weren't European, neither were they strictly Middle Eastern, and acted as a conduit for international relations, in the meantime keeping their own borders and interests safe. No one argued with them.

But this could be interesting. She was happy she'd come to see Danny Hewitt. He didn't seem to be hiding anything, and if he was, he'd have to have a replica room like this one, set up in secret, and flit between them like a master manipulator. She saw an opportunity and asked him what was going on.

'It's an arms deal.'

'Really?'

He nodded. 'Most of them are completely legal, but we need to check.'

She let him do his job and watched him with interest, noting that he dealt with pieces of a puzzle, not the whole jigsaw. The call ended.

'So, when you record a conversation, where does it go then?' she asked.

'To a desk coordinator in the colonel's office. They make the call on escalation or not,' he said. 'The other day, in fact it was Friday, I had Hassan himself on the line.' His voice fell to a whisper and Helen realised the seriousness of listening to such conversations, and what it meant to the western allies. Danny took his job seriously. She noticed his leg tap and his hand go to his pocket, where she saw a packet of Camels poking out. The poor sod was on his way out for a cigarette break when she appeared.

'Fancy a break?' she said. 'I could murder a coffee.'

He pushed back his chair and escorted her outside.

'I don't mind if you smoke,' she said. 'As long as you find me a coffee when you're done.'

He smiled at her and lit up a cigarette, offering her one, which she declined.

'So, who is the desk coordinator?' she asked.

'My encrypted emails go over to the colonel's office, and Major Graham collates them. He's our group commander and the operations officer for the colonel.'

'The second in command?' It was the man she'd met outside the colonel's office when she'd first arrived.

He nodded.

'So, have you had a chance to explore a bit?' he asked, puffing smoke.

'Unfortunately, I've been working. It's hopefully a short visit. I came to take over where Captain Thomas left off.'

'I'm sorry about that. God, that was horrendous. He was a good diver, wasn't he? That's what I heard. He was a decent bloke. I talked him through the same as you. He was more serious though.'

Helen smiled. 'Yes, it was awful what happened. What had you been discussing before Wednesday? I know the four corporals who were suspended stopped working here two weeks ago and Captain Thomas's enquiries were seemingly going well, were they not?'

'I don't know, I guess so. He seemed happy when I showed him the conversations between Hassan and his associates. He said he'd been off radar for so long that he'd obviously grown complacent, or something had given him confidence. He seems to be acting necky as hell, as if it's a big up yours to anyone listening.'

'And that's different?'

Danny nodded, stubbing out his cigarette on the grate provided. 'Come on, I'll get you that coffee.'

She followed him. 'How does the farmers' strike shut this place down?' she asked.

'Easy,' he said. 'Sometimes, they breach the fence, and then we have a security situation on our hands. The whole station has to cease operations, it's a nightmare, but the lime stickers are worse, with their nets, they sometimes get tangled in the antennas.'

'Lime stickers?'

'Yeah, the guys who poach the songbirds. They use sticky branches to trap them, and then they pickle them and eat them, it's disgusting,' he said.

'I know what they are, but that happens here on the base?' she asked.

He nodded.

Helen remembered the jar in Colonel Seaton's kitchen and agreed that it was indeed disgusting.

Chapter 18

Ani climbed into the taxi and noticed a woman staring at her from another car dropping off at the officers' mess. It wasn't a taxi. It looked like a private vehicle, because the woman was sat in the back indicating that she was being chauffeured, and the driver wore a military uniform. Tom had gone to work hours ago, but Ani had lounged on his balcony, smoking and dreaming, wasting time, avoiding going back to her shared room.

She swapped glances with the woman, who turned to watch her car leave. Ani did the same and studied the woman's face. She was English, that much was obvious by her colouring, and the way she held herself. She was also shamelessly confident, Ani judged, by the way the woman held her head and looked around. She was pretty, but something else too; she had a face that spoke to her, it was more than wisdom or happiness, more a sense of oneself. In a confused and chaotic world, it was refreshing to see a woman so grounded. But why was she going to the mess? Tom had introduced her to female officers, and this woman wasn't one of them. Besides, her pale skin suggested she hadn't been on the island long. All the officers spent their free time at the beach.

The woman's hair blew loosely around her face and then she turned away, and the car parked in front of the mess. Ani kept watching, as the car turned towards the front gate. She saw the woman get out and turn in her direction, staring at her taxi as it approached the gate. Ani turned away as they approached the exit and the barrier was lifted for her car. The guards nodded at the cabbie, who was well known to them. He was one of the few drivers allowed inside the barracks without checking his ID, because he was known by everyone here. He was kept busy by a steady stream of officers going out to town, or further afield, to get drunk and party, and often bring girls back.

'Do you know her?' she asked Artemis.

'She came on Saturday. She's staying in the mess. She's a good-looking woman,' Artemis added.

Ani could see that already and didn't need it pointing out. Tom hadn't mentioned the woman and it irked her.

'What's she doing here?'

'I know nothing, Ani, you know that,' Artemis said to her.

She sniffed, that was his line and he stuck to it. She didn't believe a word. In fact, Artemis knew more than most, and that's why he was still employed. The favoured cabbie of officers and soldiers, he had free movement in and out of the garrison. And he heard everything. They were similar beasts, she and Artemis. They traded information to live.

'Straight home? Theo wants to talk to you,' Artemis said.

It was clear that the option wasn't in fact a choice, it was just Artemis's way of making the summons sound more palatable. Theo would expect a full report from last night, and he'd want his share of any extra tips. She'd already told Tom that he couldn't give her extra money, because Theo would always find it some way or another. They were often strip searched if it was suspected they were carrying treats. So Tom, bless him, kept a stash of supplementary money for her in his room, which she could use anytime she wanted and for whatever she pleased. Of course, anything she bought had to be worn only with him, and inside his room, and if she was caught shopping too enthusiastically, she'd land in trouble. Ani was one of the senior girls and was trusted as far as any of them could be. She had no means of obvious or immediate escape as Theo kept her passport and the embassy wouldn't let her leave anyway.

She enjoyed the familiar feeling of luxury that she always experienced when she went onto the base. It tasted like pure freedom. It was sumptuous and unique. When she was in Tom's room alone, she played music and spun around to it, she read books that he ordered from Amazon and newspapers printed in London. British people complained about the most bizarre things: the weather, schooling, free operations in hospitals, and the cost of cosmetics. It was plain weird. They seemed untouched by real issues: war, informers, premature death, disappearances of young women and arbitrary power. It was a different world. The politicians, actors, influencers and commentators in the news seemed such little people. The Prime Minister was instantly forgettable and scared to make promises or announce goals. But then that was the price of being able to walk around and say what you wanted: no one listened.

Did she care? No, not really, she was just interested in the country that was to become her home. It was just a little confusing because when she asked Tom what the UK was really like, all he said was that it depended on your point of view. What did that mean? Was it up to the individual what they thought about how they lived? Was it so lacking in rules that it bordered on anarchy? At times, she thought she might have backed the wrong horse and the UK's days might be numbered, like so many other nations, but everybody said the same thing, back at the house: London was where any girl would want to be, with an Englishman.

'You're a dreamer, Ani.'

Artemis interrupted her thoughts.

'What do we have if not dreams, Artemis?' she asked him. But it was in her head. She hadn't really said that to him because everyone knew that anything shared with Artemis got back to Theo, and that would end up back at the embassy.

The short journey was over too soon and she climbed out and thanked him. He parked up and escorted her back into the building. The Blue Lantern during the day was like any other structure along the strip: it could have been a warehouse, a nightclub or a secret casino. It was a dump and closed up from the outside. They went round the back. Artemis held the door open for her and she said she wanted to smoke before she went inside. He dug in his jacket and gave her a cigarette and offered her a light. She sucked hard and leaned against the wall.

Artemis was in his fifties and had worked for his brother for thirty years. Way before she'd arrived here, Artemis had been escorting girls around the town for Theo. They looked identical, and Ani only knew the difference because they dressed differently. They both had shaggy black hair, dark skin and big pot bellies from too much food and not enough movement. Theo sat at the bar all day and Artemis at the wheel of his taxi. Ani wondered how their hearts hadn't given in yet. She'd once had a customer die underneath her during sex, and he'd had the same appearance as the brothers: overweight, oily skin and bloodshot eyes. You could tell a lot from the eyes. Tom had good eyes. The woman in the car did too.

Ani stubbed her cigarette out and they went inside.

Chapter 19

Eric chatted to one of his locally employed staff and showed him the photographs of the three men, printed off the CCTV from the Palm Beach by Major Scott. He could kick himself for falling for the story of the naval ship in Kyrenia. He'd told himself that NATO could have been doing some kind of joint exercise in the Mediterranean and using Kyrenia as a port, but the more he thought about it, the more stupid it sounded, and he felt foolish.

He held himself responsible for Paul's death, and he couldn't shake it. But at least Major Scott had given him a way to distract himself, and perhaps make himself useful, by finding out as much as he could about the three arseholes who'd duped him into taking them on the *Zenobia*.

He'd known Paul for a relatively short while, but army people made friends quickly; they had to. The first time he'd strode into his small shack on the beach, asking questions, Eric had warmed to him. He was a well-built lad, twenty years younger than Eric, probably in his thirties, excited to be on the island, so he could dive in warm water. There were all sorts of dives you could visit all over the world, but the cold ones didn't appeal to Eric, nor, he found out, to Paul. Getting in a dry suit, covering every extremity in thick neoprene, carrying the extra equipment, and all to see nothing beyond your hand wasn't his idea of a recreational dive; leave that to the pipe fitters on the North Sea, he thought.

Taking Paul on his first visit to the *Zenobia* had been a satis-fying day. Eric loved it when people, who were nervous at first, and in awe of the view of the clear water off Larnaca revealing the mighty ship under the surface for all to see, emerged from the water elated and tripped. Sure, it got crowded at times, but everybody – mostly – respected each other's turn, and everybody got their fair share of time on the wreck. The vast majority of visitors only went to the stern side, which presented itself proudly, like a sleeping dolphin, for those trained to go no further than twenty metres in depth. Certification to go deeper was the reserve of the serious, and so the other areas of the ship were quieter. It was one of the tragic reasons why all six deaths on the ship had been in the engine room. Seven including Paul's.

Eric still couldn't believe it. The man was so vital, so big of heart, and so warm. His smile was genuine and he was also good for a pint. Paul worked mostly down in Akrotiri, but he came to Larnaca Bay whenever he had the chance. They had lots of things in common, they found, and being single was one of them. Paul could have been described as shy, but Eric knew that it was more a case of him being the opposite of brash. He was an introvert, and they didn't fare well along the strip, when looking for women. It wasn't that all single ladies who came to Cyprus looking for love were after a certain type, it was just that Paul was reserved and put himself more into the background. He saved his energy for his work, and his one pastime: diving.

'They were here last week.'

Eric's ears pricked up at the news. Memories of Paul deserted him.

'What?' he asked.

The young lad was in charge of the sea kayaks. He was a trustworthy employee, who wanted to learn to dive, and Eric had promised him just that. They'd been out on training dives together and he showed promise and control. That was the most important thing: keeping one's head when in the unnatural condition of not being able to breath without something stuck in your mouth: it proper freaked people out. That, and ears.

You could either equalise or not, and it was a bit like altitude sickness: it had nothing to do with fitness. It destroyed dreams before they even began.

'When?' Eric asked.

'Monday?' Nico said.

'Are you sure?'

'Eric, you know I watch everyone around my sister.' Nico smiled. His sister, Sophia, was employed to wash the kayaks down at the end of the day, she also fitted wetsuits, made coffee and fetched doughnuts. More realistically, she served to attract much trade, especially from groups of lads on holiday. Nico stepped in if she got too much attention, and, in turn, she shooed him away.

'Go on,' Eric said.

'They were asking her questions. I noticed them because I'd never seen them before and they stuck together. They looked odd, like performers or something,' Nico said.

'What do you mean?'

'They were so ripped,' Nico laughed. 'I mean, who looks like that?'

Eric thought about it and realised that Nico was right. Everybody on every Cyprus beach had flab, wobbly bits and things that stuck out, or didn't tuck in. Eric had witnessed the bodies of the three naval men when they'd prepared to get their kit on, and they'd looked professionally conditioned, like any proud member of Her Majesty's naval forces. He'd thought nothing of it at the time because he wasn't the type of man to feel inadequate around such sculpture. He was comfortable in his own skin, exhibitionists didn't really impress him, but to someone young like Nico, they would have stood out.

'What did they say to Sophia? What did they want?'

'They wanted to buy kit. She asked me and I said no. Then they asked about diving, and I said to talk to you.'

'What kit did they want to buy?'

'A rib.'

Eric laughed out loud. 'But that's ridiculous!' But then he stopped laughing and frowned. It dawned on him that the men had been surely watching his dive shack, and they'd got to know the place. They'd selected it.

'Did they say they were on holiday?' Eric asked.

'Yes. They pointed to one of the hotels on the front, I guess the Palm Beach? Anyway, I remember them because they didn't talk to one another like tourists. I mean, they weren't joking around or talking about what they might do here, they only talked quietly, it was like they were at work, you know?' Nico smiled but Eric didn't. Youth afforded the observer more objectivity than the wise. He felt the small hairs on his arm stand up, and he knew he had to tell Helen.

'Nico, are you absolutely sure? I have to be one hundred per cent on this.'

'Yes. For sure.' Nico pointed at the photographs with confidence. 'This one spoke Greek perfectly, and this one asked me if I worked every day?'

'They asked you that?'

'I told them I had Wednesday off.'

'Oh, Jesus.'

'What?'

'They knew you'd recognise them.' His mind worked overtime, it still didn't explain how they knew Paul was planning to dive on Wednesday, or had he told someone? Eric knew, but he'd told no one. Had someone seen Paul here? Had they somehow gained access to Eric's diary? He left it by the till, every day, open and for all to see. Another wave of regret travelled through his body. He went to the diary, walking away from Nico, and flicked through it for a few pages until he opened Wednesday's appointments. In pencil, was Paul's name. Eric tried to recall when Paul had booked in, and he knew that it was the week before last. He'd done it one evening, after working at Ayios Nikolaos all day, saying he needed a breather (diving humour). Eric smiled, but it was momentary, as he realised that he might have played a bigger part in Paul's death than he thought. His hands shook as he turned the page to Monday, when Nico said the three men had visited. He shouted to him.

'Nico, what time on Monday was it?'

Nico shrugged. 'Ask Sophia, it was about ten?'

At ten o'clock on Monday, Eric was out with a party of five, on the *Zenobia*. Had they known he wouldn't be here? He had a habit of leaving the hut open, and the book was always out, because he had no reason to be paranoid about crime here on the tiny beautiful island. Now he was changing his mind about some of his routines. He saw the same pencil marks entered and knew that Paul's name was probably there, in the Wednesday slot, on Monday. Yes, it was, he remembered. Because Paul had said he had to wait the whole week to get something down at work, and, that way, he'd look forward to it even more.

If he were Helen Scott, he'd be asking questions in Akrotiri to see if three perfectly muscular and preened individuals, fluent in at least two languages, had been asking questions about the RMP officer.

Chapter 20

Major Nick Graham sat at his desk outside Colonel Bill Seaton's office. He looked up when Helen knocked quietly on the door. She knew by the look on his face that he was assessing her civilian attire. She introduced herself and a flicker of recognition passed across his face. He was either a very good actor, or extremely arrogant; they'd only met two days ago. He was the colonel's second in command, and she'd already made her mind up that she didn't like him.

'How can I help you?' he asked. 'Colonel Seaton isn't here.'

She remained standing. 'I'd actually like to talk to you,' she said.

'Please take a seat, can I get you a drink?' He was openly warm and not at all unnerved.

'No, thank you.' She sat down. 'You're probably aware that I've been reviewing Captain Paul Thomas's case notes and I've interviewed several of your men again with reference to his enquiries.'

'Right.' He waited, not giving anything away.

'Could I clarify a few things?' she asked.

'I'm not sure I can help you at all.'

'Let's see, shall we?' she said.

He sat back in his chair and crossed one leg over the other, looking at her.

'After reviewing Captain Thomas's notes, one thing that flagged up was the concern over how much access the four corporals had to complete intelligence.'

'Yes, I agree. It's pretty much impossible. I don't know how they did it.'

'Did what?'

'Passed information on so easily.'

'You're assuming they're guilty?' she asked, baffled.

'Of course, isn't that the idea? Why else are they suspended pending charges and a hefty prison sentence?'

'Is that what you've been told?' she asked.

He sat upright and took a pen in his hand to fiddle with. 'Erm, no, I suppose it's my naive assumption. Am I getting this wrong?'

'In my training, we were told to assume innocence until proven otherwise, it's even more important we do that here, don't you think? I'm getting the feeling that there's an unwritten supposition around here that they're guilty. That's not helpful in my work. Their very experienced lawyer certainly wouldn't agree with you,' she said.

'Experienced? She's barely out of primary school. That's her job isn't it, as the defence?'

Helen was shocked. 'Sorry, am I missing something here? As second in command, you must know these men quite well, does it fit with their characters? That they're fully entrenched members of a Russian spy ring, with the influence to affect drone strikes in Syria?'

He couldn't give her an answer. Watching a man in uniform lost for words was rather satisfying but she tried to rise above gloating.

'Let me elaborate. I see that once information is identified via the usual electronic channels, it gets passed back to Communications HQ, and from there collated by independent analysts, therefore it's impossible to piece together a full picture unless you have access to all the information, and a corporal doesn't have that.'

The major thought. 'But isn't it also true that they used prostitutes known to be trafficked and on the payroll of Russian businesses?'

'Of course, but men who can't keep their pants up aren't all double agents, are they?' she asked.

He shifted in his seat. She was gobsmacked that a senior officer, presumably in charge of these men's careers and welfare, could drop them so callously at the first sign of trouble.

'Who first pointed the finger at the four operators?' she asked.

He rubbed his chin and looked behind him to the colonel's door. It was a signal from his body that it was the colonel's idea.

'And yet Colonel Seaton is not suspended from duty,' she said, answering for him.

Even the very mention of a higher rank who held his next reporting card in his hand was enough to turn the major's neck pink.

He nodded.

'What about Friday?' she continued. 'A conversation between two men, picked up and narrowed down to a market-place in Aleppo? One was allegedly the voice of Labib Hassan?'

'That was Friday? I'm not sure I follow. We pick up things like that all the time, I'm afraid I can't discuss the details.'

'But I can assure you that you can. I have the highest security clearance giving me access to such things, just like you, Major, you know that.'

She passed him a piece of paper, given to her by her headquarters, at Fareham, England, giving her access to top-level conversations recorded here at Ayios Nikolaos. He scanned it quickly and Helen waited.

'Right, well, I still don't know exactly which conversation you're referring to, there are thousands, as you appreciate, I'm sure. Information like that goes straight to London, we're gate-keepers, if you like. But the colonel has the final say.'

'And did he on Friday? Was this conversation passed to London?' she asked.

'I'll have to check for you. Have you spoken to the colonel about it?'

'Not yet. I thought, as the gatekeeper, you'd know, given the profile of Hassan, and his long-standing status as a person of interest.'

'You see, that's where you're probably going wrong, here. I don't have access to the bigger picture. I'm a messenger. If the colonel thought it important enough to pass to London, then I'm sure they got it.'

'What I'm more concerned about is the seeming lapse in communications, ironic isn't it? It's true, isn't it, that your operators don't have direct access to the means by which such information comes to be a valued piece of information. They're analysts, after all, they analyse; they don't make decisions, you said that yourself.'

'Neither do we, if you put it like that. If you're telling me that a conversation was recorded and sent to London, then I'm sure you're right. I'd have to look at the particulars.'

'Easy. Here it is. This is a print-off of the transcript. It has all the details you'd need. How does this actually get to London? Forgive me, my surveillance and intelligence skills are a little rusty. In your interviews with Captain Thomas, you said the same thing, and I'm not implying anything here, just for want of clarity, I was wondering if you read them?'

'Read what?'

'The conversations?'

'No, they're in Arabic.'

'So, you rely on the translators back in London?'

'And the expert training of our analysts.'

Helen couldn't decide if Major Graham was supremely incompetent or purposefully vague. Or both. She wondered how such a generalist could be selected for such a premium role, unless it was a typical army appointment, where anyone would do – just an arse to fill a seat, so to speak.

'You have an intelligence background. And decorated,' she said. They weren't questions.

He smiled and nodded. 'Thank you, yes, I have five years to go, and pride myself on an exemplary record.'

'But, forgive me, your role here is to filter the mundane from the acutely crucial, and you can't remember this conversation?'

'Now hold on, I'm not saying I don't remember, I'm just saying that the details of it aren't what we do here. We recognise a potential communication of interest and report it.'

'But you do appreciate the level of classification such communications have? Otherwise you wouldn't be in this role.'

He tutted and unfolded his legs. He was rattled, which was exactly what she wanted because then they might get around to the truth. 'Captain Thomas was desperate to prove that we run a leaky ship. I can't personally stop analysts selling information.'

'I never said the information was sold,' she said.

'I'm surmising again,' he replied.

'Isn't it true that there is simply too much data coming through here for any operative to decipher the importance of it?'

He didn't answer.

'Major, Captain Thomas wasn't here to prove anything one way or another, and he certainly wasn't desperate. He was simply investigating why certain pieces of information had filtered through to those who should have no access to it.'

'Have you been reading spy novels, Major?' he asked. His demeanour had shifted from confusion to defence, and Helen wondered why: they were supposed to be on the same side. It was a crass joke. He was missing the point. She felt as though she were dealing with one of her cousin's children who'd stolen an extra roast potato but was refusing to own up to it. He was guilty of the classic crime of refusing to see the bigger picture, but then that was his job.

She changed tack. 'You say you've got five years of service left? What will you do then? What's the plan?'

The question caught him off guard, and he mumbled something about spending more time with his family.

'These men want to spend time with their families too, and see their children grow up, and hold down a job. How would you feel if a miscarriage of justice made that impossible for them? Does your loyalty to higher ranks override your compassion?'

He didn't follow. He was institutionalised, like an automaton. Perfect for the army but not for a case where four men's lives hung in the balance.

'The death of Captain Thomas has been elevated to murder,' she dropped the bombshell and waited. His face went pale and he sat up, finally taking her seriously. She carried on. 'You might well consider what it was that he found out that was so dangerous to have him still alive. And for it to occur while the four men were still under house arrest, or are their powers really that extensive? I'll see myself out,' she said.

He didn't stand up. And still his mouth didn't move. She could see that he was calculating his options. He was terrified of the ramifications of telling her what he really thought.

'You know where I am should you remember anything that might be important for the case.'

'Wait,' he said. He finally stood up and faced her across the desk. 'Murder? What about you?'

Now he was showing some kind of honest integrity.

'If I'm next, then we really do have a problem, don't we?' she asked.

She went to leave but turned to him at the door.

'One more thing, three weeks ago, when the strikers caused the work at the station to be shut down for three hours. Who gave the order?'

He paused. 'Is the date significant?' he asked.

She shrugged. 'I don't know, should it be?'

'Only the colonel can shut down the station.'

Chapter 21

Helen had received the news on her phone just before she saw Major Nick Graham. The death of Paul Thomas was now a confirmed homicide. It made her feel sick. She remembered what Juliana said about not leaving the ESBA without an armed guard and it made her shiver. In the time she'd been talking to Major Graham about the case, he'd never once offered his condolences to the family of Captain Thomas.

There were three things that had galvanised the decision to open a murder inquiry: Paul's toxicology report had come back as negative; the rapid rate at which Paul's regulator had suddenly run out of air was glaringly suspicious; and the absence of the line that he'd used to attach himself to the entrance to the engine room. No diver in their right mind would forget to do it and Eric had assured her that Paul had one with him, and a spare. He knew this because he'd given them to him. Both were nowhere to be found. There was only one explanation and that was that they were both removed at some point during the dive, out of Eric's view.

The findings of the coroner were that Paul had died from drowning, due to disorientation and panic, as well as sudden unexplained lack of air and him being detached from his line. It was written in black and white and was indisputable. It was now her job to find the perpetrator. The remit of her enquiries was growing exponentially, and so was the list of people unwilling to tell her the truth.

She stormed to the car and Gem looked at her out of the corner of his eye.

'What are you staring at?' she asked him.

He muttered something and looked dead ahead.

'Did you chauffeur Captain Thomas around last week?' she asked.

'Yes, ma'am.'

'Did he storm out of that office?'

'Not quite like that, ma'am.'

She slammed the door after getting into the back seat.

'Take me to Eric's Dive School,' she said.

Gem did as he was bid and pulled out of the station. He headed back to Dhekelia, past the striking farmers, who were on one of their many tea breaks. Or perhaps it was strong coffee from the north, who knew? She gazed at the ocean as it came into view and she spotted a lone swimmer in the tide and envied them their simple pleasure.

'You must hear some interesting conversations in your position,' she said to Gem when she'd calmed down.

He smiled.

'Do you know any of the taxi drivers who pick the lads up to go into town from Dhekelia Garrison?' she asked.

'The same ones tend to come and go freely,' he said.

'Where do you live?' she asked.

'On garrison, ma'am.'

'And you work directly for Colonel Seaton?'

'No, ma'am, I'm attached to the garrison transport section. The garrison and the signallers at Ayios Nikolaos call on us if they want something specific, like ferrying round VIPs,' he said.

'Have you always been a loggie?' she asked, using the pet name for the Logistics Corps.

'Yes, ma'am, I always wanted to drive trucks.'

'And you're happy?' she asked.

'Yes, ma'am,' he said.

She envied him. Sometimes, it was a relief to sit in the back of a car, anonymous, unknowing, and moving in space and time, to a destination, unaware of your surroundings. It was like a cocoon of normality amongst the confusion of what she'd witnessed so far on the island. At least he was unattached to anyone she was investigating, and thus neutral.

'What are relations like between the different regiments of the garrison?' she asked.

'Depends where you see it from,' he said. 'All units have their jobs to do, and they keep to that.'

Numerous cap badges were posted to Cyprus, simply because there was so much to do there, given its strategic importance. She knew from her time here that this was a polite way of saying that they all pissed into the same pot but tried to avoid each other's flow. The battalion soldiers guarding Dhekelia were always infantry and, as a result, saw themselves as the real strong arm on the island. However, they'd have no job if there was no one to protect. The garrison, as a whole unit, took care of the functioning of all the moving parts and therefore was seen as a type of admin centre. It oversaw education, housing, policing, security and leisure. Tom Fleet was infantry and, as such, removed from the wings of Colonel Seaton. But everybody, on paper, reported to the Commander of British Forces: the CBF. The general in Akrotiri who she'd yet to meet.

'I recognised a cabbie leaving the mess this morning. He took officers in to town on Saturday and Sunday nights, and he was driving a woman away this morning. She wasn't serving personnel.' This part was a guess, but she was backing her hunch. The woman had been inside the car and Helen couldn't see what she was wearing, but she did know that women rarely served with the infantry, even after the rules had been changed. Sadly, the culture put them off: the levels of fitness required to do what foot soldiers did, as well as the maleness of the cap badge and history, hadn't seen swathes of them coming forward to join up. And few became officers.

Helen was also guilty of gender stereotyping because the woman she'd seen had eyebrows and lashes to die for: something you wouldn't necessarily see on a woman whose agenda was showing the men around her that she was just as deserving, and as fit, if not more so, than they were, and equipped to do the job. She wasn't in the habit of judging, but it was glaringly obvious on this occasion. The woman was also young, with a mane of thick black hair, which would be a royal pain in the arse as a serving soldier. Nor had she looked as though she fitted in, or belonged there; she'd been nervous, especially when she spotted Helen looking at her, and had sunk down in her seat. Her working theory so far was that she had been a guest. Possibly Tom Fleet's mystery woman.

But more concerning than that was the similarity to a woman whose photo she'd found amongst Paul's things. Her hair was different, and it was a grainy passport photo, but it could be the same woman. If this was true, then she had a bombshell on her hands because it meant that she was a Russian prostitute on sovereign British territory. It wasn't a moral assertion or judgement, it was strategic. Nation states knew not to piss on one another's territory abroad. The ESBA was UK land; it was high folly indeed to allow a spook to infiltrate it. It simply didn't happen. So, either the tendrils of the spy ring had become entrenched inside the ESBA, or attitudes were so lackadaisical inside the enclave that no one raised suspicions. Both were scarily sobering.

'What did he look like?' Gem asked about the cabbie.

'Greek.'

'That helps,' he smiled. They both laughed together.

'Tanned, overweight, big black moustache and shaggy hair. His car was a grey Ford, number plate Kilo, Sierra, Sierra, nine-one-two,' she added.

'That'll be Artemis.'

'Artemis?'

He nodded. 'He's probably older than the garrison, he was here ferrying lads down town when I was stationed here the last time, which was ten years ago.'

'Do you know where his cabbie rank is?'

'He's an independent, he hangs out near the Blue Lantern, there's a lot of trade there.'

'The Blue Lantern?' she feigned ignorance. 'What's that? A nightclub?'

'Sort of, ma'am.'

She nodded. 'How old are you, Gem?'

'Twenty-seven, ma'am.'

'Do you have family here with you?'

'Divorced, ma'am.'

'At twenty-seven! Kids?'

'She won't let me see them, ma'am.'

'I'm sorry about that.' She looked at his eyes in the mirror and wondered what had led to his dysfunctional and stormy relationship. Hers had also broken down and she reflected that people often went in opposite directions when they really didn't intend to. 'And you were stationed here at seventeen? You've been busy. What do you do on your days off, Gem?'

'Go to the beach, cook a BBQ, hang out with the lads.'

'How old are your kids?'

'Ten, seven and five, ma'am.'

'Do you write to them?'

'What, like cards and stuff?' he asked.

'Yeah, that kind of thing.'

'I'm allowed to send them birthday cards, and my solicitor is trying to get her to allow Skype calls.'

'Good luck, I really hope you get it.'

'Thanks, ma'am. Here we are,' he said. He stopped and parked near Eric's Dive School.

She got out and didn't look back, accustomed now to Gem waiting for her no matter where she was or how long she took.

Chapter 22

'They were here last week,' Eric said to Helen.

She waited, nursing her cup of coffee. They were sat behind his office, surrounded by dive kit drying in the sun. They were out of earshot of the shop, and enjoyed peace out here, in the shady privacy.

'Are you sure?'

'Totally. Nico and Sophia – they're brother and sister – they both saw them asking questions and trying to buy a rib.'

'Why buy a second-hand rib from a diving school?'

'Exactly. Also, they booked their dive in when they knew Nico wasn't working, I presume so he couldn't identify them.'

'Paul's death has been officially elevated to homicide,' she said, letting the news sink in.

Eric bowed his head. Helen didn't know if it was because he felt relief that it wasn't his fault, or horror that he was near Paul when it happened.

'So, the heat's on you?' Eric said, looking up.

'Quite, but I'm used to it. More importantly, I want to know who can make three massive lads, masquerading as Royal Navy, disappear off this island.'

'Her Majesty's government could,' Eric said.

'Or someone else's,' she replied and Eric watched her. They both knew that if Paul's death was planned and executed by a higher power, then it had to be one with enough resources to get away with murder.

'Nico said he recognised one of their accents too. He agreed with me, and said it was Slavic. We both agreed that it was too perfect. Learned in a class somewhere. I assumed it was because they were officers.'

Helen looked at him squarely. 'You believed them to be British, now you're convinced they're Slavs?'

'I wasn't looking for the finer details of their origins when I met them, and neither was Nico when he booked them in. I was distracted. Paul was fired up and ready to go, and so was I. I didn't pick it up. I spent three years in Bosnia, and I know what Nico is saying is bang on, but admitting I missed it is killing me.'

Helen saw Eric turn away. He was torturing himself. She understood enough psychology profiling to know that humans act appropriately to their environments, as a result, when Eric was taking people diving, he didn't scrutinise their accents much. It would be exhausting to be in detective mode all the time, Helen should know. She tried to reassure him.

'They were good actors. Don't beat yourself up. How on earth would you have guessed their intentions simply from an accent anyway? That's ridiculous. Look, I'm supposed to be an expert on reading people, but everyone can get caught off guard. You have to stop blaming yourself. This is way beyond what you could have controlled. Do you know any local police?' she asked.

It averted his attention away from him wallowing in despair. She didn't need him going off at tangents, she needed him focused.

'It's not a big town. They have little to do apart from making sure the tourists keep their cool. Why?' he asked.

'The *Zenobia* isn't sovereign base jurisdiction and the red tape means I have to tread carefully when pointing fingers. Strictly speaking, this is a civilian Cypriot police matter, however, we've managed to negotiate ownership of the case, if not as much on paper, with the cooperation of Cypriot police.'

'Jesus, good luck with that. Do you know who pays their wages?'

Eric wasn't being facetious. It was a good question. Allegations of corruption on the island were never far away from matters concerning different nationalities and what they might be up to.

'This is what makes my job so interesting,' she said, with her tongue firmly in her cheek. 'Joint investigations are bloody messy, it's not ideal.'

'Should you tread on any toes that don't want treading on, it won't end well,' Eric said.

Helen sipped her coffee. 'On that light note, the Slavic accent?'

'I know what you're thinking. There's so much money here that comes from the East, Paul's killers are probably sipping vodka in Moscow by now. Have you thought about what you'll do?'

'Tread very carefully. I want to get justice for Paul, and I want to expose that motive for all to see and watch the fuckers squirm.'

Eric looked serious. 'Now it makes sense,' he said.

'What?'

'A friend of mine, who owns a shop further down,' he said, pointing along the beach to another dive shack – there were plenty along the front, and all shared business – which was enough to go around in the high season. 'He said that on Wednesday afternoon, after the accident, the dive site was closed, but two divers were seen going down there anyway.'

'By who?'

'Gossip travels fast when someone dies on the *Zenobia*. It's not common and it generates big news. I remember the last one and thinking that I hope I never have to be associated with the investigation of it.'

'Stop it, Eric, I'm getting tired of your brooding. Pull yourself together if you want to be a part of this and make a difference for Paul.'

He looked at her and a smile spread gently at the corners of his mouth. 'You don't mess around, do you?'

'Why would I? What an absolute waste of time. Are you going to keep a clear head for me or not?' she asked. It wasn't that she was being uncaring, just that, to Helen, some people responded better to a bit of tough love.

'I am. Sorry. That's it with the self-pity.'

'Now, tell me about what was seen out there on Wednesday,' she said, indicating the sea beyond them.

'It was supposed to be closed, like I said, but around dusk, a rib was spotted out there, which isn't abnormal of course. Water sports aren't going to stop here for anything, except perhaps a great white shark. The rib circled the ship and the gossip is that two divers launched off the back, surfacing about forty minutes later. That's enough time to get to the engine room and back, as well as off-gas.'

'Weren't the police supposed to be guarding the site?'

'They did, for about an hour or so. Besides, these weren't police. The port and marine police have white ribs, this was black. And I gave Paul the safety lines myself, he coiled them up in front of me and placed a back-up on his weight belt. Even if he forgot to attach himself, the lines would still be attached to his kit. Were they?'

'No. Could they have worked loose?' she asked, knowing full well what the answer was.

'Impossible. They were clipped onto him. I brought up the rear with the other two guys, and when we attached our lines, Paul's was already attached at the entrance, it was bright green, and his spare was yellow. You can't miss them.'

'And when you came out?'

'The confusion was overwhelming, my only thought was getting Paul to the surface without the bends. I still didn't know he was dead, I didn't accept it.'

'So I have to assume that whoever went to the site after the police was checking to see if any evidence had been left behind.

Did anyone get a look at them? Was it the three men who dived with you and Paul?'

'No. Those bastards probably took the lines while I was taking him to the surface.'

Chapter 23

The two Special Investigations branch officers landed at midday, on a civilian flight, two days earlier than expected. Don had told her they'd be here by Wednesday, but the sudden elevation of the case had expedited the decision. Helen gave them time to settle in and unpack and had arranged to meet them in the mess. She'd managed to organise a larger working space for them all, on the garrison, rather than the tiny box room Paul had been given. She'd personally supervised the transfer of all the files and boxes to the new office, which was more spacious, and it felt to her as though they now had a professional space to work in.

Gem dropped her off back at the officers' mess and she found them waiting for her in the lounge, drinking coffee. They wore uniform and she noticed their puzzlement as she walked in, like a civilian in her shorts and blouse.

The two officers introduced themselves with their full names and titles. She'd requested to Don that he send her two of the regiment's best operators available, and she was chuffed they turned out to be women.

'Kay, and Jen,' she said, firmly reminding them of the lack of formality inside barracks.

They shook hands.

She explained why she was out of uniform. 'I'm spending much of my time off base. I don't want to stick out like a walking target and put people off talking to me,' she said. 'We've been given an office here on the base and I've checked it out. It's decent enough – though, as you can imagine, we're not particularly welcome here. People get jumpy when you mention SIB, but that's what I want, so I'd appreciate you staying in combats, while you're here. Later, that might change, and you'll probably find yourselves needing to get into civvies.' Both women looked excited by the opportunity. 'How familiar are you with the case so far?' she asked.

Kay and Jen were serious and said little. 'We've been reading on the plane, ma'am.'

'Good. We're a small unit of three, for now, and I want you to report every detail to me personally. No outside agencies, no civilian police, and especially, no garrison commander. And no lawyer. She's called Juliana Barnaby and has been sent courtesy of Legal Aid. The suspects are under house arrest, but the elevation of Captain Thomas's death to murder only demonstrates to me that there's a wider picture here. We report only to the CBF in Akrotiri. The garrison commander here, Colonel Seaton, is still in post, despite the circumstances, and I haven't yet worked him out. He could be an interesting element to the case. No one seems overly piqued by the removal of four corporals, despite how tight-knit the regiment claims to be.'

'Smells like a cover-up, ma'am,' one of the officers said.

'Well, that's what we're here to find out,' Helen said. 'Come on. I'll show you our new office.'

As they walked across camp, passing soldiers on the parade square, Helen talked and the two officers listened. They were relatively fresh-faced and she'd read their service history. There were some three hundred military police SIB officers in the British Army and few of them were women, and Helen was acutely aware that it was on their shoulders to prove themselves. Like any organisation, women had to work harder to get their foot in the door and stay there. She questioned them about their previous cases and a sense of intolerance for breaking the law exuded from each officer. Don had chosen well.

'There are a few players here, and it's going to be tricky navigating round them. It's easier if you shut them all down and concentrate on the brief I've given you. Here's my personal mobile, that's the only number you'll use while you're here,' she said.

Vehement nodding again. Helen got the impression, and certainly from their files, that they were relatively inexperienced, but what they had done was exemplary. She fully intended to use it to her advantage. Young, recently qualified officers were much closer to their training, and the rules of engagement overseas, than their more senior old sweats. They were also less likely to be looking for instant promotion or glory.

They reached the office and Helen unlocked the door. 'Toilet down there, tea room right next door,' she added. 'Believe me it's better than the one over at Ayios Nikolaos. Right, grab yourselves a brew and I've got some reading for you to catch up on.'

The two women followed their orders and Helen felt, for the first time since she'd landed on the island, that she was among comrades. So far, she'd found herself facing a sea of hostiles, except for Eric and Gem, and the comfort she felt surprised her.

Kay and Jen came back with mugs of tea and placed one in front of Helen.

'Didn't know if you took sugar,' Kay said, plopping a small pot in front of her.

Helen smiled. This relationship was going to be just fine, she thought. Already, Kay and Jen had her back.

'Jen, read this from cover to cover. Here's one for you, Kay. When you're done, hopefully, you'll appreciate why I have to go out and visit a strip club,' she said.

Kay and Jen barely raised their eyebrows. Much SIB work was secretive.

'So, I'll see you in a couple of hours.'

'Good luck with the strip club,' Jen said.

'Thanks, I'll be sure to tell you all about it when I get back.'

Chapter 24

Gem knew where to find the Blue Lantern.

'Come here often, Gem?' Helen asked.

'It's an officers' gaff, ma'am.'

'So I heard.'

'Soldiers can't afford it.'

'Right. Drive round the block a few times, please.'

Gem manoeuvred the car and they passed the entrance to the club. It was a stone building, on the corner of a dusty block, surrounded by billboards advertising building companies and restaurants. The streets were mid-construction, like everything in Cyprus, and the road stopped abruptly, preventing Gem from doing a loop. He performed a three-point turn and went back the way they'd come, driving past the entrance again. It was a double black metal door, with posters on that Helen couldn't read. Paper blew around the step and she gazed up at the floors surrounding what seemed like the only access point. Above, the building appeared to house accommodation, but all windows and curtains were tightly shut. It had the standard appearance of every brothel she'd encountered around the world, and it made no attempt to cover it up. Whether the customers paid for sex in drinks or entrance fees, it was irrelevant.

'How do people know about this place?' she asked.

'Word of mouth,' Gem said.

'And what's that?'

'Girls. A good time. No questions,' he replied.

'Did Captain Thomas ask you to bring him here?'

'Once.'

'And?'

'It's not my place to watch people,' he said.

'Ah, yes. But you see people, Gem. Was Captain Thomas a talker?'

'No, ma'am, he wasn't as a general rule. Actually, he said please and thank you, but he didn't want to chat, ma'am, not like you.'

Not like a woman, she thought.

'Does anyone ask you what we talk about?'

'No, ma'am.'

He pulled over by the side of the road, and the cool air of the car's air conditioning soothed her; she knew full well that if she got out in the heat, she'd begin sweating immediately.

'Did you like Captain Thomas?' she asked, not really knowing why it was important. It was as if everybody's nonchalance over his death was bugging her and she wanted some acknowledgement for his life.

He shrugged his shoulders.

'Okay, let me rephrase that. Was he a decent bloke?'

'Yes.' He nodded. 'He was serious and always busy, like you. But he didn't really talk to me.' Gem held on to the steering wheel, waiting for instructions.

'So he didn't see the massive potential well of information sat in the car with him?'

'I'm not that important.'

'Well, you know about this place. What time does it open?' Helen knew it wasn't going to be early.

The car moved.

Helen was about to ask Gem what he was doing, but he was so certain of his actions that she trusted his instinct. He drove further down the street and parked behind a van delivering fresh flowers to the restaurant at the end of the street. She watched as a car pulled up outside the club, Gem watched too.

'That's Artemis,' he said.

She recognised the cabbie straight away. She sat between the seats, leaning forward with her hands on the backs of the front seats. Gem was a foot from her face. They watched as Artemis got out of his grey Ford and slammed his door. He didn't bother closing his windows or locking the vehicle. He went to the rear of the club and spoke to someone on a mobile phone, then he appeared out front again, still talking into his phone. He gesticulated with his arms and Helen watched. The black door opened and a woman appeared. The door was shut behind her and Helen saw Artemis speak to her briefly. She didn't look happy.

'Do you know her?' Helen asked Gem.

'No.'

'She was at the officers' mess this morning,' Helen said. She was sure. It was the woman she'd seen leave in the same cab. She quickly searched for something in her bag and found the grainy print of a woman's passport photo.

Artemis shoved the woman roughly and they seemed to argue.

'What's that about?' Helen asked.

'If she's a working girl, then Artemis might be taking her to a job and he's getting a cut. Maybe she's late.'

'Maybe she was up all night.' *At an officers' mess on UK sovereign land…*

'You want me to follow?' Gem asked as Artemis pushed the woman towards the Ford.

'Absolutely.'

The young woman got into the back seat of the Ford and Helen tried to study her face. She was beautiful. Helen didn't have time to analyse why she'd ended up here, just to wonder where she might fit into her investigation. For now, she had no idea, except that she was potentially providing sex to British servicemen at the same time that a prostitution ring was implicated in a spy case that had led to murder…

Artemis got back into his car and slammed his door, the woman slumped down in the back seat and plopped

144

sunglasses over her eyes. The Ford pulled away and Gem slowly manoeuvred out into the road after them. They drove along the strip and towards the single road which exited the town at this end. Gem was an impressive surveillance driver, he held back and pulled out just at the right moment to not draw attention or get too far behind to lose them.

After Helen lost count of the roundabouts they'd been round, they turned onto the main road to Nicosia.

'Where the hell are they going?' she said more to herself than to Gem.

'Should I continue?' he asked.

'May as well,' she said. She looked at her watch and figured she had plenty of time before she should return to her new recruits to see how they were getting on. Besides, they had stacks of paperwork to get through.

Twenty minutes later, they were still on the road to Nicosia and Helen could see the Troodos Mountains in the distance, and she craved their cool summer chill of twenty-five degrees, rather than the fifty she was reading on the dash.

They came to the outskirts of Nicosia and still the grey Ford kept going. The city was choked and a haze sat above its low buildings. It was almost like a mirage in the desert. The striking Kyrenia Mountains towered in the distance and she remembered back to when she'd run up there to the monastery of Bellapais. It was stunning and so quiet compared to the southern side. The huge Turkish 'fuck you' in the form of the painted flag on the mountainside always made her smile wryly: you had to hand it to them; they had balls of steel. She'd worked with the Turkish army on occasion and found them to be consummate soldiers; professional and hard.

The grey Ford turned and turned, until they were on a wide boulevard.

'Fuck,' she said under her breath, but loud enough for Gem to hear.

'What?' he asked. 'Are you all right?'

'Yes. That's the Russian Embassy,' she said.

Chapter 25

Andi Seaton drove her tax-free jeep to the stables to muck out her pride and joy: Temper, a chestnut mare that had been recommended by an ex-trainer. The island was a haven for horse fanatics, with its dry climate, wonderful trails and tourist interest. The garrison stables had seen better days because they were no longer funded by the MOD; seen as a frivolous and dated treat for officers who had better things to do. Thankfully, money had come rolling in from various fundraising events, foreign investment and friends of the ESBA. As a result, they'd rescued the stables and even expanded.

Andi loved it here. It was hard bloody work, but worth it, even if to simply evade human contact. She preferred animals. They didn't talk or have complicated emotions.

The yard was empty and the tough jobs had already been done this morning. Andi always rose early, no matter the hangover and got down here to start the day by shovelling shit. It was her private (or not so private) joke that she told visiting VIPs, to break the ice. They found it funny. She'd been home for lunch and grabbed a sandwich made for her by the cook. Thank God, that budget hadn't been cut for colonels overseas yet. Now, she had all afternoon to make sure Temper was happy and exercise her for a few hours' ride.

She checked her stirrups and secured the saddle and mounted. The beauty of riding abroad was few rules, but she still wore a hat. She was saddle-sore from yesterday's ride into the surrounding low-lying hills, but the pain soon subsided and she broke into a trot, taking Temper towards the main gate.

A car drove up the dusty track and she didn't recognise it. She stopped, naturally nosy, and more so since becoming a colonel's wife. The windows were down and she waved at the car to slow down. Instead, they sped up and gravel flew up towards Temper, who neighed noisily.

'Wankers!' she waved her fist and crop.

The vehicle drove towards the yard and she turned Temper around and cantered back behind them, catching up as they parked at an angle in front of the office, which, Andi knew was empty. Temper was unsettled and Andi calmed her by stroking her neck. She dismounted expertly and got off the horse, standing in front of the car.

'What the hell do you think you're doing?' she demanded.

Two men in suits got out, not at all dressed for a livery yard.

'What do you want? Don't you even know you're supposed to slow down for horses?' Her voice was loud, and she was angry at them.

They didn't speak but fastened their jacket buttons and looked around. They wore sunglasses, so she couldn't see their eyes. She hated that habit. The Americans did it and it drove her crazy. It meant the wearer had no manners. Eye contact was everything. For a moment, she remembered that the woman who'd had dinner with them on Saturday night was a military policewoman, and that these men might have something to do with her. Helen Scott had no humour. She'd noticed how Bill looked at her, and admittedly she was pretty, and young, but, hell, she was straight. Major Scott oozed incorruptibility and it irritated the colonel's wife. Everybody had a price, she mused.

The men continued looking around, ignoring her.

'This is private land, so if you don't mind, I demand you leave, right away.' Andi's colour was rising and she put her hands on her hips and glared at them. But the men seemed oblivious.

She looked around for help, but the yard was deserted, as it usually was this time of the day. Sometimes, the young volunteers were so quiet that one might only assume it was empty, but this afternoon, it actually was. The tiny hairs on her arms stood up.

'Right, I'm calling the garrison guards. I suggest if you know what's good for you, you'll get back in your vehicle and fuck off.' The impertinence!

'We're looking for Mrs Andrea Seaton. We were told she'd be here, who are you?' one of the men finally said. His arrogance confounded her but stoked her interest. They sounded foreign. Perhaps they were looking for her husband.

'I'm Andi Seaton.' She jutted out her chin.

Temper kicked the dust and pulled against her leash, so she walked her to a tying station. The mare yanked and whinnied, but Andi secured her and walked back to the men.

The man who'd spoken looked her up and down and she was unaccustomed to the lack of respect.

'My face is here,' she said, pointing to her own chin.

The other man laughed and shook his head.

'Mrs Seaton, we have a message from your investors.'

'My what?' Andi demanded.

'The people behind all of this,' he said.

The other leaned on the car and lit a cigarette.

'Put that out! The horses don't like it!'

He continued smoking.

'Let me be clear. The people who enable you to stay here have a message for you and you're to come with us now.'

Andi laughed out loud and surprised herself with the absurdity of it. She looked towards the office and went to make a step in that direction, but the man who spoke blocked her way.

'Get out of my way!' she hissed.

Temper kicked ferociously and Andi turned to calm her.

The man who was smoking opened the car door to her.

'You must be crazy if you think you can just drive in here and take me away! It's kidnap! Help! Help!'

She made a dash for the office, but something tripped her. Temper squealed loudly, and Andi hadn't heard her do this for such a long time that she instinctively got up and went to go to the horse. Temper was so-called because she used to pick fights with other horses and her squeal, a vocal talent common in horses, was part of her building aggression. Until she met Andi. The man who was smoking blocked her path and she felt trapped. Panic began to close slowly in on her and she realised what a precarious position she was in. She had no idea who these men were. She had less clue as to how they'd got onto the garrison and thus here to the yard, and she was alone.

'You can make this easy or you can make it difficult, it's your choice,' the other man said.

Andi breathed heavily and looked from them to Temper and back again. She chided herself for tying her horse to the station, if she'd left her free, she could have mounted and sped off.

'Who are you?'

'Just the drivers.'

She looked inside the back of the car and fear enveloped her. Control deserted her and she went to sprint away. She was a fit woman, surely capable of outrunning two middle-aged men?

Not so. They anticipated her thoughts and she felt a heavy weight catch the back of her legs, then a hand grabbing her jodhpurs. Another pair of hands were on her in seconds and the noise of her struggle, coupled with the whine of her horse, made the confusion worse. She felt her hands being tied with something and then she was lifted and shoved into the car. Her knee caught on the door and she squealed in pain. The doors slammed and they set off with a screech and a cloud of dust, leaving Temper chomping at her tethers.

Andi screamed, but it was half-hearted because she knew there was no one around. The man who'd been smoking was in the back seat with her and he forced his arm around her neck, immobilising her. His strength amazed her and she stopped struggling, knowing instinctively that it was in her best interests. All she could do was sit limply and smell the tobacco on his breath.

Chapter 26

'Sit down, Fleet,' Major Graham said.

Tom fidgeted. He was understandably nervous. This was his chance to put a case forward for marrying Ani. He told himself over and over that it wouldn't be the first time, and not the last. It happened all the time: soldiers and officers alike, posted overseas, fell in love. That was all.

But she was Russian. It was complicated.

Which is why he was sat in front of the colonel's eyes and ears, and not some warrant officer, chewing the fat over the details and choosing their quarter of marital bliss, back in Blighty.

'I've read the reports. It's the opinion of the battalion that you need to give this some airtime.'

All army officers spoke in code. It was like an ancient rite. But it was most annoyingly deployed when trying to avoid the plain truth. Airtime was a euphemism for no.

'Sir?'

'Look, lad, we all understand how one gets carried away with the locals. There's nothing wrong with that, son, but marry her? Do you even know her?'

'I do, sir. She's a trustworthy and good woman.'

The major snorted and Tom's hackles went up. He didn't like the senior officer at the best of times, no one particularly did. It wasn't that the major was of deficient character, he was simply aloof, but then Tom guessed that was his job. Most senior officers became wankers in good time. Would he one day?

Unfortunately, this senior officer held Tom's future in his hands. Tom fiddled with his beret.

'She still takes clients?' the major asked.

Tom expected this, but there was something about the major's tone that made Ani sound contaminated.

'Yes, sir. It's her job, but if I can give her some reassurance, then she'll stop. She's scared of them, sir. She daren't go against them unless I can guarantee her safety.'

'Guarantees? Doesn't that sound suspicious to you? Do you talk to her about your job, Lieutenant?'

'No, sir! It's not like that.' Tom's stomach felt heavy. He knew this would be the route they'd take – after all, they had to be careful. But Ani wasn't like that. This was different.

'I'm sorry, son, I've got some bad news for you,' the major said.

Tom watched the older man get up and pace about a bit, before going to a filing cabinet. He waited anxiously. But then he'd waited so long, another few minutes wouldn't hurt. He'd met Ani the first week he was stationed here and they'd been together ever since. He took precautions, of course, but only against things that Ani couldn't control. He used condoms. As soon as she was his, she could clean herself up and he wouldn't need to. They wanted children.

The major finally spoke as he held up some paperwork. 'These are previous applications, from both soldiers and officers, to marry Miss Anastasia Lebedev. Seven in all, over the last five years.'

Tom's mouth fell agape.

'I'm sorry to do this to you, Tom. The colonel is regretful too, but we see this kind of thing all the time.'

Tom flushed.

Major Graham placed the forms on the table between them. 'Read them,' he said.

Tom shook his head, taken aback.

The major continued. 'They were all like you, all in love, all convinced of her authenticity. They were all turned down because of the same reason.'

'Because she's Russian, sir?'

'No. Tom, that's where you're misreading our intentions here. I've nothing against her nationality, it's her history that worries the colonel and I. No, we believe – and have always believed – that Miss Lebedev is an informant.'

'That's ridiculous,' Tom said, standing up.

'Lieutenant, remember where you are, son.'

Tom swallowed hard and sat back down. He could be court-martialled for insubordination if he wasn't careful. Was Ani worth his job? He searched his heart. Being with her had been like a drug. For months, he'd breathed her in, consumed her and become intoxicated by her, finding himself hopelessly and powerfully addicted over time. Did he really love her? But, he also had to ask himself if he truly believed her capable of being a spy.

'If you've calmed down, we have an alternative suggestion which might just help you out, and us.'

'Sir?'

'Well, simply put, son, we need to find out what she knows. This RMP officer snooping around is making everyone nervous. No one wants to find out that the Intelligence Corps at Ayios Nikolaos has been compromised. Major Scott would like to prove otherwise of course. She's the type. All glory and no substance. She's in the mess, yes?'

Tom nodded.

'Keep an eye on her, Tom, and carry on seeing Ani, but we'll give you a few pieces of select information for you to plant when the time is right. We'll soon know if she's an informant or not.'

'And the RMP officer, sir? If she interviews me?'

'She might ask you questions about your job and I'm sure you can make that about as interesting as it really is, can't you?' he laughed.

Tom found himself laughing too. Inside, though, he was crying. Part of him didn't believe what the major was telling him about Ani.

'By the way, Tom, just look at the most recent application to take Anastasia Lebedev home as a wife, will you?'

Tom didn't want to see the photos of all the men Ani had duped. It was too raw and too painful. It was bad enough seeing her with clients at the Blue Lantern, but fellow officers? Even if they were on the island years ago and he didn't know them. He felt a fool. He fingered the top file and saw the name of the officer who'd applied to take Ani as his wife. He also saw his photo.

It was Victor, and the application had been made three weeks ago.

Chapter 27

'Hi, sorry! I got held up with something, but, hey, that gave you more time, right?' Helen shut the door behind her. The small space was hot, even with the window open. But at least there was a breeze. They heard shouts and commands from the parade square and it made Helen feel as though she was back in basic training. She fanned herself.

'Jen found a fan,' Kay said.

'Ah, good job!'

Helen put her things on her desk and gulped from a bottle of water. She felt grimy, but that really was of no consequence compared to her trip to Nicosia.

'Right,' she said, pulling out her chair. 'What do we think?' She was keen to get somebody else's opinion.

Kay and Jen looked at each other.

'Who wants to go first?' Helen asked.

'We've compared notes. We figured you were busy and got our heads together.'

'Good. Shoot.'

Kay took the initiative and Helen surmised that she was the more confident of the two. Perhaps she was the articulate one and Jen had the ideas. Helen liked the combination. It was always good not to have too many chiefs to spoil the flavour of the inquiry.

'If we take the week that Captain Thomas was working on the case of the leaked coordinates for the strike in Aleppo, then, working from the scope of his analysis, it's a fairly large group

of people who were aware of what he was doing. He interviewed the four servicemen, and if we assume that all partners
discuss their worries with their spouses, let's include their wives
too. Then you have Colonel Seaton and Major Graham. The
major is unaccompanied, but Colonel Seaton no doubt shares
everything with his wife, or let's assume at this point to be on
the safe side. Then we have the grapevine. The whole garrison
was aware that the on-island SIB representative, Paul Thomas,
was here asking questions, which means we have to consider the
serving personnel here on base. Apart from that, it's whoever
has contact with outside agencies.'

'Narrows it down then,' Helen said sardonically.

Jen spoke, acknowledging the irony. 'We have to look at
who would want to avert an attack on Labib Hassan. His
entourage, seemingly only ten minutes from the order to deploy
the smart bomb from the unmanned US aircraft above Syria,
took an unexpected diversion, according to sources on the
ground. That means the information got to him quickly and
directly. It was precise, confident and from a secure source. Has
London been ruled out?' Jen asked.

'I'm assured that with encryption, transparent data searches
and whereabouts on the day, that it is impossible that the leak
came from London: they wouldn't have had time. It had to have
come from somebody watching Labib's movements in real time
and privy to his conversations running up to his rendezvous at
the planned attack site. The Special Forces on the ground had
confirmed his every movement in the run-up to that meeting,
supported by printouts which I have seen.'

'So, we go back to the four servicemen,' Kay said.

Helen looked at her. Fresh eyes were a wonderful thing. It
was a fact that the four Intelligence Corps soldiers had manned
the operations room at Ayios Nikolaos in the twenty-four hours
leading up to the air strike, not including the times it was
closed down because of striking farmers. Labib had slipped away
and the operation had been restarted from scratch. Helen felt

for the Special Forces on the ground. Their mission was to follow, gather intelligence and track the movements of targets, all the while remaining incognito and melting into the local population. Sometimes they were out there for years, doing everything it took to get close to a target. Their efforts were unsung, secret and unrewarded. To lead a major power to the whereabouts of a high-profile mark like Labib Hassan, and for it to be scuppered last minute was maddeningly frustrating. And it had happened twice in the last three weeks. They were the true labourers in such a war; working underground, churning over the terrain, making it passable for the rest of their fold.

She also knew, from being attached to such units in the past, that information was incredibly slow to feed back if anything went wrong. They would probably have no clue that the reason their intelligence – information they might have worked for a year to get – wasn't followed through was because of a snitch on their own side. They would be bitterly disappointed. It's what had led to Grant packing it all in.

'Can I introduce my spanner now you're up to speed with the basic events?' Helen said.

Kay and Jen looked at one another, awaiting her bombshell.

'On the day that Labib Hassan literally dodged a bullet, there was a particularly disruptive farmers' strike on the road between Dhekelia and Ayios Nikolaos – are you familiar with them?' Helen asked.

They both shook their heads.

'They happen every summer, for long periods, and occasionally, they disrupt the well-oiled productivity of Ayios Nikolaos. Now, the coordinates were agreed twelve hours before the strike, from intelligence on the ground. But when that arsenal was being dropped, the station was locked down, because farmers had driven their vehicles onto ESBA land, and Colonel Seaton shut down the station for two hours, while delicate negotiations took place.'

Kay and Jen were quick thinkers and it didn't take long for them to catch up. They stared at her for more information.

Helen sat back. 'I think we need to face the possibility that Colonel Seaton might have a past that interests the spooks here on the island. If they have a lever to control him, we need to find it. It'll likely be in the usual places: his dick, or his wallet, or both.' Helen tapped her foot on the desk and rested her cheek on her hand. 'What are the most plausible routes for information travelling into Syria in real time?' she asked.

There were three main answers. The first possibility was it went directly from a technical operator, here at JSSU, which is what Colonel Seaton was effectively accusing his own men of, and that was technically impossible. The second was somebody in higher authority who'd switched sides and was being paid or blackmailed for a general picture, and this would have to be someone with the highest level of access. The only person fitting this description was Colonel Seaton himself. The third scenario came directly from the defence lawyer, Juliana Barnaby, and now, after seeing the girl from the Blue Lantern taken to the Russian Embassy in Nicosia, was something they had to turn their attention to: a moll. Helen had checked her passport. Her name was Anastasia Lebedev.

'Have you heard of Mata Hari?' she asked. Neither of them had. She told them about her history, and her death and compared her to the honey traps of Northern Ireland during the Troubles. She also told them about the Blue Lantern, and the young woman's visit to the Russian Embassy in Nicosia.

'The driver didn't hang around, and he left alone, so she was dropped off there. I also saw her leaving the officers' mess early this morning. I know it's a well-worn path, the sound of soldiers' boots to a Cyprus strip club, but it's happened before. The Cyprus seven in the eighties.'

Jen knew all about it. 'They were able to sue the MOD after the trial because of their unlawful treatment during the investigation here on island.'

'And all seven were acquitted,' Kay added.

Helen nodded. 'There was no doubt that they were involved in some after-hours activities, which is frankly their prerogative, but the case collapsed because of assumption. Assumption that because they were doing one thing, they had to have been doing the other. Foolish indeed.'

'Hasn't our screening got a bit better since then?' Kay asked.

'You'd like to think so, but alas, the promise of sex is still better than an MOD wage, last time I checked.'

The three women shared the joke, but it wasn't light-hearted. It was deadly serious. The whole premise behind serious security vetting was so that, no matter what the enemy offered you, you wouldn't be tempted. But didn't everyone have a price?

'My problem with all of this, and I wish I could talk to Captain Thomas right now, to see if he was thinking along those lines before he was killed, is that none of the four servicemen had access to a full picture, and what would be their motives? They're all in deep shit with their wives. If they were promised a better life elsewhere, wouldn't they have gone by now? I did clock quite a profusion of luxury goods and holidays, but they can be explained with good housekeeping. I've requested to seize their bank accounts, here on the island, as well as those back in the UK to clear that up. Meanwhile, we've got to get closer to the Blue Lantern, but we need to be careful because it's outside the ESBA. I'm not happy sharing this information with Cyprus police, simply because their economy is more reliant on Russian investment than it is on summer pounds from Britain. But I want the place watched. Any volunteers?'

'I'll do it,' Jen spoke. Helen admired her enthusiasm. 'My background is surveillance,' Jen added. 'I don't need anything fancy, just a notepad and pen, and a camera.'

'Done,' Helen said. 'You'll need to get out of that uniform.'

She briefed them on the update from Eric's Diving School about the sightings of the three men posing as Royal Navy officers.

'The water around the *Zenobia* wasn't even cordoned off for twelve hours after Captain Thomas's body was pulled from the water. A rib was spotted there that evening, with two divers going down for forty minutes or more. They weren't registered at any dive school along the strip, because Eric confirmed to me that they all closed out of respect. And it wasn't a police rib. So either it was dark tourism, or, the more likely scenario, they were checking the scene to make sure nothing had been left behind. It's professional. That's what I'd do. At the time of Captain Thomas's death, Eric would have spotted any foul play, so they had to pretend shock and come to the surface along with him and face the authorities. Prelim enquiries into the three men were woeful, and they disappeared, via the Palm Beach. Eric Dukakis also assures me that the profile of the two divers who were seen that evening over the *Zenobia* didn't match the physiques of our three actors.' Helen shuffled her notes. Her case files were growing by the hour. 'Kay, from landing at Akrotiri, and getting here, have you had any contact with any personnel on island?'

Kay thought about it and shook her head. 'Just the driver.'

Helen had sent Gem to collect the SIB officers, so she was happy that no one knew they were here yet. 'Fancy a visit to the Blue Lantern?'

'As a punter?'

'Can you pull it off?' Helen asked.

'Sure,' Kay said.

Chapter 28

Tom Fleet kicked the sand and his foot connected with a stone, however, he wore his heavy black patent leather service shoes and so, apart from the grainy dust getting into his socks, it didn't cause him any pain. He kicked harder.

A child booted a ball close to him and he stared at it, not at first understanding where it had come from, then the child ran up to him and stopped. Tom watched him and looked around. He saw a few families on the beach, not many tourists ventured this far down to Dhekelia beach; it was mainly army families who used it, though it was public. Diners waiting for their superb fish and chips from Lambros restaurant often sat about or paddled in the shallows, but by and large, it was quiet.

'Why are you dressed like that?' the boy asked.

Tom went to the ball and picked it up. 'Here you go, fella. I'm a soldier.'

'Cool.' He took his ball. 'Manchester United,' the boy said.

Tom laughed: it was the international communication of children everywhere, and the first English they learned.

'Ronaldo?' Tom said. The boy nodded and beamed, then he ran away with his ball.

Tom watched him and mused how simple life was when you were only three feet tall, but he couldn't allow himself to wallow in self-pity. He was torn between the safety of who was waiting for him back home: a fiancé, a girl who'd make a good wife, and a family who'd never know he was contemplating marrying a prostitute; and Ani – all eyes, breasts and thighs. He sniffed and realised that his dick had taken over his head, and it had been that way for months. He'd spent hundreds, if not thousands of pounds on her body, and having it all to himself, so he thought. Now, he'd been told that Victor had the same designs. How long had Ani strung him along? What nights did she fit in his colleague? What happened on the nights they were both at the club and Tom was given first go? Did she wait until the early hours and finish herself off at Victor's, before climbing back into his own bed?

He felt sick. It was ridiculous. He took his beret out of his pocket, plopping it on his head. He wiped away sweat from his brow and walked back up to the road, his shoes sinking into the sand. His feet chafed against the grit that had filtered through his fine socks and he stopped to take off his shoes and tap them out. Then he walked towards the mess.

It was quiet. The coolness circulated around the thick walls, testimony to the quality of the engineering of the building itself, when the army could afford to treat their officers like valued members of the human race, willing to give their lives for their country. The fact that it remained was pure luck. The MOD couldn't afford such riches today. The silver they ate off, the crystal they drank out of and the art depicting past glory were all fading trophies, like his own mood.

Vic was sat in an armchair, reading the *Daily Mail*, imported every day, one day late, in the British Forces mailbag. It was curious how news from home paled into the background when one was surrounded by sun and sex. The stories never changed, and consisted of celebrities trying to shock, politicians straining to shout the loudest and society generally growing more distant by the day. Maybe that's why he'd fallen for Ani? She wasn't part of home.

Tom took a deep breath and went to the bar for a glass of water. Refreshed and ready, or so he thought, he went to his friend, or the man he had assumed was his friend at least.

'Mate, look at this,' Vic said, when he saw Tom striding over. He flicked the paper around and showed him an article on the recent events in Afghanistan.

Tom wasn't interested. He'd never served there, neither had Vic. He didn't react, but sat down heavily on the opposite armchair.

'You all right?' Vic asked.

'No, mate, I'm not.'

'What's up?'

'I was in Big Willy's office this afternoon. With Major Graham. We were discussing my application for Ani to become my wife.'

'And how did it go?' Vic asked.

'Are you fucking kidding me?' Tom said, incredulous.

'What? Am I missing something?'

'Apart from the other God knows how many poor fuckers she's had propose to her in the past, yours was the one that hurt the most,' Tom said.

'What are you talking about?' Vic asked.

'What? You're going to deny it? Do you think I'm that stupid?'

'Deny what?' Vic asked.

'He showed me your application to marry Ani.' Tom's words stuck in his throat. His friend wasn't taking this seriously. He knew that officers went to the Blue Lantern, and he wasn't stupid; he also knew that Ani would never turn down business, but Vic's betrayal was a blow.

'Mate, I have no idea what you're talking about. Why would I want to marry a hooker?'

Tom's blood boiled over. So, it was a joke. This whole thing was a set-up. Vic had applied to marry Ani to make sure that Tom didn't, plain and simple. Tom knew that his body language was aggressive because Vic kept looking at his fists, which were clenched, to the point of his nails biting into his skin.

'Why would the major tell you that? It's bullshit, Tom. I swear.'

Tom didn't know what to do. He looked into Vic's eyes and they were earnest. Then he thought of Colonel Seaton, whose history of integrity was sketchy, to say the least. The guy managed to get over a hundred grand spent on his house, when the whole island suffered cuts, and no one knew how he did it. Then there was the question of the local contractors he employed who monopolised all civilian work on base. Big Willy benefitted nicely from all of them, from kitchen fitters, to gas engineers, to gardeners. But why would he get Major Graham to lie about Ani?

'Wait a minute, tell me everything from the beginning,' Vic said, leaning forward and folding his paper away.

Tom took a deep breath and did as he was asked.

When he finished, Vic rubbed his chin. 'It's a lie, mate, you have to believe me. Apart from the fact I don't fancy her, I've never fucked her… I wind you up about it, sure, because you're so in love with her, and I think you're making the biggest mistake of your life. But I haven't been near her, I promise, mate. But if Big Willy is feeding you cow shit through his sidekick, he must be doing it for a reason.'

'What do you mean?' Tom asked. 'I was interviewed by Major Graham.'

'Big Willy's mouthpiece? He does nothing without checking first. Think about it. Why would she not be allowed to accompany you back to Blighty? Maybe she's needed here, if you know what I mean. I always told you to be careful what you told her.'

'I didn't tell her anything!' Tom said.

'Mate, forgive me for pointing it out, but you're not the only one who shares her pillow. If she poses no risk, then why make up some bullshit to put you off?'

'That's exactly what he said,' Tom said.

'Who?'

'The major. He said my application was turned down, along with everybody else's, because they think she's an informant. They want me to keep an eye on her.'

'There! I fucking told you!' Vic said.

Chapter 29

Colonel Seaton poured a very large brandy.

His wife had been dropped off right outside their house by a taxi driver. When he'd seen her jeep wasn't there, he'd thought she'd been shopping, or to meet a friend for coffee in Larnaca. She often went out unannounced. What did he know of her habits? She could come and go as she pleased. Then he'd remembered that she'd said she'd be at the yard all day, tending Temper and all the other waifs and strays she cared for. Andi liked to see herself as some kind of horse whisperer, saving abandoned animals, and she did a damn good job. She was self-sufficient and hard; perfect army wife material. But why return in a cab?

So his shock when he saw her face was genuine. And she had been limping.

She was still shaking, and hadn't stopped since walking into their kitchen through the back. Andi didn't like using the front door when she wasn't expecting guests; she saw it as a frivolous waste of time, going through all of those rooms to get to the place she loved best: the garden. She'd much rather leave all that to the staff and settle in her favourite chair on the decking, overlooking the recently trimmed bushes, and beyond, down to the beach. The house was built cleverly, with the view in mind. It was the best on camp, and so it should be. The colonel was the most important man on the base and so he needed to show this with his status as a homemaker. They'd had all sorts of guests visit them since taking over the post almost two years ago. They'd applied for an extension to the posting. A position this good was like rocking-horse shit and he'd argued his case to the MOD, saying that the relations he'd built were invaluable and relied upon him staying garrison commander, at least for another two years: the usual tenure. It was a blatant abuse of the rulebook, but out here, in the sunshine, the rulebook often got lost.

But now he asked himself if it was worth it.

'Drink this,' he said gently, handing her a brandy in a beautiful locally handmade earthenware goblet. It was decorated with flowers and birds, they had a whole set.

She took it with both hands and steadied herself.

'What else did they say?' he asked.

She'd said very little since coming in and heading straight for the drawing room, taking a seat by the large open fire, which wasn't lit until Christmas, and then it was only a ceremonial nod to home. He'd known something was seriously wrong when she didn't go out to the garden. He'd managed to get a little out of her, in so far as two men had come to the yard and demanded she go with them right away.

'Why didn't you call security?'

'They threatened me, and handled me,' she said through tears.

Andi never cried, unless a horse or dog had to be humanely dispatched. She didn't even shed a tear when their children left for boarding school, keeping a stiff upper lip to set an example for them to be strong. Not so with animals, and not so right now. He'd never seen her like this before. She drained the cup, he went to get the bottle and poured another.

'Jesus, that's better. Bill, what have you done?' she asked him squarely, staring into his eyes.

A creeping feeling tingled up his spine. He went to the cupboard and got himself a glass, pouring another large brandy and draining it.

'What do you mean? Why are you asking that? Has this got something to do with me?' he asked.

'I've been given a very specific set of instructions. I had to memorise them. They are for you. If you don't follow them...'

She held her glass out for him to refill. Her hand started to shake again. He put his hand out to still it, lest the drink spill. Her hands were as cold as death. He knelt before her. She looked at her hand, where her jewellery usually graced her long fingers casually but indulgently too.

'Where are your rings?'

'They took them.'

'So this is robbery! I'm calling the garrison police!'

'No! Bill. Listen to me. You can't tell anyone.'

'What the hell! No one tells me what to do, Andi, I will find them both and have them thrown in an island jail for the rest of their lives.'

'No you won't,' she said simply.

He stared at her. She sipped the brown drink, slowly this time, and took a deep breath.

'At first, I thought just that, a robbery or assault.'

'They assaulted you?'

'No. They didn't. They weren't interested in that. Just you.'

'Me?'

'Yes, Bill, you know what I'm talking about, don't you? The money. The flights. The trips. The hospitality and holidays and jewellery. All of it. I'm not stupid. I've always known. The people you have over to the house. I'm always polite and leave at the appropriate time, but I know that you shouldn't be doing it because I know you don't talk to me about it. You're ashamed. Is this about the money or the prostitutes?' she asked.

'Andi, there never was—'

'Oh, Bill, I saw the photos, remember? It will never go away, will it?'

He knew she was watching him, as he got up and walked to the fireplace, as if about to deliver a chapter of Dickens on a chilly winter night.

'I had no idea it was this serious,' she said.

'Don't you even dare!' He spun round and attacked her full on, with his glare and accusatory eyes. She burst into tears. He put down his glass on the mantelpiece and put his hands in his pockets.

'How dare I?' She looked at him, begging him with her eyes to open up to her and admit it was over. But she knew he wouldn't.

'You said yourself, you're not stupid, you know what I have to do to keep us safe,' he said.

It was an admirable attempt, but she wasn't some new kid on the block, looking for reassurance, he knew that much. She'd lived with Bill half her life.

'Listen to me, Bill. Whatever you have done, it has to stop. We need to tell the MOD that you're being blackmailed. They can sort it out. We'll go back to London and start again, slate clean and fresh.' She motioned around her. 'I don't need all this, they're just toys. I really think it's time we got out of here.' He could tell she was scared and defeated. Her earlier belligerence had been wounded pride: now reality was setting in.

He watched her and turned away to the window. It was clear that he was in thought for long moments until he turned back to her.

'Andi, tell me exactly what you were told. It's for the investigation, yes? We need to give them all the details,' he encouraged her. She relaxed a little.

'Right, yes, for the investigation. So, let me remember, it's coming back.'

'Start at the beginning.'

She nodded, nursing her glass like her life depended on it.

'Two men came to the yard and I was alone. I told them they were on private property, I asked them how they'd got in, but they became threatening. Temper was tied up and she was whinnying. Oh God! Temper!'

She placed her glass down, and got up and ran across the room. He followed her and caught her in time before she got to the door, blocking her way and grabbing her arm.

'Andi, calm down, somebody else can go and see Temper.'

She looked at him oddly.

'Come on, carry on with the story. This is important for the report I have to send, so I can get extra security at the gate. I'm sacking whoever was on the gate today and I'll have them removed from their jobs.'

Locals were commonly employed by the sovereign base to fill all sorts of roles, including some in security. It was madness but had been like that for decades. It improved international relations between the two nations and generated income.

'I need to see if Temper's all right, Bill,' she said again.

'Of course you do, but tell me what you remember first or it will fade. I have experience of these things, trust me.'

'Trust you? Are you kidding? Jesus, Bill, this is all about you.'

He backed away from her and splayed his arms apart, as if proving his innocence. Then she saw his brow knit and a cloud of anger come over his face.

'Don't play that game with me, Andi. You knew full well what we were getting into. This is a step too far, but they must want something. What is it?'

She gawped at him, mouth open wide, and what colour she had left in her face drained away, despite her fabulous tan.

Now, she looked away.

'They showed me pictures of a dead woman.' Her voice was deadpan. 'They also said that I would end up like that if I didn't communicate successfully to you the importance of not losing your nerve right now. They said you would understand when I told you that we need a sacrificial lamb.'

Her husband turned away.

'Bill?'

He didn't answer. He was deep in thought, so she left quietly and took a set of keys from the table by the door. She closed the front door gently and got into the spare jeep; they had several. She drove towards the yard, across the exercise area and towards the scrubland in the distance. It was slightly elevated and the view was serene. There was no hint of tourism or fuss up there and as she got closer to the gate, excitement built inside her to see Temper, and give her lots of apples and carrots. She gripped the wheel harder and put her foot down. Dust flew up behind the wheels and spread for a dozen yards behind the vehicle, which tottered along the bumpy track.

The gate was wide open and she hoped that someone else had rescued Temper from the afternoon heat and given her some water and food. As she neared the stables, there was only her abandoned jeep parked up, there wasn't another car in sight, or any sign of a human being. The sky was orange and the air cooler and shadows danced in technicolour across the arid sand. And then she saw it.

'No! No!' she wailed. Her voice whipped away into the empty air.

She screeched the jeep to a halt and jumped out, rushing to Temper, who lay on her side, on the floor. White foam was stuck to her mouth and lips and her eyes were open and staring. Andi found an artery and felt for her heartbeat, but there was none. She stared up to the sky and beyond to the beach, but there were no answers there and no redemption. And no going back.

She buried her head in Temper's mane and lay down with her, holding her gently and whispering, 'I'm sorry.'

Chapter 30

Theo Charalambous sat at the bar, in his usual place, and ordered a Coke. Somebody had once told him that he drank too much of the dark caramel soda and he'd told them to fuck off, in Greek of course. But the general language of the Blue Lantern was English. And this was a beautiful irony.

His wife had bought him a fit watch and he wore it because it made her happy. But he never looked at it. Occasionally she did and told him that his blood pressure was way too high and that he needed to lose some weight: perhaps get off his bar stool once in a while. But that's where he was happy and he'd been sat there for the best part of ten years. It was still early and only a few regular drinkers sat with him, but they sipped expensive beer and wine, bought in exchange for the day shift peeling off their scraps of clothing as they frolicked on the polished counter top, slipping around poles and kneeling down to wiggle their wobbly bits into eager faces. He took no interest in it and paid little attention until the later punters arrived who brought the serious money.

A waft of air behind him caught his attention and he turned to the door. Artemis, his brother, strode in and took a seat next to him.

'Is it done?' Theo asked.

Artemis nodded. They shared a joke in Greek and laughed.

'Look at Irena trying hard to get noticed,' Theo said to his brother. 'She wants a night shift.'

'She'd scare everybody off,' Artemis joked. The brothers preferred women with flesh on their bones, but the

171

higher-priced ladies were always the skinnier ones, in the western style, with large breasts and small waists, and a lot younger. They'd always said when they were growing up that they'd go into business together and make their mother proud. It hadn't quite worked out how they imagined, but they had jobs that paid well and came with certain perks. Their mother had a nice new swanky house in the Troodos foothills and both men had been gifted homes close to the oceanfront. Their tastes were modest, and they'd been told that this was what kept them trustworthy: they weren't greedy. But what more could a man want than food in his belly and time to walk along the beach, watching their grandchildren play in the sea? They knew they'd never get rid of the British from their beloved island, but, piece by piece, they were becoming limited to this tiny base at the end of the Larnaca strip. And the Brits were too terrified to get involved in local politics anyhow. They left each other alone. As long as the American planes were allowed to use the airstrip at the other end of the island, and launch their pathetic campaigns to the east, the rest of the territory was theirs and theirs alone.

'She's easily replaced,' Theo said, referring to the subject at hand. Girls like Ani came and went. They meant nothing. There was a steady trickle of imports from Moscow, flights arriving three times weekly. Now it was done, he could get back to business as usual.

Monday nights were slow and Theo didn't expect any serious business for hours. The girls were easily bored. Only those who behaved themselves were allowed to venture beyond their rooms above the Blue Lantern. Ani had strayed too many times.

A woman appeared behind the bar, she nodded at the brothers, to signal that Ani's things had been distributed between the other girls, and her bed made ready for a new arrival. Artemis nodded and ordered a drink. Theo watched a silent football match being played in Paris. The return leg would be played at Nicosia at the Pancyprians Stadium. He pushed the tray of pistachios to his brother and they peeled the nuts from their shells, discarding the hard husks back onto the tray. A blatant foul made them both wince. The woman behind the bar glanced up and shook her head, taking no interest in the beautiful game whatsoever. An import of the British that was decent, along with driving on the left, and chips.

Artemis saw a flicker of movement out of the corner of his eye and nudged Theo. A man, who was clearly intoxicated, was getting too close to one of the dancers and the girl had given the signal that he hadn't paid. Artemis walked slowly around the bar to the man in question.

'You had enough, friend?'

'Who the fuck are you?'

Artemis didn't recognise the man, but he was obviously a Brit, alone, and off his tits on booze. No one at the establishment had any problem with drunk men paying for the girls, but that was the thing: they had to pay, and up front. 'You don't pay, you don't get to sit here. That's the policy, otherwise you can leave, my friend.'

Artemis was shorter than the man, but wider, and had the advantage of being sober and mean as fuck. His knuckles were as fat as a bowl of moussaka, but that's where the comparison ended. Nothing about Artemis was fluffy and light, and he made sure to wear heavy gold rings on the fingers that made contact best. He put his hands on his hips and called over the girl in question. She whispered into Artemis's ear, who speedily got the man round the neck with his huge forearms. The guy struggled, but he stood no chance. He was uncoordinated and weak. Artemis dragged him off the stool he was barely stuck to and easily manoeuvred him towards the door. Theo continued watching the match.

Artemis kicked the door open with his foot and dragged the man out into the entrance, where the evening doorman was doing pull-ups on a bar above the door. He dropped down and raised his eyebrows to Artemis.

'He won't pay for the girls,' Artemis said.

The man spluttered and coughed. 'I can pay!' he said. Artemis set him free and the man wriggled to his feet. 'Look, fellas, I was about to go to the cashpoint, come on, give me five minutes.'

'Fuck off,' the doorman and Artemis said in unison.

The man scowled. 'This place is a shithole anyway.'

The doorman moved towards him and the man stumbled backwards and edged out of the door, letting in a piercing shaft of orange evening light, warm air and dust.

'Don't come back, we look after our girls,' Artemis said.

The doorman shoved the man out of the door and slammed it shut.

'Don't worry, boss, I remember all faces,' he said to Artemis, who went back inside.

'Make sure if he comes back, you break his legs,' Artemis instructed.

'Yes, boss.'

Artemis went back to his brother to ask when Katerina would come again. They had business to discuss with her.

Chapter 31

Helen sat on the wall which bordered the officers' mess garden. It was about as far away as she could get without having to make conversation. She didn't want to engage with anyone, knowing full well that she would have to get to know Tom Fleet better at some point, when he turned up. She'd looked for him after dinner, and even knocked on his room door, but he wasn't here.

She watched the sea. Crystals of blue and purple danced on the surface and the sun finally disappeared behind the horizon, and the furnace heat subsided. It had been a long but productive day. Her body was tired. A breeze wafted upwards towards the camp and it moved her blouse over her skin. Lights flickered all along the strip, which curved round like a bay out of a magazine shoot. It was a perfect horseshoe and for a moment Helen wondered what had caused its faultless shape: years of steady erosion? An ancient volcano? It was mesmerising.

As the day wore on, she'd become more in awe of Kay and Jen, both utterly dedicated officers, and the relief only added to the sensation of her body letting go of some tension. They would be at the Blue Lantern by now. Each taking a role. Kay inside and Jen outside, watching. Helen was satisfied that they both knew their professional limits. Besides, she'd asked Gem to keep an eye on them. British soldiers weren't generally armed when off the ESBA, but there was safety in numbers. She'd do it herself, but her face had been spotted all over the ESBA in the last couple of days and she trusted few. Her decision to include Gem in that small circle had come when he'd held his hand out to her when, this afternoon, she tripped when she got out of the car, rushing to get to the mess, and Gem had caught her. It was a small thing but said a lot about him. It was something that Helen had learned many years ago about people's compassion.

The lights of a car caught her attention and she decided that she fancied a walk. She had everything she needed: phone, ID, wallet and lip balm. The evening was seductively mild compared to the daytime and she understood why people who lived in hot countries came out at night to party. She removed her sandals and carried them in her hand. The lights of the strip burned brighter as she walked along the beach. She could barely hear any noise, apart from the waves breaking on the shore, and the swish of a car engine rushing past, up on the road. As she got closer to the strip, she heard music and laughter: the sound of holidays.

A few businesses were in full darkness, finished for the day, but the tavernas, discos and bars were filling up and coming alive. She looked towards the row of dive shops dotted along the front and noticed that a light burned in Eric's. It made her happy that she had a friend to visit and she decided to walk there. As she got closer, she realised that the light was coming from the rear of the shop. He'd be sipping coffee, no doubt. She smiled to herself and walked up to the back of the shop.

'Hi,' she said quietly.

Eric jumped and spilled his coffee.

'Shit, sorry, I didn't mean to startle you,' she said.

He got up and assessed the damage and laughed. 'I don't expect beautiful women to sneak up on me in the middle of the night,' he said.

Helen let the compliment go. She found tissues and handed them to him. He thanked her and wiped up the coffee. It had only splashed on his leg.

'I wasn't sleepy,' she said, by way of an attempted explanation, suddenly feeling foolish that she'd intruded.

'Is your manservant with you?' He smiled.

Helen shook her head. 'I walked.'

'Should I make a new pot?' he asked.

'Do you mind?'

'Not at all, I could do with the company. I thought I was done for. I shouldn't underestimate you, I'm sure you can take care of yourself,' he said.

'You know that might not be too far from the truth. What I mean is, you need to watch your back.'

'Well, I've got you. Besides, what do I know?' he asked.

'You've been asking questions on my behalf, maybe you should stop. For your own safety, I mean.'

She took a seat and watched him fix coffee using a silver percolator on the stove. Her father had one and it reminded her of home.

'You don't prop up the bar at the Palm Beach and get smashed on cocktails?' she asked. 'What else is there to do here?'

He nodded, acknowledging that many of his peers did just that. 'I don't think diving and drinking mix that well,' he said.

'You're right. I was hoping to get a tour for old times' sake on the *Zenobia*, would you take me?'

'Now?'

'No, don't worry. My night diving is a bit rusty, I just thought you should get back in the water.'

'Nice try. Don't worry, I will. I've done about as much as I can here, so I need to get back to work soon.'

'I've held you up,' she said.

'No, not at all.' He stirred sugar and milk into the cups and handed her one. 'I'll take you out there when you're ready. I had you as someone who never stops working,' he said.

'I'll take that as a compliment. I'm on a tight schedule. I've been given a week to find out what happened to Paul, and I feel as though it will run out before I get to the bottom of it.'

'Has it crossed your mind that you'll be next?'

She nodded, sipping the hot coffee, and trying to relax. Being around Eric was as close as she got to downloading and unwinding, which was ironic given why they'd met. He was easy to be with and she figured it was his age. He exuded calm, but she knew that he was still rattled by Paul's death.

'Did Paul ever tell you about the Blue Lantern?' she asked him.

'You're joking? Paul was the straightest guy I knew. He was all copper and duty. He didn't approve of clubs like that, he thought them all dens of money laundering and told me he'd love to close them all down.'

'If only we still ruled the island,' Helen chipped in.

Eric laughed and stretched in his seat. 'Tell you what, why don't I take you out tomorrow?'

'You serious?' she said.

'If I want to find out what happened to Paul, I need to keep you sweet. Here, bright and early before you start work?'

Helen's sense of obligation to her mission warned her to say no, but she also knew from experience that if she got here early, they could be done by nine a.m. Besides, she'd reached several dead ends today. She couldn't build a case on supposition. The plan she'd hatched between herself and the SIB girls was only a goer if she got permission from back home. Feeding information to intelligence operatives and the commander of JSSU was a serious undertaking and she needed to back her case with solid evidence, of which she had none. Yet.

Her phone buzzed. It was a text from Kay, whose task it was to pose as a punter at the Blue Lantern. She was working late. The text was lengthy and began by apologising for disturbing Helen if she was asleep. She was anything but, and read it with interest. It would appear that the woman identified by Helen at the officers' mess, and who'd been tailed to the Russian Embassy, still hadn't showed for work.

'I'm spending a fortune on cocktails. Planning to leave as soon as I can make an excuse for not paying for a private dance,' Kay wrote.

Helen appreciated the good humour, but she also felt guilty for putting her officer in a tricky position, but then the woman had offered. Helen had worked undercover many times and knew the risks. Sex was a language; that was all; it was used for bartering and gaining information. And as an undercover officer, one had to avoid it with more ingenious excuses every time.

'Be careful,' Helen texted back. 'Is Jen still outside?'

'Yes. Don't worry. I've got what I need. The taxi driver and the manager are brothers. All the girls are terrified of them.'

Helen took in the information and put her phone away.

'Still working, I see. Have you got a waterproof phone for tomorrow?' Eric teased her.

'I promise I won't bring it. When you say early?'

'Six?'

'I'm glad you're ready to go back in the water,' she said.

They clinked their coffee mugs together and Helen went to leave.

'I'll walk you back,' Eric said. It was a fair walk, but they could see the lights of camp glistening across the bay. It would take perhaps twenty minutes.

It was a chivalrous gesture but one that didn't offend. Helen knew that it was also an excuse to spend some more time together, and she didn't mind at all.

Chapter 32

Kay sat in the Blue Lantern alone. She wore a summer dress, and pumps, with a thin cardigan. She didn't look like an average punter, but then who did? The stereotype of the fat desperate and lonely man looking for girls wasn't usually what you found in these joints. Women frequented them too, either to enjoy the show, because watching a woman's body gyrate around a pole was captivating and sensual, or because they preferred to sleep with women than men. It didn't much matter, because paying customers all spent the same cash.

She greeted the doorman with a smile and he opened the door for her, admiring her figure. As she expected, there were other lone women inside, sat in dark corners, some of them accompanied by escorts, and some just drinking. And watching. The bar was full, so she was sat at a table already occupied by two men. They'd joyfully accepted when she'd asked if she could join them. They made small talk, but Kay, whilst being polite, gave nothing personal away. Her story was that she was sizing up the joint to surprise her friends, who were there on a hen party. The two men happily gave her their assessment of the quality of the place, compared to others along the strip, and Kay acted impressed. They talked about the costs involved and if the club might do some deals. The men doubted it, but then if they were a large group, clubbing together, surely it was worth it for her friend? Kay agreed.

'Here she comes, sorry, love, we need to watch this,' one said, falling into mesmerised silence as a young woman strutted onto the bar and approached the pole. Helen had given her a bunch of Cypriot pounds, and she got through them at a rapid rate. Getting comfortable took time. Every time she was served a drink, she came up with better ways of disposing of it: either taking it to the toilet, filling up the men's drinks when they weren't looking and too drunk to notice, or simply pouring it into the fake plants behind her.

She clocked the layout of the place: the fat man at the bar who she knew was Theo; the number of girls; the people who came and went, and their motives. For the most part, they were punters, but occasionally, somebody walked in and went straight across to Theo to tell him something.

A girl approached her and sat on her knee. Kay went along with it and bought her a drink.

'You want a private dance?'

'I was waiting for somebody. I want Anastasia,' she said.

The girl stiffened a little.

'I'm sorry, I didn't mean to offend you. I don't know what she looks like, I was just told she was amazing, I'm sure you are too.'

The girl smiled. She was young, definitely not yet twenty.

'She's gone,' she said.

'Gone? Where?' Kay asked.

'Just gone. So, you have to have me.'

And that was how simple it was. The girl offered her a private dance.

'Is your boss watching?' Kay asked.

The girl nodded and smiled, without looking towards the bar.

'He watches how many private dances you have?' Kay asked.

Another nod.

'I'm guessing it's the fat bloke at the bar? Come on, I'll buy a bottle of champagne, just to get you in his good books,' Kay said.

The girl was delighted and cuddled close to Kay. Her skin was sticky and her hair, on closer look, was unwashed. The girl was semi-delirious too and Kay knew she'd been taking drugs of some sort. But none of what she was witnessing was about to crack any spy rings, or even pique the attention of the local police: it was a normal evening along the strip here, so she'd been told, an ordinary life for this girl, and the other twenty or so sitting on people's laps and exhorting money out of guests.

The drugs worked in Kay's favour, because the girl almost nodded off, and Kay propped her up, pretending to talk for the sake of her boss. Not that he looked around often, he was more interested in his tapas. But it did afford her the opportunity to watch.

Kay had learned to observe at airports, with her father, travelling to and from her grandmother's house in France. She'd been flying for as long as she could remember, and her father always made sure that they played games at the airport to keep her interested. They made up stories about them and Kay had done it ever since. It stoked her appetite for intrigue and honed her skills of perception to investigative levels. It was no surprise she'd entered some kind of detective career. She'd toyed with the general civilian police, but it somehow didn't tick the same boxes as the army, when she'd approached them at her careers fair at university. The travelling clinched the deal, and here she was, amongst strangers doing what she did best: scrutinising people.

She'd learned to read a room, as soon as she entered it, and take in each person's position in it as well as their character and contribution to what was going on. Theo, at the bar, didn't move or say much, but she knew by his body moves, that he was one hundred per cent in charge. The girls changed their body language as they walked past him. It would be imperceptible to the untrained eye, but not to her. Then there was the woman in the suit who joined him late into the night. They were wrapped in intense conversation, and seemed to argue. The woman was a negotiator of some sort; Kay knew this by the way she held herself and tried to reason with him. Theo treated her with confident nonchalance. She got the impression that this was a mistake, and he was treating her this way because she was a woman, not because of what he seemed to pretend to know of her position.

When Kay looked at the woman's face, she saw impatience and something else. It wasn't like a wife, or a lover, after a tiff. It was the look of superior knowledge. It was as if she was trying to give Theo a chance. But he kept rejecting it. The woman gave it her best shot, it seemed, until the door opened and Theo's brother joined them. Kay watched as the woman's body stiffened and she got off her stool and gathered her few belongings, as if this was a business meeting, not a social call. She drained her water glass and said something to Theo, ignoring his brother. Kay watched as Artemis returned the frostiness and took her stool as she got off it, and walked out of the club.

Kay turned to her date for the night, and saw that she was asleep. Kay poked her and she stirred. She felt sorry for the girl, and another came over, realising the girl would soon attract the wrong attention if she wasn't earning money.

'Can you put her to bed?' Kay asked. The woman nodded. 'Make it look as though I'm taking her to a private room,' Kay added. The woman nodded again. They held her up. The two brothers looked round, but the brightness of Kay's smile and her loud order of another bottle of champagne, despite the last one, at over one-hundred-and-fifty Cypriot pounds, having been poured into a planter seemed to satisfy them. They went back to their beer and tapas.

Out in the dingy hallway, Kay helped prop up the young woman and handed her to the older of the two. Their eyes locked. An understanding passed between them. Kay got out another hundred pounds and gave it to the woman.

'She made me happy,' Kay said.

The older woman thanked her.

'She won't get into trouble?' Kay asked.

'No,' the woman shook her head.

'I like her. I liked Anastasia too,' Kay said.

The woman nodded. Her face was grave.

'Is she ill? Tired?' Kay smiled.

'No. She's gone.'

'What, she's left?'

'Yes. Not coming back,' the woman said. 'You go, I take care of her.'

Kay left them and went to the exit. She had what she'd come for. Before she'd taken her seat at the club, she'd checked the camera on her jacket; the angles, the lighting and the battery. She checked it again now and got into the back of Gem's car.

'Back to the mess?' Gem asked.

She turned to where she knew Jen had been parked. She saw her behind the wheel, and they gave each other the thumbs up.

Jen text her. 'Call it a night?' she asked.

Kay agreed.

'Yes, back to the mess, please, Gem.'

Chapter 33

When her alarm went off, at five a.m., Helen forgot where she was again, until the sweat along her breastbone reminded her that she'd unconsciously flung open the window again in the night. The air-conditioning unit whirred, unused to having to work against the warm air flowing freely in through the curtains. Helen got out of bed and closed the window and the air-con unit calmed down, seemingly thanking her. She dressed quickly, second-guessing herself and feeling guilty about promising to meet Eric. Damn it. What was it that the wellness team said about mental health and burnout? Her sense of commitment chided her for even thinking that she needed a break, after only being on the island barely three days. She pushed the thoughts aside and reminded herself that no one would be up now anyway. Not here. Apart from fitness tests and weighted marches across local terrain every few months, the garrison wouldn't get going until gone seven.

She put on a bikini, packed in haste just in case, and then a pair of shorts and a T-shirt. She pulled trainers onto her feet and tried to remember the tenets of diving. It had been years. Had she perhaps given Eric an overinflated impression of her talent? Probably. Well, she was sure she was in good hands. A tiny voice in her head reminded her that the last person to dive with Eric Dukakis had died tragically. 'Fuck off,' she told it.

By the time she arrived at the dive school, Eric was already there; he might not have even left, after he'd walked her back last night, and they'd chatted about their time in the military, and their lives. He was divorced. He had two kids. He loved his life here: he was free and happy. Before Paul's murder.

In return, she'd told him that she'd never married, though once come close, and she had no kids. There she'd stopped short of telling him about the baby she'd lost. She'd told him that she didn't have time for kids. It was different for women in the military: they had to choose between life and career. She didn't want the pressure that came with being a working mother: working like you weren't a mother, and mothering like you didn't work. She omitted to tell him that her hand had been forced.

Eric was all smiles and, for a moment, she forgot why she was on the island. After all, that's why he was taking her out on the *Zenobia*: to forget. It seemed like a brutal irony that the site of Paul's death was her choice of a leisure spot, but it wasn't about that – in fact, from what she'd found out about Paul, he'd approve.

They checked their kit and Eric walked her to the rib, which he'd already packed with tanks, fins and other equipment. She watched him in his element and hoped that today he'd begin his journey back to his old self, when he dived, because it was in his blood. She wanted to be a part of his getting over Paul's death, not the reason why it lingered. She could see, because it was abundantly obvious, that Eric was a professional and took safety seriously, which was why Paul's death, on his watch, hurt so bad.

The sea was flat calm and there was no one else about apart from a single waterski boat that pulled a couple along behind it. They fell into the water regularly and needed setting back up every few minutes. Helen preferred being under the water.

They'd had a chat about the depth and pattern of the dive. All she wanted was to go to the stern side of the ship that was surface-facing, the port being on the seabed at almost fifty metres. She'd be happy seeing a few fish and practising her technique. To Eric, the request was second nature and she could tell he was looking forward to it.

He chose a short wetsuit for her and she slipped it on to her waist, keeping her T-shirt on. He already wore his, open to his shorts, and he wore no top. She often wondered what it would feel like to be so body confident: strutting around, tying ropes and fixing stuff with half your body showing; it must be the most liberating thing in the world. But then one had to have the taut muscle structure to get away with it in the first place. He did. His torso was tanned, as it should be spending so much of his time in this sun. Her skin was pale in comparison, having spent a measly two weeks in the French Alps.

They didn't talk much on the way out, as the sound of the engine and the spray from the sea drowned them out. Helen faced the direction of the sunken ship and allowed her hair to flow freely and the sea to give her a soaking. Thoughts of the investigation were paused for now, and she knew that as soon as she touched the shore once more, in an hour or so, it would all come rushing back.

Eric slowed the engine and Helen saw something in his face that she hadn't seen since she'd been here. If nothing else, this had forced him to face what he was most scared of. For that it was worth it.

'We've beaten everybody,' he said.

Each dive school had its own buoy and they bobbed about with the wake from the single rib, even though it was tiny compared to some of the boats out here during the day. Otherwise, the water was untouched and the sun shone directly down to the depths, where Helen could see the outline of the ship. Her stomach flipped with butterflies. She forgot about her inhibitions and her natural sense of excitement took over as she stripped off her T-shirt and stood up in the rib. Eric clipped the rib to the buoy and pulled up his wetsuit. She zipped hers up and pulled on her kit for final tests before they went over the side.

'You're shaking,' he said to her as he passed her buoyancy jacket.

'I'm anxious but excited,' she said, and it was the truth. She couldn't wait to get down there, but, at the same time, she knew that her buddy was surely worried himself.

He covered her hands with his and fastened her weight belt tight, making her body pull towards him. He concentrated on his own kit and then it was time to test the tanks one last time before their descent. She took long deep breaths, but not too deep, because hyperventilating at the surface before a dive could be fatal. She was trying to calm down so she didn't suck too much air and disappoint him. A rookie would last twenty minutes out here, she hoped she'd last longer with the air they each had. She had no doubt that Eric would breathe like he did on the surface and she knew that it wouldn't be the case for her; she was too fired up and felt too alive. The exhilaration she already felt threatened to overwhelm her, but she got herself under control and they sat together on the side of the rib. A final spit into her mask and a suck on her DV did the trick and they fell backwards off the rib.

She'd forgotten how blue the water was under the surface. It was almost magical in its infinity. Visibility must be fifty metres or more. She looked down and the colours of the metal below had turned orange, green and purple with the years of a hostile takeover by the ocean's flora and fauna. She could already see fish down there, who'd made it their home.

They agreed to descend, with thumbs down, and she adjusted her buoyancy and they started to go down. Eric checked on her frequently and she got the distinct impression that he'd never leave her side. She gave the okay sign and focused her attention on him.

In a few minutes, they were past the six-metre mark and heading down to ten, then fifteen, then within touching distance of the deck. Fish scattered as they descended and Helen looked up to the surface, seemingly untouchable above them. The bright blue surrounded her and her breathing slowed as peace engulfed her.

Eric held her hand gently and pointed out parts of the ship, still discernible after all the years she'd been assaulted by nature. It was funny how ships were supposed to be on top of the water, splendid in their finery, but, down here, the *Zenobia* looked comfortable in her slumber, as if she was meant to be there. It was a lazy repose, like one of those snow globes at Christmas, with the scene behind glass, shaken by children to reveal the hidden world inside.

As the animals parted for them as they drifted along, using their fins sparingly against the lenient current, Helen recognised the colours and shapes of most of the fish; she saw huge groupers, ugly with their downward pouts staring at her; silver sea bream, darting this way and that; bright wrasses, of all colours, injecting blazes of neon; and great amberjack, easily mistaken for tuna.

Helen looked around, to the rear of the ship, where the sea turned dark because the light reflection off the wreck faded, and Eric pointed to the propeller. It rose up like a giant monument and her pulse began to creep up. Maybe they'd see a turtle or a moray eel?

Swathes of grass wafted up from the twisted metal and they swam closer.

Grass? Helen's head was playing tricks on her. There wasn't any seagrass down here, or reeds, or anything else resembling what might have been taken for weeds that commonly resided in ponds, not sea water. Then Eric stopped and grabbed her hand. He'd seen what she had at the same moment, and a thrill of excitement rushed through her as she guessed that it might be the tail of a huge eel. As long as it wasn't the gaping jaw end that she encountered, she should be okay.

They swam closer, but then the black swathe of grass-like hair parted and revealed the face of a beautiful young woman. Helen let out a gasp of air and, for a moment, she thought she might spring to the surface, horrified by what she saw. Was she imagining it? Panic threatened to overwhelm her, but the warmth of Eric's hand, even down here, without the heat of the sun, brought her back to her senses.

It was a woman down there.

Suddenly, Eric was in front of Helen's face, forcing her to look at him, calming her down and focusing his eyes on her, pointing to his air gauge. He was telling her to slow her breathing. She came to her senses and reality thrust into her brain, waking her up to what she was witnessing. She allowed Eric to check her air and he was happy that she was safely within limits. He shielded her, but she needed to look. She gave him the okay sign and they turned around, staring at what they'd seen, not quite believing it.

Helen saw clearly now that the black mass of reedy material was human hair, and it swished about in the current. She stared at the woman, almost hoping that she was still alive, somehow wondering if she was swimming down here. But a cheeky grouper came in for a nibble and knocked the woman's head to the side. Helen cringed and batted him away as gently as she could. He was only looking for a meal.

Eric got out his plastic board and pencil and began writing. As he did, she went closer to the dead woman. Her hands were bound behind her back and she was tied, by her feet, to what looked like a rusted ladder, which might have served a purpose many years ago, out here on the deck.

'Shall we take her up?' Eric wrote.

Helen shook her head. She took his pad and pencil and wrote her reply.

'We shouldn't move her. Don't touch her.'

Helen gave the thumbs up sign, meaning they should ascend. Their dive was over before it had really begun. Then she realised what she must do.

'Camera?' she wrote.

Eric looked at her oddly, from behind his mask, but then she saw understanding dawn on his face. He nodded and pulled out his underwater camera from the pouch at his hip. He handed it to her and she shook her head, pointing at him. He nodded and got the camera ready, waiting for her instructions. She pointed at the woman and gave a signal to click a shot when she was ready, making sure her hand was in place, pointing to various points on the woman's body, for reference later. Eric did as he was asked and once Helen had what she thought was a comprehensive assessment of the woman's body, she signalled they should go up. She paused in front of Eric as he put away his camera and wrote on his board. 'Are you okay?'

She held both his hands and looked behind his mask, into his eyes. He returned her grip and shrugged his shoulders in response. All she wanted was to talk to him, in real terms, not through code. It was such a sterile moment, when what they both needed was an organic connection. But that had to wait. Her head raced with the cruelty of Eric's situation. She'd witnessed plenty of dead bodies, and studied them, but Eric had two thrust on him, in under a week, in the most horrendous circumstances.

They had to off-gas at the six-metre point, given the depth of their dive today, and they hung about on the guide rope, not looking at one another, just into the blue beyond and down to the woman, drifting below them. They hadn't seen her on their way down, but now they couldn't take their eyes off her. Finally, they were ready to ascend back to the rib and they broke the surface and clambered back into the boat, not speaking for a long time. They just knelt there, after pulling themselves over the sides, and ripping their DVs out of their mouths, gasping for air – real, true air – and staring ahead, trying to process what they'd seen. They threw off their masks and fins and sat in stunned silence for seconds or minutes, it wasn't clear. Helen ripped off her jacket and the tanks clunked on the rib base, Eric did the same, and busied himself with tying them up. Then he came back to her and lifted her head.

Helen looked at him and her breathing finally slowed. 'What the fuck?' she said. 'Are you all right?' she asked, he was shaking and he hadn't said anything. 'Eric?'

He gasped. 'Yeah, I'm okay. No! You know what? No, I'm not okay! Jesus fucking Christ, what was that? Did we just see that?'

Helen nodded and held onto him. The movement of the water caused them to hang on close, and they bobbed up and down, catching their thoughts.

'I know who she is,' Helen said.

'What?' he replied.

She looked at him and nodded, pushing her soaking hair away from her face.

'She's from the Blue Lantern.'

Chapter 34

The coastguard was quick to reach the small rib, and they brought two divers, like Helen had told them to when she made the call from the radio on Eric's rib.

They spoke in English. She explained who she was and they agreed that she could hang around while the body was brought to the surface. Helen had no idea what their protocol was regarding death at such depths, and if the scene would be secure or examined quickly and closed off, or if at all. All she could think about was how badly the crime scene had been handled after Paul's death. That's why she'd asked Eric for his camera. This was no diving accident, nor had the woman gone for a leisurely swim at twenty metres and caught a chill. This was murder. And a message. This girl was supposed to be found, and quickly. The *Zenobia* dive site was a busy and public place.

Helen's head rushed in all directions. She had to call Don at HQ, and let him know. The woman who was being pulled from the water, into the white police boat, as other dive boats circled, angry that their slots were delayed, was a potential suspect in her case, and she was last seen at the Russian Embassy in Nicosia. The last thing Helen needed was a clash of international interests, but that was what she was facing. It was now confirmed that she couldn't avoid the fact that another nation was at play here, on the island, and it had something to do with leaked intelligence, and how close Paul had got. Helen needed answers and she knew that she'd find them at the Blue Lantern. But how?

She looked at the body as it was dragged out of the water, and knew that was how people ended up when they talked to the wrong people. She'd have to get to Tom Fleet first before anybody else did, but perhaps it was too late already? News could have leaked via one of the dive boats nosing around, and his own life could be in danger.

'We need to go,' she said to Eric.

'Are you done?'

She nodded. 'They won't give me anything. It's a civilian death, and nothing to do with British sovereign interests. I'll be closed out of the case. Which is why we need to get those photos downloaded as soon as possible.'

'We can do it on my personal computer at my place,' he said.

Helen signalled to the police coastguard in charge and he agreed that she could go, they had statements from both of them. She hadn't mentioned in hers her thoughts about the death of the woman being linked to Paul Thomas or the Blue Lantern. She took one last glance at the woman's body and Helen remembered her in life, in the back of the car, driven by a man called Artemis, pensive and afraid being driven away from the officers' mess.

Eric stripped his wetsuit down to his waist and Helen did the same. Out of the water and in the sunshine, the salt dried on her skin and made her itchy. She gulped from a water bottle and sat back, holding onto the side of the rib as Eric sped them to shore.

Once there, they both emptied the boat of kit in silence.

'So much for a relaxing dive,' he said.

She lugged kit to the back of the shop and took a hose to rinse it off.

'Look, this is getting bigger than I thought, I don't think you should be involved,' she said seriously.

He carried on rinsing the kit and turned to her, with the hose running in his hand. 'Bullshit. I am involved. And if bodies keep turning up that were somehow linked to what you're 'doing, then it won't be long before they start looking for you. They might already be doing that, right now. Are we being watched?' he asked, looking around. 'Maybe, probably. I'm not bowing out now,' he said.

They finished cleaning in silence. Helen no longer thought about what her white skin looked like against his walnut glow in the morning sun. She went about the tasks, concentrating. It felt good to get the salt water off and she stood hosing herself, deep in thought.

He brought her a mug of steaming coffee and she turned off the hose and took it gratefully.

'I'm glad I was there, and I'm grateful I was with you,' she said. She put her cup down and looked at him, and he came closer. Their bodies touched and she put her free arm around his middle. His body was warm and she leant her head into his shoulder.

'I don't want you out of my sight,' he said, holding her closer.

She looked at him and smiled. 'I can take care of myself,' she said.

'I don't doubt that,' he replied. He kissed her forehead lightly and she held on as tightly as she dared, for now. She wanted to end it like this: afraid of what might happen if she stayed. Her thoughts were muddied and she didn't know if it was because of Eric, or just that she'd discovered a dead body at twenty metres under the sea.

He ran his fingers up her back and held her hair gently, and she allowed herself to be lost in the moment: just briefly, because it felt good. Time stopped because it had to. She couldn't make sense out of what had happened, and, right now, she didn't have to. She raised her head and he pulled her closer still. Their lips were centimetres apart and then he bent his head and kissed her.

A noise startled them and they unlocked their embrace and stared towards it. It was Nico.

'Sorry,' he said.

Eric put his hands on his hips and Helen stood back.

'There's a police van here,' Nico said.

'I'll handle this,' said Helen.

Chapter 35

The Troodos mountain air was clear and thin, a welcome diversion from the heat of the shore. Colonel Seaton drove alone: an activity that he wasn't used to on this island, unless he was asked to, as he had been this morning. He was more accustomed to being driven, sitting in the back of a vehicle like a lord; but this was private business. He'd left Andi in bed, still shocked by her ordeal – in fact, she'd threatened to leave. He'd begged her not to; to consider their position and contemplate their life without the prestige and privilege that they were bestowed here, in Cyprus, even if it could be misinterpreted and seen as above and beyond his job requirements. In the army, integrity was the all-important buzzword: one led by example and that's why they were untouchable, untainted and unreachable. Taking presents, gifts, bribes or other means of supplementary income was a strict taboo for good reason.

But Colonel Seaton was above such trivia. He considered himself a pivotal link in the chain of international relations, and his decisions were based purely on furthering the interests of his regiment as he saw it. The MOD wasn't here on the ground, witnessing the intricate conversations and deals that went on anywhere in the world between nations.

Or that's what he told himself, and his wife, who remained in bed, terrified and betrayed.

He was angry. His hands clasped the wheel as he drove and he remained oblivious to the stunning scenery out of his window as he passed ancient churches nestled in the hills, their verandas hanging precariously over the mountainside, looking as though they'd fall at any moment, laden with their blooms of jacaranda and cyclamens. He opened the windows, as the choking heat turned cooler as he gained height. The air was cleaner and clearer up here. He wore civilian clothes and felt distinctly average in his corduroy trousers and open-neck shirt. His uniform provided him with the power he required to leverage himself between volatile nations. Here, he was simply a man, and it felt distinctly uncomfortable.

As the car proceeded up the mountain road, he looked for a familiar sign that led him to a large white house at the end of a private paved road. The first time he'd come, he'd been taken with the grandeur of the place, but now familiarity had sucked awe from him, and it was just a house. The cars parked outside were impressive, but they didn't put him off. He was a soldier of the British Army, warrior of the greatest nation on earth, his hand was his bond, and his word his honour. But still his heart rate betrayed him and, before he realised, he was sweating and his shirt stuck to the back of the seat. He was flustered, but the irritation with his body's display of weakness only served to irk him more. By the time he pulled up, watched, he knew, from several windows above, he was in a flap and wished he hadn't come.

A man in a dark suit, with an earpiece and a bulging shape under his jacket, appeared from the shadows and approached him, stony-faced. *These Russians*, he thought, *they take themselves so goddam seriously*.

He turned off the engine and smiled, showing his hands and communicating that he was unarmed. Good god, he wished he was allowed to be armed, cutting about up here, in bandit country, meeting savages, but his country's paltry rules of engagement forbade it. He didn't feel in any physical danger, but his anxiety was heightened nonetheless.

The man was humourless and there was no point talking to him. He was frisked and allowed to pass. He made his way to the rear of the house and only now sucked in gulps of mountain air, realising its calming properties. Another nameless, characterless man in a dark suit beckoned him and showed him into the cool interior of the residence. He was told to wait, not verbally, but by way of a curt and familiar nod.

The hall was large and airy, and minimally decorated, stoic in the absence of luxury, and starkly different to the offices of other nation states, who adorned their departments with glorious nods to the past: great paintings of battles, trophies stolen from indigenous peoples, and opulent rugs and furniture gifted from grateful satellites. Not the Russians. They had no need. He stared at a portrait of Vladimir Putin and shivered slightly at the man who stared back at him.

His body was ready to fight. He'd done nothing wrong. Somebody, somewhere, had screwed up, not him. He'd kept to his side of the bargain, if that loose term for a deal could be applied here; it was a flimsy arrangement, but he meant to keep it. He fiddled with his shirt collar, not wanting to sit, and not being offered the option. These Russians kept you waiting in uncomfortable positions for any length of time they fancied, he was used to that at least. It was just their way. They liked to be in charge. Well, he thought belligerently, no one was his master but Her Majesty the Queen, and he answered to his conscience alone.

Another curt nod interrupted his paranoid thoughts and he was led into the study of Secretary Dimitri Bugov. Like the hallway, it was a sparsely decorated room, soulless almost, and reminiscent of the photos he'd seen of Cold War European checkpoints. He stifled a nervous laugh as he took in the unspoken significance of the lack of comfort. He wished he could think of a joke to lighten the situation, but he couldn't. Besides, Secretary Bugov wasn't known for his humour, just his remoteness. Somebody with such emotional distance was a waste of one's comedy anyway.

'Secretary,' Colonel Seaton boomed. He strode across the room and stretched out his hand. The secretary glanced at it and nodded. Seaton withdrew it and put it into his pocket gingerly.

'Sit,' the secretary ordered.

Seaton did as he was told, instantly regretting his acquiescence.

'This problem,' the secretary began. 'It is awkward for us.'

Colonel Seaton was momentarily furious at the secretary's lack of deference to his title. It served to remind Seaton of where he was. On paper, Secretary Bugov was sat in an office in Moscow, in Lubyanka Square, working for the Federal Security Service of Russia. He was what states termed an undeclared diplomat; in other words, they weren't on the official employee website of the Russian Embassy in the host country: they were supposed to be somewhere else. In this case, nowhere on any document relating to Soviet–Cypriot relations was Bugov's name to be found. He simply wasn't here. He had the title and rank of someone who'd raise eyebrows with enemies of Russia in host states, and so he was simply left off. It wasn't unusual, everybody did it, and so they were entitled, but Seaton knew that no one in London or Washington knew he was here, on the island.

'I'm assuming you're referring to the inquiry into the death of the RMP officer?' Seaton said.

Bugov nodded. He wore full uniform, and it intimidated his guest, rather annoyingly. Seaton knew that the secretary's stripes and adornments were awarded mainly for turning up to party meetings, unlike British army decorations, which were granted for time served in real battles. The irony that Seaton hadn't come closer than perhaps ten miles to the vicinity of a real live combat situation in twenty years was entirely lost on him, and he wore his medals with pride, despite the lack of them, three of them being Queen's medals for turning up on Jubilee days. Today, being in civilian clothing, made the absence of rank more visible and thus more bothersome.

Bugov waved his hand nonchalantly. 'Whatever. You have a keen-eyed detective from London on his case?'

'She's a lone operator, Secretary.' Seaton didn't mention the two new SIB officers who'd turned up to help Major Scott.

It was protocol to have paper-pushing lackeys on hand for something fairly significant. After all, an officer had died, and London needed answers.

'But a lone operator who is asking too many questions. In the interests of national security, she may get in the way.'

A trickle of cold sweat formed at the base of Seaton's spine. He daren't touch it, lest it soak through his shirt and the secretary suspect he was nervous.

'I will deal with her. She'll be wrapped up and off the island within the week,' Seaton said.

'I do hope so. If not, she will become collateral damage, like her predecessor.'

Seaton's heart began to race and his body felt awkward. He was used to standing for hours, in his younger days, on the parade square, in front of his troops, as a junior officer, but here, before this man who he knew would not think twice about ordering the murder of another British Army officer, things were quite different altogether. The air seemed to have been sucked out of the room and there was no noise, just interminable silence, as Bugov looked at him. Seaton decided to take a stand.

'Your officers weren't exactly subtle,' he ventured.

Bugov didn't react straight away. But a slow grimace, a sort of smile, spread creepily across his face.

'Those officers have been sent back to Russia. They are being dealt with via the proper channels. Now, what I want from you is a timeline. I am a busy man. I have other things to do, which concern me greatly. Weak links in my chain are tiresome to me, and my brief is very clear. I thought I could count on you, Colonel, can I not?'

Seaton hated the lack of transparency when speaking to high-ranking officials from other nations. Men, and sometimes women, who wouldn't think twice about betrayal. A British Army officer's word was his reputation, but, unfortunately, this did not count in other cultures. He'd worked with men and women from every nation on earth, virtually, so he knew when he was dealing in veiled threats, and it bored him to distraction: why couldn't everybody just be honest like him? They were all supposed to be singing from the same sheet.

'Have I ever let you down?' Seaton asked.

'You are still alive.'

Seaton didn't know whether to laugh or cry, or run away. The finality of the statement hit him. No one got a second chance.

He swallowed hard.

'Couldn't we have had this conversation over the phone?' he asked.

'No. We could not.' Bugov took an envelope from his desk and took out its contents. He spread dozens of photographs across his desk. They were all of Major Scott. 'How is your wife?' Bugov asked.

It took Seaton by surprise. 'Well, she's in shock. Was it quite necessary?'

'Yes. If it gets too much for her, then I have arranged for her transfer to Moscow – all expenses included, et cetera.' He waved his hand again.

A heavy feeling spread across Seaton's gut. 'Wait a minute, what are you talking about? We never agreed—'

'Agreed? Colonel, you speak as though this is some kind of diplomatic arrangement that we signed on TV. Take a long look at yourself. You are a traitor.' Bugov moved closer. 'You belong to me now. And so does your wife. Do your job, and we will protect you. It is too late for you to return to your mother country now. The line is crossed. Either you serve Russia, or you don't.'

'Hang on, I never signed up to serve anyone! I—'

'You what? You give away secrets behind the back of your country and you want thanks? In my country, we have a saying that the squirrel never runs from the bear. I will explain.'

Seaton went to speak, but he was shushed by his host, who held up his hand.

'Interrupt me once more and I will revoke my kind offer of a life in my beautiful country. The squirrel, you see, is very clever. Everybody knows that. But the bear is ruthless. He knows that the squirrel steals his food, but he shares because the squirrel takes only what he needs. Thus, in times of crisis, the squirrel doesn't run because he knows he will have enough to eat. If he did run, then the bear would take this as a betrayal and, well, then we all know how that ends.'

Seaton couldn't speak. He couldn't breathe. For the first time in four years, the gravity of what he was doing hit him. He was at first outraged, and all sorts of ideas rampaged through his head: go to the authorities, tell them everything (nearly everything) and say he was being blackmailed. Then doubt set in and he realised that he had been outmanoeuvred. His shoulders hunched forward and he faced the reality of the difficult conversation with Andi about what their life might look like.

But then a tiny sliver of defiance crept back in, showing how conflicted his mind was. Rage screamed at him to fight back and put this stupid arrogant man in his place. They were, after all, on paper about the same rank. However, the secretary had probably been awarded his, rather than earned it, for doing somebody a favour. It was the worst kind of bestowment. Seaton had no respect for the man, and less so for the nation he represented. To move there – to defect – was unthinkable. Dear God, how was he to explain all this to Andi?

'You are conflicted. Don't forget that in the time it takes the squirrel to betray its own instinct, the bear has already blocked the path.'

All the fablesque poetic bullshit was hurting Seaton's head and he wanted to laugh, and he would have done had he not seen first-hand what people the secretary had behind him.

A tiny flicker of hope descended on him and he thought he could talk his way out of this with Major Scott. He could go to her and tell her he'd been threatened; that he'd gone along with it at first to protect Andi, and now it had got out of hand.

The door opened behind him and it was obvious that he'd outstayed his welcome. This irked him further and he held his shoulders squarely and puffed out his chest as he walked to the door.

'There are too many squirrels in the woods, but only one bear,' Bugov said.

Seaton strode out of the room and was shown out to his car. He got in and slammed the door, deciding to make a detour to Nicosia to get a decent meal and clear his thoughts before making his way back to Dhekelia Garrison.

Chapter 36

'I don't want to do that! Good God, Bill, just tell them no!'

'Jesus, Andi, I'm losing patience. These people are not some jerks who hang around in teenage gangs, they're killers! Look how easily they took you,' he shouted. He hated having to raise his voice, and he was reminded why, as his wife's face crumpled. Next came the tears.

People who forced him to lose control lost his respect, but his wife was different. Women in general had to be treated distinctly, they were sensitive creatures, and none more so than Andi. She talked a good game, but was fragile, if the truth be known. Which is why he'd never discussed the finer details of his relationship with Secretary Bugov; she didn't even know his name. It was his way of protecting her, he guessed. Now, he felt the weight of every decision he'd ever made dragging him down to depths he had no way of managing.

He regretted the day he'd met the secretary, at a diplomatic party thrown by the High Commissioner, in Nicosia. Statesmen hobnobbed wherever they were posted, it was the way of life for men on the ground like him. Recently, more women had been taking prominent roles in governments across Europe, to his embarrassment. Females simply didn't understand the intricacies of international relations. They brought feelings into everything and it simply wasn't appropriate. Action was what built and stabilised nations, not hugs and biscuits. If it was up to Brussels, every important meeting from Asia to South America would be wrapped in cotton wool and they'd all be doomed. Only men could truly grasp the language of nationhood. He treated his wife gently.

'Andi, come here darling,' he soothed.

She stopped unpacking the shopping from the Naafi and stood at the counter in the utility room. Normally, their staff performed such menial tasks; how the hell they'd merge back into British society when the time came, one never knew. But the prospect was infinitely more alluring than trying to forge a life in Russia. It was just a few bits and pieces, such as a bouquet of flowers and some proper spread for their bread, not this local goat's butter that everybody seemed to think was fashionable. He watched her. She turned around and her eyes were glassy.

'I just thought it was all right, you know? Making friends with these people. I didn't think it would lead to the problems we're having. A few well-placed words at dinner, and the odd boat trip. How did it get to this?' she asked. They both knew that her sentiments were grounded in delusion. They also both knew the real reason he was in the secretary's pocket.

Andi had a great way of papering over tricky issues with her soft words. He didn't think he'd ever given her the impression that they were exemplary diplomatic missionaries, but if that's how she wanted to play it, perhaps he'd underestimated her. He was also thankful that she hadn't dragged the whole business of the photographs up again. Years ago, that's all she could do; she was hurt and blamed him. She was stung and embarrassed by his behaviour and the pain inside her had lingered on, until one day, he couldn't remember which, the gifts and freebies masked the shame of having a husband who was caught with his pants down. Literally.

He'd been set up, obviously, and for a time, he'd ignored their advances. But then they'd involved Andi, and she'd seen the colour images in all their glory. That was the last straw. That's when he made the choice between his reputation and his career.

'Darling, these things go on all over the world. What we've done is not new. We haven't invented the wheel here. But we might be made an example of. Like that colonel who got banged up for inflating his children's school fees for years: it's an outrage, but sometimes you have to fall on your sword,' he said. He realised from her face that he'd used the wrong analogy. 'I didn't mean that literally, I just meant that sometimes the do-gooders in Whitehall want a fall guy and this time it might be me. What I've done is not wrong, but we may have misjudged the severity of a few issues,' he said as kindly as he could. Even as he spoke, he realised that he was trying to convince himself, not his wife.

'Severity? Have you done something serious? What about the house in Split? The children? My pink sapphire? Do you think we'll be held accountable in some way?' she asked.

They'd been gifted a beautiful villa on the Adriatic, near Split in Croatia, only last year, and the children had met them there from university. The water was turquoise blue and they felt like they deserved that life. A whole generation of servitude surely warranted some perks? His stomach sank at her mention of the children. He'd massaged a few school fees too but had managed to cover them up, thanks to a few favours here on the garrison. He felt the frustration of being caught out keenly. It was unfair. Officers had been playing the game for centuries. It dated back to the time of Metternich, Bismarck and Wellington. Countries rose and fell on their deals with others. That he should be the one to somehow be blamed for the shift in tidal opinion, thanks to the woke generation, horrified him and made him want to seek an alternative to telling the truth.

The truth. That would only lead one way: a military tribunal and court martial. He stoically believed that his dealings with Secretary Bugov were, on the whole, harmless, but he accepted that, on paper, it wouldn't look good. That only left him with one choice: take everyone down with him.

The defection option was looking more and more attractive, but he'd have to secure passage for his children too. What was Moscow like this time of year? he wondered. Surely it couldn't be that bad?

'Darling. I've made arrangements for the children to spend the rest of the summer here. I want them close, in case—'

'In case what?' she said through her sniffles. She looked thoroughly miserable, as if her life savings had been raided.

'Well, in case it doesn't look good at the MOD, and I find myself in the position where I'm used as an example.' He said it as breezily as he could.

'Example? For what? You're excellent at your job. What you have done for this island has been an almost impossible task! They should be thanking you!'

'I know, darling, but I'm afraid not everyone might agree with you.'

'Go to that woman and explain everything! Or is she a traitor too?'

'Who?'

'The officer from London. Helen. She's a good sort. She admired what I'd done with this place, she gets it, the need for those in charge to fit in and entertain to a certain level. I saw it in her eyes; she'd love to be in our position. Get her on board.'

Bill sat down heavily. Andi was not only misreading the severity of their situation, but also everyone around them. 'How about a new start with the children?' he suggested softly.

She rounded on him. 'What?'

'Well, I was thinking maybe, if it looks like I might be hung out to dry by my own side, then—'

'Go over to them? The men who kidnapped me! Run away? Bill! How could you suggest such a thing?'

'It might be the only way to keep what we have. Otherwise, imagine me going to prison, you in a terraced house in Bulford, not being able to afford university fees, begging for favours,' he said.

Her eyes flickered. It was working. She'd been pacing up and down the kitchen, and now she stopped and stared at him. He could tell that he'd got under her skin. The seed had been planted.

'Where?' she asked. 'Anywhere but Russia.'

'The north?' he replied. He meant Northern Cyprus. It wasn't such a fantasy. It was a rogue state, declared independent in 1983, only recognised by Turkey. He had to say something.

'Kyrenia?' Her face brightened.

He shrugged and felt like a traitorous bastard.

She spent the next half an hour, before the afternoon shift for dinner arrived to cook and tidy, blabbering on about villas near the beautiful port on the north coast of the island. She googled swimming pools and artwork and it kept her busy and happy. Meanwhile, Bill went to his study and closed his door, and began tracing back the deals he'd made over the last four years of service here on the island. Maybe his glory days were finally about to come to an end, but not in a ceremony at the palace with the Queen pinning his knighthood to his chest, but in a rather different scenario altogether.

Chapter 37

Jen sat outside the Blue Lantern in a rented car. She'd been here all morning. She'd been talking to Kay about her experience at the club last night when Major Scott called and told them the news about the young prostitute. They were still in shock.

She wore civilian clothes, which were more comfortable than combats, but she felt as though she was naked, without her armour, and she was hot and discombobulated. She kept shifting in her seat, and wanting to talk to somebody. She tried to concentrate on her job. This is what she'd joined the RMP for. This is how she'd imagined her career, spent tailing nasty foreign criminals in the interest of national security for her homeland. She'd romanticised it, yet, it wasn't quite as glamourous as that, given the smell of tobacco in the car, the remnants of discarded McDonald's, the heat and the dust, and her gloomy mood. Now, with another body linked to their case, it made her jumpy.

All they had on Artemis Charalambous was that he'd lived here on the island all his life, gaining a relatively mediocre education from high school, and had done odd jobs for mechanics and painters until he began working in bars as a doorman and became a cab driver, some thirty years ago. His licence was up to date, and he was registered with the island's tourist board as part of the list of drivers serving the Larnaca area. He appeared on the websites of numerous hotels, as a local and trustworthy driver, and Jen had a photo of him on the passenger seat. She also had one of his brother for reference because they looked like identical twins. She knew from their profiles, given to them by the civilian police here on the island, that Theo Charalambous was older, by six years. Side by side, they were difficult to tell apart, but Artemis dressed a little smarter than his older sibling.

Jen knew that the local police were difficult to work with, and it wasn't a surprise. Major Scott had briefed both she and Kay on how tricky it was to investigate a crime when the geographical parameters they worked with encroached on Cypriot soil. They'd been given what little information they had on the brothers, who'd found themselves in minor scrapes for the last thirty years. There were traffic infringements, scuffles, problems with drunk tourists and the like, but nothing serious, or that's what they'd been told at least.

Artemis's grey Ford was parked outside the club and Jen waited. This was her task for today: find out where he went and who he met. Surveillance was dull and she filled her time by assessing her boss. Her first impressions of Major Scott were positive. She was a woman, which was a good start. Jen had only ever worked for men in the RMP and she'd always wondered what it might be like to have a woman in charge; the problem was that they were hard to come by, especially at a higher rank. It was all she and Kay had talked about on the flight over. At first, when they read the name of the officer in charge, a flicker of recognition had taken a while to settle and then they realised that the sense of familiarity was justified. They'd both heard of Major Scott, but there were a couple of male officers with the same surname and so it was only when Kay mentioned it that it hit Jen. She was on her way to work for the Wrench.

Army regiments were small, like little communities, and gossip travelled fast. Chatter about a woman who'd made her name in some of the harshest theatres of war around the world was something that women in the RMP discussed frequently. In fact, she was their inspiration. Neither woman would have probably even gone for the SIB course if it hadn't been for Helen Scott opening the way. They heard that she got her nickname of Wrench because she could turn her hand to anything, just like the multitool.

Jen and Kay agreed that it was their ambition to be like their idol one day, but both had been apprehensive about meeting her. That was the problem about meeting your heroes: they never quite matched up to one's dreams. However, so far, Helen Scott was everything they'd hoped she was. Jen had imagined her to be physically tough, given her record and the way she looked after herself; they had also seen her be mentally robust, intelligently shrewd and capable of inspiring the type of work ethic that Jen was showing right now: sitting outside a club in the baking heat waiting for a short fat man in his fifties to emerge, and there was nowhere she'd rather be.

Thoughts of her heroine were interrupted when Jen saw Artemis swagger out of the club, from the back entrance. There were plenty of cars parked along the street and he paid no attention to Jen's. He walked, or waddled, with the confidence of somebody who had no enemies. She watched as he fiddled with something in his hands and he dropped his keys. He looked annoyed and bent over sluggishly to retrieve them from the dust. It looked to Jen as though he might actually topple over like those Weebles that wobbled from her childhood, but, sure enough, he made it back upright. He paused and placed his hand on his hip. He looked so out of shape that Jen thought his days were numbered. He was classic heart-attack age, and shape, and his face, though dark with a life in the Mediterranean sun, was pasty. He seemed to gain his breath back and Jen wondered how people let themselves go to such an extent. The guy was a mess. His T-shirt stretched over his gut and she looked down to his feet and felt sorry for the flip-flops supporting his huge weight. She almost heard them groan.

But she wasn't fooled. His forearms were bigger than her calves, and his shoulders wider than the seat she was in. She shrank into the shadow of her vehicle and watched him shuffle to the Ford and open it. It sank down to the pavement as he got in and started the engine. Her adrenalin kicked in as she realised that this was it: she was actually about to follow somebody for a live case. Her desk jobs in the UK so far hadn't given her the opportunity to do something like this. She'd investigated drunken soldiers, thefts of traffic signs, even domestic-abuse cases, but nothing like this: a real chase. A murder case, no less, and one of their own. All of her skills as an operator came into play and she checked her distance before she pulled out on his tail, making sure that no one was joining him.

Jen sent Helen Scott a voice note on hands-free, telling her that Artemis Charalambous was on the move and she was shadowing him. She gripped the wheel and held back, not wanting to blow her cover. But she seethed with excitement. All the pieces were coming together and she was tracking the man who had probably taken Anastasia Lebedev to her death. She felt part of a lone warrior team, far from home, seeking justice for a murdered woman, and that of one of her colleagues too. She hadn't known Paul Thomas, but she knew one thing: he didn't deserve to die. Whatever he'd found out about the relationship between the British armed forces and this club, he'd taken to his death, but she had no doubt that Helen Scott, with her help, would find out what it was.

Chapter 38

Tom drove and Victor sat in the passenger seat. He believed his friend. But he didn't know who to trust anymore. Captain Graham had sat in front of him, looked him dead in the eye, and told him that his friend and brother in arms had applied to marry Ani. It was a lie. But why?

There was only one way to find out and that was to speak to Ani herself. He'd seen her just yesterday morning but hadn't been able to contact her since. He figured that it was a mixture of her being busy and also a little miffed at the way they'd parted yesterday. She was also limited in the amount of time she had access to a phone, those bastards controlled her every move to make sure she was making money. They'd argued about her clients. Again. But the weekend had been one of the best he could remember and he knew that he was in love with her. The girl he'd left in England, waiting for him to come back and marry her, paled into the background when he was with Ani. Back home, as a young lieutenant, possibly soon to be captain, embarking on life independently and watching all of his mates getting married, his parents assumed he'd be next. Everybody expected it. But he'd been with Freya for three years and never experienced the intensity of feelings he had when he was with Ani. He knew, deep down in his heart, that he was only with Freya because she looked the part: an army officer's wife; dependable, smart, attractive and, most importantly of all, resilient. That's what they all looked for wasn't it? Someone who could withstand the moves, the tours, the job of a dependent spouse, packing boxes, having babies and celebrating milestones alone. Always alone. It took some kind of woman to marry into that. But Freya was just that. And that was the problem: she was too perfect. It was as if she'd been packaged up to be a good wife and he hated it. His mother had helped him choose the ring and they'd already talked about the wedding. He knew that they were planning it as he was fucking Ani, every weekend, discovering depths of pleasure he never knew existed. He couldn't go through with it. He'd taken down all his pictures of Freya, and rarely talked about her. But his mother had called early Sunday morning and asked about the wedding. Ani lost her shit and it had taken him an hour to persuade her that he was pulling out of it, and to get her to agree to stay with him another night.

He felt bad. She'd got into Artemis's cab miserable and he saw that Helen Scott witnessed it. Why was he surrounded by intelligent women out here where everything was supposed to be so simple? A fling with one, an interview with the other. Women saw bloody everything. Major Graham's instructions to him sat heavy on his shoulders. He felt allegiance to his flag, but he couldn't stand the man, and he rather liked Major Scott. It was a dilemma that he hadn't yet worked out.

'Great day for a waterski, mate,' Victor interrupted his thoughts and it was welcome because he could feel himself becoming maudlin and he hadn't even seen Ani yet.

Tom nodded towards the sea, it truly was a beautiful day. 'Are they police boats?' Tom asked, pointing towards the water.

Victor followed his gaze and squinted. 'Looks like it, I wonder if there's been another diving accident. It's not my thing. I'm glad we got that one out of our systems.'

They'd joined the army dive team at Dhekelia early on in their tour, for something to do, and it was an adrenalin high at first. But then Victor had freaked out twenty metres under the water and tried to rip his DV out of his mouth. Later, he'd said he imagined himself near the surface and wanting to breathe real air. The instructor said it was nitrogen narcosis and usually happened at much deeper depths, but with beginners it could happen at any depth. It could have been the way he was breathing, but it didn't really matter what the cause was; it put Victor off for life. They'd barely discussed it. After all, what man wanted to admit that he couldn't hack a sport that revealed one's true masculinity by its very daring? It was like sky-diving or motorsport: the nearer to death, the better. Twenty metres under the ocean, death was always close by and Victor's body had said no. It wasn't an easy thing to admit, but Tom appreciated his honesty.

'Just shows how dangerous it is, mate. It's not natural, breathing under all of that water,' Tom said.

Victor agreed.

They drove on in silence until they reached the turning for the Blue Lantern. During the day, it was deserted, while the girls slept, but they'd both been in for a pint or two at this time, when they weren't working. Postings abroad could get tedious when you missed your family and your home comforts. Their mates back home assumed it was like a holiday with sunshine and girls at every turn. Sometimes it could be like that, but for the most part, it was worse than working at home because you still had to wear the suffocating uniform in the heat, with no let-up until you knocked off and went to the officers' club beach at sundown to cool off.

'Artemis isn't here, he always parks out front,' Tom said.

He parked and they got out of the vehicle. They looked up to where the girls lived. The curtains were always tight shut, not only for privacy but also because the girls kept crazy hours and slept for most of the day, with fans blazing. The last thing they wanted was to be reminded of the midday sun.

Tom tried Ani's mobile again. It was dead.

'God, she's really pissed at me this time,' he said.

They walked round the back. The back door was always open and they knew the doorman, who was huge and not to be reckoned with. He sat on a sunlounger, smoking. He nodded at the two lads.

'Nothing doing today, boys,' he said.

'What? It's shut?'

'Deep cleaning, apparently.'

Tom and Victor looked at one another and shrugged.

'Have you seen Ani?'

The man's face didn't change, but he shifted his body to make himself upright and he pulled his shades over his eyes, shaking his head. Tom got the first hint of something not being right. This guy was usually their best pal, because they tipped well, like rock stars in fact, the girls were that good.

'Can I go and see her?' Tom asked, revealing a Cypriot note in his hand.

The doorman took it but shook his head. 'No one's to go in, pal.'

Tom looked at his hand where the note just was, but couldn't think of anything to say. 'Robbing, thieving bastard' might not make the doorman happy.

Victor stepped in. 'Can you go and get Ani and ask her to come and talk to us?' he asked.

The doorman placed his sunglasses on top of his large bald head and got up. 'You're interrupting my rays, boys. Another fifty.'

He looked at them and Victor produced the note.

The doorman disappeared and they waited in the red-hot sun. It was almost midday and the streets were deserted. The beaches would be heaving by now, and both Tom and Victor imagined chilled daiquiris at a pool bar, and a cool dip, maybe at Makronissos, up the coast, towards Ayia Napa, which was always quiet. Tom licked his lips as if anticipating a drink. They both wore uniform, as they were on an extended lunch break. To be fair, as platoon commanders, they could take a break anytime they wanted, as long as they weren't required by the colonel for something. They looked odd in the middle of the deserted street, two officers in combat uniform, loitering outside a strip joint, but this didn't register with the doorman or anyone else who happened to walk past. Only tourists might glance over and this wasn't a daytime haunt for families on holiday. They waited.

The doorman came back and spread his hands. 'She's not home,' he said.

'Where is she?' Tom asked.

The doorman spread his hands again.

'Come on.' Victor pulled Tom's arm.

They walked back to the front of the building and Tom bent over to pick up a couple of stones. He threw them at a window: the one he knew was Ani's. Victor kept a lookout to see if the doorman heard. Tom threw more stones and there was movement at the window. Curtains were pulled open and a face appeared. Tom knew her; she worked there. He waved. She shook her head and made a warning sign with her hands. Tom stared at her and she opened the window. She leant out.

'Ani's not coming back,' the girl said. It was more than a whisper but not loud enough to rouse the doorman from his sun chair.

'What do you mean?' Tom held his arms apart in a desperate gesture. He couldn't understand.

'You need to forget her,' the girl said.

'What?' Tom asked. This time it was louder and Victor told him to keep it down.

'You want to get us all in trouble? Fuck off and don't come back!' The girl shut the window and closed the curtains.

Tom stood with his mouth gaping open. Victor came to his side.

'Let's go, buddy,' he said.

Tom looked at him.

'I'll drive,' Victor said.

Chapter 39

Helen scrolled through the photographs on Eric's computer screen.

They hadn't talked about this morning. When their faces had been so close she could smell the cologne on his chest, seeping from his body with his warmth. They hadn't touched, or discussed running to the bedroom that was right next to the sitting room, door slightly ajar, beckoning them as the sun rose through the windows and shone upon the computer screen.

His place was a small, modest house, a short walk from the dive school. After talking briefly to Nico and Sophia, who were busy hanging up wetsuits for the day, they'd carried on undressing and changing, glancing at one another but never at the same time. She could feel his eyes on her, many times, but when she looked up, they had sought another place, elsewhere.

Two stories high and slender, the house sat in between other similar homes, all pointing towards the horizon, waiting for the sun to warm them, like sleeping animals waking up slowly. They were all painted white and the windows were large, to make the most of the stunning views. There were steps up to the front, and planted jacarandas in full bloom, pregnantly overflowing onto the cream-coloured tiles, petals blowing around gently in the warm breeze. The entrance was through two giant sliding doors, framed by translucent white curtains that wafted as Eric had opened them. The sitting room led out the back to another comfortable seating area, with a huge TV and computer station where they sat now. At the very back was a shower room and a well-fitted kitchen. It was cool inside and Eric told her he didn't need air conditioning apart from at night. The image of them laying together in bed, with the shadows of white and grey dancing around with the light wind off the Mediterranean, sat between them and they changed the subject. Upstairs were three bedrooms and another bathroom, and Helen had been up there to use it, peeking into the other rooms as she went. She couldn't help guess that his was the largest, with the unmade bed, all white in décor, like the rest of the house: confirming that Eric lived alone. She wondered if his two kids visited him. The whole house made her feel at ease and she breathed steadily, noticing that she hadn't felt as peaceful during the whole length of her stay here on the island.

He brought her a coffee and placed it on the table beside the computer, on a pretty coaster, the only colour in the room, except a few cushions and paintings. She still couldn't get warm, despite the temperature outside creeping up already. Salt still clung to her skin and it made her feel sticky and unclean. Her hair smelled of the ocean, and so did his. Eric suited the permanent look of somebody who was in and out of water all day, like water sports instructors all over the world, who graced their beaches: he was most comfortable in shorts and T-shirt, with shaggy hair and sunglasses plopped on top of his head.

'I'm going for a warm shower, you're welcome to have one, I'll shout when I'm done, and leave everything out for you,' he said.

She looked up at him and it was the first time they'd properly locked eyes since they'd kissed. She smiled and nodded. 'Thanks, I will.'

He left the room and went upstairs. She had work to do and the sun caught the gems on her right hand, glinting in the light, a sparkling reminder of the man who'd given it to her. She thought about Grant for a moment and wondered if he had found himself in the company of a woman, in their house perhaps, looking at him with eyes that begged him to come upstairs. He was a free man, he could do what he wanted, she thought. Being with Grant was the last time she'd been intimate with any man and she thought of the moments, the whispers and the movement of their bodies, in the chalet in the Alps, when they'd promised always to be there for each other. She looked at her phone and was tempted to call him. If anyone's brain could make sense of all of this, it was his, and, more than that, she trusted him with her life, but her innate stubbornness prevented her.

She looked back at the screen and took in the images of Anastasia's body. The woman was nowhere to be found on any government website or search engine: she was harmless and insignificant. But Helen was convinced that she'd been murdered as some kind of collateral. A search of Russian Embassy members, up in Nicosia, had also served up nothing. There was no shady character with an interesting history that flagged up anywhere she looked. Phone calls to London confirmed there were no reported movements at the embassy recently that would indicate anything out of order. Of course, foreign nations embedded in other countries were always up to something. There would be a handful of personnel up in the border city that shouldn't be there – undeclared diplomats – who travelled incognito around the world, carrying out the secret instructions of their motherland, but Helen found no intelligence along those lines. Relations between Russia and Britain in Cyprus were tolerable if wary: they'd both benefitted from their histories on the island, economically and strategically. But sometimes, lines were crossed and old animosities reared their heads. Of course, Putin didn't like the West's stance on Syria, or Ukraine, but that wasn't anything new. But something in her physiology warned her that the death of this woman was somehow connected to the murder of her colleague.

Helen had learned to trust her gut when she'd been posted to Afghanistan for the second time. It was something to do with the way all animals react to stress and the human race had distanced itself so much from its own natural instincts that few people listened to their bodies, thinking the animal form unreliable and primitive. But that was the whole point. Millions of years ago, animals had become adept at sensing danger, and it was no different for humans, we just simply ignored it, or tried to argue or reason our way out of it. It was a bit like walking into a room full of strangers. If she stood still for not even a second and allowed her instinct to wash over her, she could pretty much figure out very quickly who was who.

She listened to her instincts now. Anastasia had been strangled. She could tell by the bruises around her neck that Helen hadn't been able to make out underneath twenty metres of water. A phone call to the local police officer, who'd offered his card on the boat, confirmed that they were not about to share information on this one. She was too late, even two hours after the discovery: somebody, somewhere, had been told not to cooperate with British forces and her hands were tied. This was a sovereign nation, and outside the ESBA, Helen had no jurisdiction whatsoever. The Cypriot police were not obliged in any way to share what they'd found. They'd also told her that, unfortunately, a few key CCTV cameras that might have caught the three so-called navy men in and around the Palm Beach area had stopped working in the last few days. It was all part of the challenge of working inside hostile states, though she never viewed this island in those terms, up until now. Their only motive for withholding vital information was that somebody, somewhere had made that decision. Why? To protect something usually.

She was well aware that behind the scenes, back in London, and no doubt elsewhere, in diplomatic corridors, her case was being discussed. Her orders, she'd been told by Don, in no uncertain terms, were simply to follow procedure and bring or drop charges on the four men under house arrest. Added to that, thanks to Paul's autopsy, it was now a murder investigation, however, that's where her remit ended. Any involvement of theories concerning government spies and diplomats was well above her pay grade, but that didn't stop her being curious, and irked at the same time. Don would tell her to calm down, that it was none of her business and that diplomacy would carry on regardless of what her investigation flagged up. 'Just do your job and get the paperwork done and get home,' she heard him say. She concentrated on the photos.

Anastasia had been naked when she was discovered this morning. Her eyes were open and she'd looked like a mermaid, ethereal in her beauty, had Helen not known instantly that she was dead. Her skin was paler than snow and shone like a full moon in the dark background of the depths of the sea. The ship, the sea's wealth of flora that had grown over decades and the disappearing blue of the water all framed her completely and Helen had been able to lock this image into her head. Anastasia also had bruises around her face: she'd been beaten. Her dark luscious hair caught Helen's attention and she enlarged the image, realising that the waves of black silk had been tampered with, bits were missing and Helen froze the frame. Some of her hair was significantly shorter near her crown and Helen had seen it before on corpses. Anastasia had been pulled violently by her scalp, or had lost hair during a struggle, she guessed. She zoomed in on her mouth and realised that the dark hole of her mouth wasn't shadowed like that because of the dark, it was her tongue that protruded ever so slightly and Helen noticed that it was bulbous: another sign of strangulation. Helen hoped the woman had been already dead when she was strapped to the side of the *Zenobia*.

Apart from those signs of violence, the body was at peace, surrounded by the life of the sea, and Helen thought she looked like one of those figureheads on the bows of ancient ships. The Vikings used menacing mythical creatures, the Egyptians used birds, and the Phoenicians used horses. The Brits used women. They were guardians of good luck and protected the sailors within, and kept them safe. This is how Helen would remember her now.

A small flicker of memory, of the woman in Artemis's taxi, jumped into her head. Jen was on him. Helen had seen Artemis deliver Anastasia to the Russian Embassy, but it was another nation's sovereign turf and none of her business. Anastasia, in the context of her own enquiries, was simply background detail. Context.

Helen heard a noise and realised that Eric was done in the shower and had joined her downstairs. He was dressed, in another pair of shorts and a T-shirt, but this time with a sweater over the top. To the locals, only when the mercury tipped forty was it truly hot. Eric might as well have been a local, he'd lived here for twenty years.

She stretched. 'I think I'll take you up on that offer, then I need to go. I'll be quick.'

'Helen…'

She stood up and turned to him. 'Not now,' she said.

Chapter 40

Artemis drove out of Larnaca, towards the mountains.

Jen followed, sticking to her strict rules of engagement when tailing suspects. It was taught in all expert evasive and surveillance driving courses: don't set patterns, don't get too close, allow them to get out of sight, and the like. The traffic was relatively busy and she guessed it was the tourists flocking to the mountains to escape the heat of the beaches.

Artemis was a slow driver and it made it tricky to hang back as much as she'd like. He stopped at a gas station, and at a roadside stall selling ice cream. Jen was puzzled and she texted Helen Scott. Her subject didn't seem to be heading off to a job, and this was no local taxi journey. He hadn't yet picked anyone up and he seemed to be happily heading up to the hills.

Major Scott replied straight away and told her to be careful and report back when the target finally reached his destination.

Jen's hire car was a standard navy colour and it was pretty dirty now from the dusty roads, so she felt as though she blended in quite nicely. She changed the radio station when she got bored and tried to find something playing pop music instead of reading the news in Greek. She was capable of picking up snippets in French and Spanish, but this language was impossible; however, the tone of the sentences did keep her entertained. They spoke quickly, like all DJs she guessed, and she tried to work out what they might be talking about. Somehow, their accents fitted the weather, but she couldn't work out why that might be so. Maybe it was something to do with the deep resonance and the occasional laughter. She figured that British radio presenters were fairly bland in comparison, and that too matched their own meteorological conditions.

She tapped her fingers on the steering wheel and turned off the road occasionally, to allow the driver in front of her to get ahead. At no point did Artemis appear to look into his mirrors or seem agitated by anything at all. In fact, she heard him singing through his open windows. He threw the ice cream wrapper out of his car window and Jen wasn't impressed. She tutted to herself.

They passed signs for villages that she couldn't pronounce, deep into the foothills of the island's peaks. She too had her windows wide open and she noticed the air getting cooler. This was no ordinary job for a taxi driver; that was for sure. She wondered if she should turn back. She sipped water from the bottle on the passenger seat and saw that it was running low. Then she noticed Artemis turn off up ahead. She checked her satnav and followed the car off the junction, as slowly as she could. Once off the main road, it turned to little more than a dirt track and was lined with Cypress trees. It was hardly wide enough for two cars and she held back as she watched Artemis's car in the distance.

She sent a message to Kay giving her the GPS coordinates of the junction, so she didn't feel so alone. Up ahead, she saw Artemis turn again and she travelled along the road until that point, turning to the right, like he had. The road was barely a track and it took her through trees to a sharp corner, where the road swept around and revealed an opening in the thick trees, exposing an outstanding view of the valley below. She lost sight of Artemis's car and checked her position once again. She was near a tiny village called Kykkos, but apart from that there was nothing else for miles. The air from the valley wafted through the car and she was struck by the peace and beauty of the place.

She steered the car back onto the road and carried on. The road steadily ascended higher and she was afforded another grand vista of the valley below and this time, in the distance, she could see the coast. Soon, the road narrowed even further and she took it slow. After another mile, she slowed as she spotted some kind of dwelling behind the thick treeline. It was above her on the right, and accessed by a tiny track, which she would have missed had she not been travelling so slowly. From the track below, she could see Artemis's car and she breathed a sigh of relief that finally she could report back to where he was picking up from. She sent another message to Kay, thankful she had phone coverage up here. The place was about as isolated as she could imagine, but it was distractingly pretty. Birds sang happily as she turned off her engine and used binoculars to assess whether she could walk up to the property from the rear without being detected.

Her vehicle was conveniently tucked under a shady canopy of bushes and well off the main track. Jen got out and locked the doors, taking the keys, her phone and miniature binoculars in her pocket. She was glad that she'd dressed sensibly, in shorts and trainers, with a loose shirt. She'd almost nonchalantly worn flip-flops in the heat, but they would have been impossible in this undergrowth.

She crept upwards and closer to the house. As she got nearer, she saw that it was a large property, built of wood, with impressive balconies overlooking the incredible valley below. It appeared deserted, and she heard no sound. Her footing was steady and she took care to take her time. She spotted Artemis's car and the main entrance. Maybe this was his summer retreat and the guy was on holiday?

Finally, she was close enough to see through a ground-floor window but she saw nothing but the interior of a fine house that seemed happily nestled here for many years. She saw no people inside. She crouched down and thought about what to do. She checked her phone but there was no reception and so she popped it back in her pocket. Her brief from Helen Scott was to tail the guy. She'd done that. Maybe the property would be important in the future, but, for now, regrettably, she made the decision to head back to Larnaca.

She turned towards the direction of her car, down the steep slope, but she hadn't got far when she heard a sharp crack, like a twig breaking. She turned around.

She faced the barrel of a pistol. It was a Makarov 9 mm. Her heart stopped as she concentrated on the small black hole pointed at her face.

A man spoke English with a Cypriot accent. 'Who the fuck are you?'

Chapter 41

Theo Charalambous had never met the secretary himself. He only ever dealt with the woman who visited him at the bar at the Blue Lantern. Of course he knew of the man. Katerina had told him about her contact at the embassy. Theo didn't much care who he traded with, it could be Mickey Mouse for all he cared. But when Katerina came into the dark lounge today, she called him by his name.

'Secretary Bugov wants to speak to you,' she said.

Theo spread his hands. 'If he pays me, I'll talk to him. I don't care for rank and status, that's what the Brits do. Pitta?'

This was the way Theo communicated: through food. Katerina was always offered plates of it, but turned it down every time.

She shook her head. 'He wants to talk now.'

'Why the rush?' Theo asked. 'I have all this to finish.' He waved his hand over the bowls being brought to him at the bar. Katerina was all business and no fun, with her immaculate suits and dour expressions.

The doorman had told him that two British officers had wanted to talk to Ani earlier. They'd gone away, seemingly buying the deep clean ruse. He had no time or inclination for meddling. If those boys got any closer, they'd have to be sent a message loud and clear. Boys from the base got into trouble all the time here in Cyprus; they couldn't help themselves. Their masters wouldn't give a damn about them should they get roughed up. Since those scum Green Jackets raped and murdered a young girl back in the nineties in Ayia Napa, the

British were jumpy about their soldiers getting into any kind of trouble on the island. No one would take their side when it came to it. Unless they were inside the Queen's gates, they were subject to local rules. They'd better fuck off and stay fucked off, or else.

Theo liked the word fuck in English, it was satisfying and rolled off the tongue like a good cough. He used it often.

'He's not coming here to meet me?' Theo smiled mischievously. Even Katerina smirked. It was the first inkling of a sense of humour he'd ever seen in her. He'd once thought Katerina the sort to dabble with him sexually, but she'd quickly put an end to his amorous attentions, years ago. She was all work. Probably a lesbian, he judged. He no longer thought about her in a carnal way and it made things easier. If he ever fancied a fuck, then he had the girls upstairs. He shifted on his chair and lit a Camel.

'You're going to die of a heart attack, Theo, before you even retire,' Katerina said.

'Retire? What's that?' He laughed and pulled out a seat for her. She remained standing. 'I can't concentrate when you're so tense,' he said.

She put her hand on her hip. 'Look, something has come up and we need to step up. It's important. Look in there,' she said. Her eyes flickered towards the envelope she'd placed on the stool that he'd pulled out. He hadn't even noticed her doing it. He'd always suspected she was some kind of kick-ass spy, or something. Like Lara Croft. Hot and lethal.

He blew smoke and wiped his mouth on a napkin. He put his cigarette in an ashtray and picked up the envelope, peeking inside. It was a ton of cash; that was for sure.

'It's not enough,' he said.

'What?' Katerina looked gobsmacked and he liked the way her mouth fell open.

Theo stopped eating and stubbed out his cigarette. 'Look, do you think I'm stupid? I've been feeding you information for years now, and suddenly people are dying and there's an investigation up at the base. That means the Brits are jumpy. That means that whatever it is I'm passing to you means as much to them as it does to you, right? Like I said, I'm not stupid. I want more.'

Katerina paused and he liked the way she didn't know exactly what to say straight away. She was thinking and he allowed her some time. He looked at his watch and at his phone, as if bored. Artemis had contacted him telling him they had to move from the house near Kykkos, in the mountains. He knew he was on the right track with Katerina.

'I'll meet your Secretary Bugov, but only here. Out there,' he nodded to the door. 'Out there is too dangerous. I assume he's here with diplomatic immunity? Yeah, well that doesn't apply to me, so he comes here or nothing. I'll get him what he wants, but don't forget that this place is being watched. I'll leave it up to you as to how you get him in here undetected. That's my final offer,' Theo went back to eating.

Katerina looked at him and to the bar, where a girl was practising her pole-dancing moves.

She left and closed the door gently behind her.

Theo lit another cigarette and ordered a lager.

Chapter 42

Helen sat in the back seat and Gem drove.

She'd been summoned to a meeting in Akrotiri with the Commander of the British Forces for the whole of the Island, the CBF himself, and she was apprehensive. She had little to give him, apart from conjecture. She couldn't help the feeling that the four corporals being stiffed for leaking secrets to the enemy were innocent. It wouldn't be the theory he'd be looking for, but then she might be underestimating him. She didn't know the man. She'd read his service history. A two-star general, he'd seen some action in his time. He'd commanded premium posts and was highly decorated.

She couldn't work out if her nerves were because of the case, and the developments that seemed to be piling up daily, or the worry that the CBF was about to hamstring her with more demands. The RMP was essentially independent; it had to be, otherwise how could any military misdemeanour possibly be investigated without prejudice? But, and it was a big but, like any giant institution, there was a huge difference investigating the crimes of an individual compared to when the finger was pointed to the establishment itself. Individuals were dealt with swiftly when they fucked up. But accuse the whole institution and, suddenly, people close ranks, doors shut, and you had an almighty battle on your hands. Helen had a feeling that she was in the middle of a war that was about to get messy. She was used to it of course, and that's why Grant had left the forces. What she hoped wouldn't happen was that those in power high above, untouchable compared to other mere mortals, wouldn't come to some sort of diplomatic settlement and forget that Paul had died for it. She looked at her ring and knew what Grant would say. He'd tell her to get to the truth and shout it from the rooftops, regardless of what the cowards in Whitehall might say.

Her gut told her that the CBF would be after some kind of diplomatic solution. The British had been embarrassed in front of their allies; they had to be seen to be doing something about it.

The news that had kicked it all off in a different direction was the intelligence she'd been told this morning, as she sat at Eric's computer, that the three men who'd posed as British Naval officers, and had probably murdered Paul, were now known to have boarded a flight to Moscow on Sunday. Colonel Murton had given her the heads-up. Don knew as well as she did that pressure might be brought to bear to close the case quickly and move on. But it wasn't 1985 anymore. Inquiries were made public for a reason: accountability. Institutional corruption wasn't tolerated. Somebody's head was about to roll, but she wanted it to be the right person. The character trait – needing to find justice – had plagued her all her life and she knew that it could sometimes cause her to be isolated.

It was still her investigation and so Don acted in full faith, sharing the information with her. It had come from MI6. Movements of known operatives around the world were monitored all the time. The three men were paid-up employees of the Federal Security Service of Russia. It almost made her want to vomit when the news was corroborated in black and white. Her worst fears had as good as been confirmed: this was a diplomatic game. Paul had died as collateral waste.

It meant that she almost wanted to miss her summons today to Akrotiri, for fear of what she might be ordered to do, or worse: not to do. She'd asked Don, when he'd called her, why they were bypassing Colonel Bill Seaton. After all, the man was in charge of the Ayios Nikolaos listening station where the leaks had originated from in the first place.

'I'm afraid that's one thing I've been told I can't divulge at the moment, Helen,' he'd replied.

'That tells me everything I need to know,' she'd said back to him. He'd remained silent and she knew that Colonel Bill Seaton was suspected of collusion. But what did they have? 'Okay, Don, I was thinking my next move would be to feed the colonel some strategic information from a source I've developed at Ayios Nikolaos. Fake information – to see if it's acted upon.'

'I would say that's a very good idea,' Don had told her.

So that's what she planned. The young corporal – Danny Hewitt – who'd been so helpful when she'd asked how the station worked was somebody that Helen was convinced she could trust, or at least, use. She'd already instructed him to let her know when and where Labib Hassan popped up over the airways, and Danny had been true to his word, bypassing the colonel to give her the news first. In her capacity as chief RMP investigator on the case, as well as the station being on British soil, she was fully within her rights to demand such action, and Danny had impressed her. As far as Danny knew, Labib's movements were hotting up. In other words, he was taking risks where he hadn't before. It was as if he was acting with impunity, as if he knew he was protected from above. Not by God, but by false information resulting in missed opportunities to blow him to smithereens from one hundred thousand feet.

Her phone rang and it was Kay. 'Ma'am.' Old habits… 'I'm a little concerned about Jen. She ended up in the Troodos Mountains, near a small village called Kykkos, and that was two hours ago. I know the signal can be inconsistent, but she was checking in with me every half-hour, and now I've heard nothing for the last hour, and her phone's dead.'

Helen absorbed the information; she didn't want to overreact but armed with this new information about active and lethal operatives on the island, a knot formed in her stomach. 'Give it another hour. The only thing I can do, short of you driving up there yourself, is get the local police to send a car up there to see if she's in trouble. Do you have an address?'

'The last message was from a residence, but no known address as it's in the middle of nowhere, but I do have GPS coordinates.'

'Good, give it an hour and get back to me. I might be in my meeting then, but something tells me I won't mind being disturbed,' Helen said. They hung up.

Gem drove steadily, like all army drivers. He was super careful and Helen almost wanted to grab the wheel from him and drive herself. She had shit to get done. For something to keep her occupied, she called the chief of police for the Larnaca area and was put through to an underling. It was expected. These things usually took time. She didn't have a professional relationship with the man, she'd only been on the island for three days, but relations were usually good between the forces police and the island department. Normally, they worked towards the same goals. Finally, she was put through and she asked him about the murder of Anastasia Lebedev.

'Murder? She drowned,' he said.

Helen's stomach sank to her toes. 'I'm sure I'd drown too if I was beaten and strangled, and tied to a ship twenty metres down,' Helen said.

Gem looked in his rear-view mirror and she sighed.

'I don't know where you're getting your information from, Major Scott, but I can assure you that's not the case. The woman was autopsied this morning and the results are final.'

'That was quick,' Helen said.

Even in London, it was like pulling teeth trying to get an autopsy on a murder victim. Twenty-four hours was considered an emergency.

'Our policies and procedures may be quicker than what you're used to,' he said, satisfied with himself.

Helen rolled her eyes. 'Can I see the autopsy report?' she asked.

'Why?'

'Because I found her while working on a case for the British Government,' she said. She knew it was futile.

'Pure coincidence,' he said. 'It's Cyprus jurisdiction. Thank you for finding her and bringing her to our attention.'

It was final.

Gem approached the gates of the Akrotiri base as she hung up. There was no way she'd ever see the file on Anastasia Lebedev. Deep down she'd known it, that's why she'd taken the photographs. At least she had proof of how the woman had died, should anyone ever care to ask.

They were ushered through the gates and Gem drove straight to the offices of the CBF. Helen was now in a thoroughly bad mood. She was furious that it appeared that she was being slowly locked out from certain conversations. Weren't they all on the same side? She was also despondent that some people's lives mattered more than others.

She was shown into a formal waiting area and watched as army and air force personnel pranced up and down carrying files, not speaking, rigid in their agendas. Their uniforms were pristine, and they walked like they had rods up their arses, which, she guessed, she did too.

She was shown in to the general's office and stood in front of him.

He looked up from his desk and introduced himself. 'David Street.' He almost shook off her hand, but she was used to it. The higher the rank of soldier, the more keen and desperate they were to show it. 'What a mess,' he said. 'No uniform?' he asked, looking at her state of dress.

She wondered if the mess he was referring to was somehow connected to her skirt, shirt and soft trainers. She looked down, worried for a second.

'I'm spending a lot of my time off base, sir. I'm sorry,' she added. She could kick herself that she felt so awkward.

'No, that's not what I meant. Yes, I know you're working very hard. I hear you. You just stick out like a sore thumb round here, that's all.'

'With respect, General, in combats, I'd stick out like a sore thumb out there.'

He nodded. 'So, the case. I've been briefed by London. I fancy it won't be long until the island's crawling with your colleagues, and I wager it might go further than that, to the government's lawyers. So, where are we?' he asked.

'Sir, with respect, I work for the Special Investigations Branch, in my current capacity, so I can't divulge—'

'Oh, I see, we're going down that route? Cut the bullshit, Scott.'

Helen was taken aback. This was not protocol at all. If she was ten years younger, she might have succumbed to such bullying behaviour, but not now. He was just a bloke, with a few medals, trying to intimidate her. What was it about a uniform and a title that made men think they could push people around?

'This has caused a ruckus all over the place. I want to know what's happening on my island,' he continued.

His island... Jesus.

Helen tried to keep her cool. 'I'm sorry, sir, if you are privy to something I'm not. I haven't been told—'

'Yet. You will be.'

He got up out of his chair and paced up and down.

'All right,' he said. He seemed to have calmed down. 'Your investigation is specifically to ascertain if a crime has been committed at Ayios Nikolaos station, which is under my jurisdiction. What we have here, though, is an international incident where I have been ordered to intervene and decide if these offences are a police matter or of vital national security. I need your cooperation.'

It made sense to her, now he explained himself. He was trying to get her to share what she knew, which was unorthodox at this stage of an investigation by the SIB, because he was having pressure piled on him from somewhere else to protect Britain's reputation abroad: a different matter entirely.

'The Chief of the General Staff has become involved. The Defence Secretary wants answers.'

Helen processed the information in her head. Don had warned her that something was afoot. She hadn't imagined it went this high. For a minister to get involved, British political interests had become involved. This was a new development and she realised that she was way out of her depth.

'Sir, I might point out to you that the handling of the Cyprus Seven in the 1980s came unstuck because protocol wasn't followed.'

'Yes, I'm aware of that!' he barked at her. It didn't matter how angry or entitled he got, Helen couldn't budge her brief. The enquiry had to be independent otherwise it wouldn't stand up in any court, military or other. She appreciated the severity of the Defence Secretary's involvement, who oversaw all policy inside the MOD, but this was, and had to remain, an autonomous investigation. 'I can see you're one of those moralists,' he said.

'The integrity of the case hinges on its self-determination. If I get dragged into politics, we won't have a leg to stand on should we need to deliver this in the public arena. What about his family?' she asked him.

'Whose family?' he asked, defiantly.

'Captain Paul Thomas, sir. The RMP officer, my colleague, who was murdered.'

'Ah, yes.'

He sat down heavily. He rubbed his eyes.

'Sir, if I may, I feel as though I'm stumbling round in the dark on this one. My brief is to investigate Captain Thomas's death. If it's not done properly, then the perpetrators will never be brought to justice.'

'That's my point, Major Scott. It's not in the national interest that they ever are.'

Chapter 43

By the time Gem dropped Helen at Colonel Seaton's house, it was gone four o'clock in the afternoon, and Jen was still off radar. Helen had managed to secure a Cypriot police squad car to check on her, and the number plate of her hire car had been passed to them. She could do no more, short of drive up there herself, and what good would that do? She came to the grim conclusion that she was about to perform a dance between two sovereign territories, and Jen was caught in the middle. She could be lost. She could be hurt. Or she could be out of battery power. Surveillance took time, and checking in every five minutes was something that was impractical. Kay was young and inexperienced, and Helen had to be the leading example by keeping calm and level-headed. A rare moment of self-doubt caught her attention and she wondered, now, if she should have asked Don to send a couple of old sweats from Special Branch instead. But it was on her head.

Andi Seaton answered the door. She looked like hell.

'Hello, Andi, may I come in?' Helen asked.

The colonel's wife was hesitant. She peeked from behind the door, as if she were protecting herself from the horrors of the outside world. Like somebody in isolation, she looked pale and tired.

'It's not a good time,' Andi said finally.

'I'm afraid it's a bit important. I'll keep it brief. Are you feeling okay?'

'I think I've got summer flu,' Andi said, widening the door so Helen could enter.

The house was dark; Andi, or her waiting staff, not having opened any curtains. It was the time of day that some army wives called the witching hour. Army life was tough for spouses. Helen had seen it before. Those attached to army personnel always set their game faces in public, it was part of how they coped. But the constant requirement to look happy and in control was wearing and she could see it all over Andi's face. The woman wasn't in the mood. And she didn't have summer flu: whatever that was. Hiding was the only known antidote.

Helen walked into the entrance hall and Andi closed the door behind her.

'No staff today?' Helen asked.

Andi looked around warily. 'Day off. Are you looking for Bill?'

'Actually, I came to speak to you. Colonel Seaton has been extra busy recently and there are a few questions I have that you could help me with.'

'Such as?'

It was quite clear to Helen that she wasn't going to be invited further into the home.

'I think you live and breathe his job, don't you?' Helen said. She didn't wait for an answer. It was her opening shot. Andi was at a loss for words, and Helen could tell that she regretted letting her in. 'Where is he?' Helen asked.

'I thought you wanted to talk to me?'

'I do, I was just making sure he wasn't here, that's all. Are you sure you're all right?'

'I've had a rough few days, bad news from home.'

'Oh, I'm sorry,' Helen said, not believing a word. 'Andi, can I speak frankly?'

'Something tells me you're going to with or without my permission.'

'The colonel's wife is like the mother of the regiment, is she not? You get to know all the boys very well, especially abroad, when you have them round for drinks and they confide in you in the early hours. I know, I was one of those soldiers once. Though, it's a bit different for women. There's something about the way a man missing his mother confides in an older woman.'

'Where's this going?' Andi demanded.

'The four men suspended from their jobs at Ayios Nikolaos. You know them well? I'm struggling to find any reason for them to remain suspended, and London agrees with me. Why was the finger pointed at them in the first place?'

'Bill doesn't discuss that with me.'

Helen noted the colonel's wife's body stiffen and her jaw set. 'Really?'

'You know you're bang out of order coming here and insinuating—'

'I'm not insinuating anything, I'm simply asking you your opinion of four soldiers, who I know you know well, because they're on your wall of fame, on the stairs.'

Andi's mouth fell open and she touched her throat absently. 'That means nothing.'

'Really? I think back to my quarters and what I put on my walls. Let's go and refresh your memory, shall we?' Helen walked past her towards the stairs.

'What are you doing?' Andi followed her. She didn't seem so poorly now. The mask of innocence was falling off, and the colonel's wife was truly rattled.

'Here we go, and who is this man?' Helen pointed to the photograph she'd spotted when she'd attended the house for dinner on Saturday night. 'I recognise him from somewhere. He looks important, and the way the colonel is laughing beside him, and the fact that you eulogise it by giving it pride of place, says something to me,' Helen said. 'What was the evening celebrating?'

'I have no idea who he is,' Andi replied. 'Please leave – in fact, I'm calling my husband.'

'Call him, I'm sure he'll remember this man.'

Andi didn't move and Helen pressed on.

241

'So, these four corporals. Decent enough chaps, aren't they?'

'I'm proud of all of the men who serve under Bill,' Andi said.

'And they're loyal?'

'Of course!'

'Loyal enough to risk their jobs by lying?'

'Get out!'

'You need to be more careful what you post on Facebook, Andi,' Helen said.

'What?'

Helen showed her phone. It was something she'd done as a matter of course, when investigating the four corporals. People have a terrible habit of bragging, generally, and the most common way was posting pictures on social media. They just couldn't help themselves. It gained instant envy and recognition, and that made everybody feel better.

'This is you in the Maldives? Oh, and this is you in LA. This one's my favourite, you and your three children, who go to private school back in the UK, courtesy of the taxpayer, all in Sri Lanka. Very expensive holidays, wouldn't you agree? And all in the space of one single year.'

'I have money left by my dead father. How dare you come in here and question where I get my money from!' Andi's chest was turning red.

'Whatever I've implied, you just confirmed,' Helen said. 'Your father is alive and well. You forget, Andi, that you belong to the military and we know everything about you. Where did the money come from really?'

'Get out of my house!' Her face was twisted with fury and Helen knew this was the real Andi.

'But it isn't your house, is it? In fact, it's my house, because I pay taxes.' Helen was pushing her because she knew it was the only way to get the truth out of the woman: by goading her into a natural emotional reaction, without reason or recourse to thought.

Andi marched down the stairs and towards the back of the house. As she did so, Helen popped the framed picture off the wall and behind her back. She went towards the door, letting herself out.

Helen slammed the car door as she got in and asked Gem to take her back to the mess. Once there, she went into the lounge and hunted for what she wanted. Attention to detail was the pivotal difference between somebody who investigated and somebody who simply did a job. She found what she was looking for. A similar photograph, framed and hung amongst an arrangement of other photographs of VIPs laughing and chortling their way through countless dinners sipping from silver and crystal. She popped it off its hook and went to her room.

The man's face wasn't familiar, but that wasn't the point. She just knew, when she saw the picture in the mess on Sunday morning, after she'd had dinner with the Seatons, that she'd seen him before and now she knew where. The man was clearly highly thought of: the regiment would have thousands of photos to frame of their choosing, so why choose this one? The man was surrounded by sycophants in both pictures, and Helen had already noticed that on his left lapel, in an otherwise dull and boring ensemble, he wore the emblem of the Russian security services. It was a tiny metal badge that the man evidently wore with pride. It was a stupid mistake. The pin was shaped like a shield, with a golden sword behind it. Two golden eagles held a ball and sceptre, with a knight in the middle. The symbols replaced the old hammer and sickle, and Russian star. The agency took over from the KGB over two decades ago, but ostensibly it was the same organisation, just with a friendlier name.

She emailed the pictures to Don Murton and asked him to find out who the man was and if he had a position here on the island.

Chapter 44

As Helen rushed down the stairs at the mess, she saw Tom Fleet arrive with his icy colleague, Second Lieutenant Victor Cobb.

All three paused and Helen read tension on their faces. The job had to be done at some point, so she greeted them and asked if they'd accompany her to a quiet room, where the snooker table was. No one was playing. The men would be finishing work and getting ready for tea, taken in smart casual formality, in chinos and shirts and ties. The two officers were wary but followed her.

She closed the door and turned to face them.

'Off duty?' she asked.

They looked at one another and both went to speak at the same time. Helen held up her hand and allowed Tom to speak.

'We had some time during lunch and went into town,' he said.

'It's almost five o'clock.'

'We finished early.'

She waited and looked at Victor. He said nothing.

'You don't know, do you?' she asked. They looked at one another.

'What?' Tom asked.

'When's the last time you saw Ani?' she asked Tom.

'Yesterday morning when she left the mess,' he said. 'We went to the Blue Lantern to find her.' Finally he owned up and Helen felt sympathy for him.

'She wasn't there,' she said. It wasn't a question and Tom heard it.

'You know where she is?' he asked.

'She's dead, Tom,' Helen said. There was no way of dressing it up.

She allowed them their few moments of disbelief and frantic questions, and she appreciated that she'd get no sense out of them until the news sunk in.

'What?'

'How do you know?'

'Where is she?'

Victor comforted his friend and Helen saw true warmth there. Tom was a good-looking and intelligent young man and he had his whole life ahead of him. He'd get over this, but not right now. She waited until the questions ran out and they were both properly listening to her. She pulled up a chair and suggested they do the same. Tom held his head in his hands.

'She was pulled out of the sea this morning. She was found on the *Zenobia*.'

'What?' Victor asked.

Tom continued to nurse his head. His eyes were red and Helen was touched by his obvious affection for the girl, but she also saw him as incredibly naive. There was something so raw about his emotion that she knew, in that moment, that he truly loved her. Or at least he thought he did.

'It's my belief that Ani was some kind of collateral damage in the case I'm investigating. Tom, you need to tell me everything about her: what she said, who she knew, and especially what she told you about the Blue Lantern.'

'Where is she?' he asked.

Victor lay his hand on his friend's shoulder.

'She's in police custody at the general hospital. The police won't release her body. It's out of my jurisdiction.'

Helen wasn't about to tell him that she was the person who found her, and that she'd taken photographs to prove how she died, and that the Cypriot police weren't sharing any inform-ation, calling it an accidental drowning. Why anyone would believe that a woman would go for a morning swim at twenty metres below, on her own, was laughable, but that was the story, and Helen could do nothing about it.

Victor cottoned on first. 'She was killed?'

Tom looked up between his fingers, anger turning to rage. He stood up. 'Murdered?'

Helen stood up and went to him, pleading with him to take it easy. 'Tom, your anger will not bring her back, but it could ruin my investigation, and I'm determined to find out who did this and why. You have to trust me on this.'

Victor was stood up now too, trying to calm his friend, and agreeing with Helen. 'Mate, she's right. There's nothing you can do anymore.'

Tom strode to the cue rack and took one, smashing it against the table. Helen gasped and stood back, Victor took the pieces out of his hands. Tom went to stand against a wall, and couldn't face them. Victor turned to her and they each knew they were in agreement. Tom had to control himself.

'Neither of you can talk to anyone, please promise me this. The more you're involved, the more you're in danger yourselves. I don't want you leaving the base.'

'Major Graham told me to keep an eye on her,' Tom said, through tears.

'What?' Helen said, surprised. 'Why?'

'He thought she was trying to get to Britain for a reason. Not to marry me but as some kind of informant.'

Helen raised her eyebrows.

'That's not all,' he added.

Vic looked at him. Helen waited.

'He also told me to watch you as well,' he said.

'Me?' Helen said. 'Am I dangerous too?' she asked. He didn't answer.

'We went to the Blue Lantern to find her this morning,' Victor said.

'Who was there?'

'They said they were deep cleaning and were closed. A girl leant out of the window and told us to forget Ani.'

'So they all know. Victor, stay with Tom. Make arrangements for your platoon sergeants to take on your work for tomorrow, make it casual. The colonel is tied up all day, he won't even notice. I'll smooth things over.' She told a white lie, having no clue where the colonel was, or what his plans were, but knowing he wouldn't be thinking about the discipline of his subalterns right now.

Victor nodded at her. She went to Tom, who was fuming.

'Tom,' she said softly. He faced her.

'Why?' he asked.

'She knew something,' Helen replied.

'About what?' he asked.

'You tell me,' she said.

'She was desperate to leave here, and live in the UK,' Victor said behind her.

'Did she ever mention the Russian Embassy?' she asked both of them.

'Russian Embassy?' they said in unison.

'I know she was taken there yesterday.'

'Wait,' Tom said. 'There's a woman who hangs about the Blue Lantern, always in a suit, looks proper businesslike, has something to do with running the place, has Theo eating out of her hands, and she's Russian.'

'How do you know?'

'Because Ani told me.'

It wasn't the first time that Helen had heard about the woman in a suit. Kay had seen her too. And photographed her.

Chapter 45

The journey to Ayios Nikolaos was short but predictably tedious, with the farmers still blocking parts of the road. With her ID, they let Helen through. They weren't there, after all, to disrupt British operations, just cause a headache. But she knew now that they could be used to cause more than that, should their actions be manipulated.

'Gem, what are the ESBA police doing over there?'

There was a scuffle to her periphery, and it didn't look like farmers they were talking to. It was a group of casually dressed men, holding sticks and baskets.

'They're lime stickers, ma'am.'

'Catching songbirds?' she asked.

'Yes. Their nets are a nightmare, they threaten the dishes.'

She looked towards the base, where the satellite features could be seen plainly. They sat like whitewashed Greek stone homes against the bright blue sky, even at this late hour. Orange was creeping into the hue, and it was rather beautiful.

She watched as the ESBA police talked to the men, and they turned to stare back at her. The group of men stood with their sticks suspended and unmoving as they passed by. Some of them chewed sloppily, like the gunslingers of the Wild West masticating their snuff. Helen realised that they were actively producing the bird-lime required to make the sticky substance used to catch the birds.

'Does it happen often?' she asked.

'What?' Gem asked.

'The nets getting stuck in the dishes,' she said.

248

Gem shrugged. By now she was used to his body language.

'Can you remember the last time it happened?'

'Couple of weeks ago. The authorities never do anything about it. These guys are dirt poor. They rely on the trade of the small birds. I tried one once, it was quite nice, but it's cruel, isn't it?' Gem said.

Helen pushed away her repulsion. Gem wasn't being callous, he was telling her he'd tried a local delicacy; that was all.

'Why are they allowed on ESBA land?' she asked.

'They've been here forever. The Brits are not about to kick off ancient farmers and bird catchers, it would cause an outrage.'

He was right.

'Unless they cause a real problem,' she added.

Gem shrugged again.

The gaps in her investigation were laid out in front of her. She had her answer to what had been bugging her the whole time the four corporals had been held under house arrest. The fact that they couldn't possibly pass intelligence in real time suddenly made sense to her. They didn't need to. What was important was that for certain periods of time, no one could pass anything. If the listening station was out of action, then no one would know where Labib Hassan was during that time. He could operate undetected.

And only Colonel Seaton could suspend the workings of the station. Perhaps he could make sure the stickers were undisturbed too.

She watched as the police chatted to the group; there were no arrests happening, they were simply talking.

She instructed Gem to drive on.

At the station, she went straight to the operating room where Corporal Danny Hewitt worked, and she knew already that he was on duty.

'Corporal,' Helen said. She surprised him.

'What are you doing in here? Sorry, ma'am, I didn't mean to be rude,' he said.

She sat down next to him, pulling a chair up. 'My phone is off. So, any intel from Syria?'

'Hundreds of coordinates,' he said. 'Actually thousands.'

'Very funny, you know what I'm talking about. Our friend Labib Hassan, how's he doing?'

'Reckless.'

'In what way?'

'After years off the grid, he's swanning about like he owns the place.'

'He's not scared of the sky anymore,' she said.

'Ma'am?'

She turned to him. 'Danny, I need you to do something for me.'

'Of course, ma'am.'

'It comes from the highest authority.'

He nodded gravely.

'I want you to give Major Graham false coordinates.'

He swallowed hard and looked around, but the other operators had seen Major Scott before; they didn't look up from their work, and they wore headsets which meant they couldn't hear a thing.

'It's an order.'

'Yes, ma'am.'

'Good. Stay here on duty, and I'll be back with further instruction. I don't have to remind you that you are, as always, bound by the Official Secrets Act. This goes no further, not even inside this room.'

Chapter 46

As she left the station, Helen heard from the local Cypriot police that the squad car sent to the Troodos Mountains had located a residential address at the GPS coordinates given, but nobody was home, and there was no car on site matching the description of Jen's hire car.

A heavy feeling spread across Helen's gut.

She called Colonel Don Murton.

'We have an SIB officer missing.' She got straight to the point.

'Outside the ESBA?' he asked.

'Yes.'

'Jesus, Helen.'

She waited.

'Tell me everything.'

She gave him a brief outline of what Jen was doing, who was involved and her suspicion that Anastasia Lebedev had been delivered to the Russian Embassy by the same man who Jen was following.

'And you let her go alone?'

'We didn't know then what had happened to Lebedev. I had no reason to see him as capable of being an accessory to murder.'

'The High Commissioner is meeting with the Russian Ambassador tonight.'

'What?' Helen spat. 'So, they're going to cover all this up, aren't they?' she asked angrily.

'Calm down, Helen. Now we know that an officer is involved, it can be part of our terms.'

'Jesus, Don. As easy as that? Why should anyone listen to you? What have we got to bargain with? Zero. All we've done is bust their little racket, they won't budge.'

'They can't risk the murder of an officer.'

'They did last week!'

'Helen, the file on Captain Thomas's death is being closed and sealed. He had a diving accident,' he said. She could hear the pain in his voice.

'You fuckers,' she spat.

'Helen,' he pleaded.

'Don't *Helen* me, Don. What about his family?'

'Okay, what about his family? What would you rather if it was your fucking son, Helen? A diving accident or knowing the terror he might have seen as his air was taken from him at fifty metres? How could his mother ever live with that? How could any mother be expected to take that? Put yourself in her position. You're all rules and revenge. How about some compassion for her?'

'By lying to her?' They were both shouting now.

'By softening the blow,' he yelled.

'So you can all go back to playing your diplomatic game? And no one is ever brought to justice for it? Fuck you.'

'Fuck you back, Major Scott.'

Don was used to Helen's temper. He stayed on the line. They both knew she was right. Morally. But reality didn't work like that; it had nothing to do with ethics. She closed her eyes and thought about the baby son she'd lost. Luke. How could she bear to know he was killed by strangers? Wouldn't she rather think that he'd been taken by a cruel twist of fate? Tears stung her eyes.

'You're right,' she said finally.

He said nothing. Helen sniffed and Gem passed her a tissue from the front of the car. She took it and blew her nose. He drove slowly and she heard vague shouts outside of the vehicle. The farmers were chanting. Fires were burning: campfires for the night shift. What were they gaining from staying out all night? The local press was here, interviewing men stood on tractors. Behind them, she saw lime stickers poking the trees from a distance. The ESBA police had gone.

'This place is fucked up, Don.'

'It's a drop in the ocean, Helen. You know, as do I, that the island's stability is more important than the chief of ESBA police hand-picking his force, or a refurb on the colonel's house.'

'But it's not just that, is it? An officer of the British Army was murdered.'

'You're going to have to take that one on the chin, Helen. We can't risk an international incident.'

'Of course you can't, Don. And what if it was me?' she asked him.

He didn't answer straight away.

'But it's not, is it? You're not going to take any more risks. I'll authorise an armed guard to take you up to the Troodos Mountains to find your officer. Meanwhile, we'll pressure the ambassador to produce a peaceful solution.'

'Via the High Commissioner? Did you find out who the Russian Security Force guy is in the photos? I'm sure he's shared plenty of local delicacies at the High Commissioner's residence in Nicosia.'

'Now you're surmising because you're angry.'

'What else do I do? I'm doing it to you because I know when I finish this conversation, I'll never have the opportunity again.'

'We did identify him, yes.'

'And?'

Don sighed and sucked his teeth. Helen waited.

'He's called Dimitri Bugov, and he's not listed as on the island, and he never has been.'

'Brazen bastard. He's on a picture I took from Colonel Seaton's hallway too.'

'Helen—'

'Don't, Don. If I have to leave Paul's death alone, then allow me this. I want that shithead off the island, that's the least we can do.'

'What about the life of your officer for now? Anything more is a bonus. But you're right, his cover is blown. They'll remove him anyway. He's certainly failed in his mission now he's been identified. Poor bastard will probably be assassinated before he leaves Cyprus soil anyway, that's how they deal with failures in Russia.'

'What a pity we haven't got the balls – there are scores of senior officers who'd be on my list.'

'Get your anger out, Helen, this is your opportunity.'

'Oh fuck off, Don.'

'I hope my name isn't on your list,' he said.

Her mood lightened a little. Don had taken her under his wing and watched her career blossom. She'd saved his life in Baghdad. It was recorded in no official reports, but Don knew that it was her who'd taken the shot that had made the difference between his life and the sniper who would have killed him. That's why she got to speak to him like she was sounding off at a wayward husband. It was a good trade-off and she knew Don was never offended by her honesty. She suspected he rather enjoyed it. Don was an expert statesman and had been taken out of the field after his brush in Iraq, to hone his skills elsewhere.

'No, it's not, Kofi.' On more than one occasion, after telling him to fuck off, she'd nicknamed him Kofi Annan in a more than scathing manner to goad him.

'What about the Russian woman who was photographed at the Blue Lantern?'

'We're working on her,' Don replied. 'Right, get your arse out there and smooth this over. The financial accounts of the four corporals are ready for your assessment too, our fraud department has been working round the clock.'

'What about Colonel Seaton?'

'He'll be charged with school-fee fraud and removed off the island, once we've got solid evidence.'

'If you can find him,' she said.

'Why?'

'I haven't seen him since I was offered cocktails at his pad on Saturday night. His wife is jumpy. Something is going on there.'

'Well, what are you waiting for?'

Chapter 47

Gem drove Helen, and two armed officers followed in a car behind. It was nine o'clock when they left the base and headed to the Troodos Mountains. She knew what she was looking for. Any soldier worth his or her salt would leave traces of themselves at a volatile scene, but she wanted to see it for herself.

Surprising, but welcome, was the news that, via some diplomatic manoeuvring, Cypriot police were also looking for Artemis Charalambous, on some trumped-up traffic violation charge. They'd passed details of his family properties to the ESBA police, who'd delivered it to Helen at the mess. She'd taken the information, at her small office, in shock. Kay was there too. They were busy discussing things that Jen might have had with her to identify herself should she get into trouble.

An ESBA police officer had knocked on the door and delivered Helen an envelope. Inside was a whole file of information on Artemis Charalambous. By the time she looked up at the door, the police constable had disappeared. She and Kay had devoured it, looking for properties within a radius of the Troodos Mountains, and found that the villa near the tiny village of Kykkos, where Jen had last checked in, belonged to Artemis's mother. Mama Charalambous must be a wealthy woman, Helen thought.

'Likely story,' Kay had said out loud.

Helen had smiled. 'Our first break.'

Helen had insisted Kay stay behind on the base to plough through the financial accounts of the four corporals. Helen knew Kay wouldn't sleep until they heard from Jen, so she might as well give her something to do.

The lights from the vehicles lit the way, on the dark streets. Road lighting was woeful on the island but not really essential. The volume of traffic didn't merit the cost. It just made the journey resoundingly eerie. They left the glare of the Larnaca strip behind them and soon they were on the road to Troodos. Helen opened her window and felt the cool air of the evening refresh her. She closed her eyes and faced the rush of air.

'You alright, ma'am?' Gem asked.

'Just thinking, Gem.'

She needed to find something to prove that Jen had been inside the villa. It was international leverage: something that couldn't be argued away diplomatically. It could be solid proof that a citizen of the United Kingdom was held by a known criminal. She wanted no wriggle room. If anything happened to Jen, it couldn't be explained by an accident, because she'd raised her disappearance, on active duty, and her suspicions to a senior officer, and she wasn't letting this one go, and Don knew it too.

No one wanted a stink on their hands.

The endless dark road made her weary and she wanted to rest her eyes for a moment. But the next thing she knew, Gem was shaking her. They'd arrived at the villa, which was even more remote than she'd expected, and surrounded by forest. Her first thought was frustration with herself for being unprofessional and she looked about her, taking in the area around the house. They were on a virtual dirt road, in front of a grand house. It was pitch black and after her eyes adjusted, she realised that there were no lights for miles. They used torches.

The two armed officers got out of their vehicle and approached her. She knew their weapons were on safety, but they shouldn't have to use them. They wore body cameras. Helen felt secure in the belief that no one in their right mind would challenge British soldiers, with automatic weapons pointed at them, out of a theatre of war. But she was still nervous and her heart rate seemed to double upon waking and becoming alert. Gem stayed in the vehicle outside.

The two soldiers went ahead, and approached the building, which was in complete darkness. The front door was large and surrounded by ornate climbing plants, it was stunningly beautiful, and well-tended. Whoever lived here, or looked after the place, couldn't be far away. The door was unlocked and Helen almost couldn't believe it. Houses like this in the UK, or almost anywhere else on earth, would be locked up, gated and under surveillance, but here, in the middle of a Mediterranean island, where neighbours had grown up together, security was lax.

They went in and the two soldiers cleared each room. The movements of their bodies reminded Helen of the countless times she'd done the very same thing in theatre, on operations. They shouted 'clear' every time they exited a room, and it didn't take long to establish that no one was home, just like the Cypriot police had said.

'No lights,' said Helen.

They used the torches loaded onto their weapons, and Helen used a handheld unit to search the property.

'Touch nothing without these,' she said, passing out gloves.

Helen approached the main sitting room and the ethereal light cast by the torches made it seem like a world lost in an apocalypse, and they were the last survivors on earth looking for signs of life. Shadows bounced off surfaces and made ornaments glow. Nothing seemed out of place. They searched the kitchen and Helen scoured the cupboards and cabinets for signs of her officer.

Upstairs, they found beds made and welcoming, as if a family had just recently walked out. For a moment, Helen questioned if they'd got the right address. In the third bedroom, Helen noticed an indent in the mattress and went to it. The soldiers pointed their weapons in her direction and she could see the bed clearly. Instinct told her to kneel down and she did so. Their light was sure and steady. She peered under the bed and held her own torch firmly. She lay fully on her belly and squinted into the spectral gloom. Something glinted.

She shuffled further under the bed and reached out in front of her.

'Bingo,' she said.

Before she left the base, Kay had shown her a ring. Every officer in their business needed something personal to leave at a scene, should they find themselves compromised. Kay and Jen had bought matching ones at Heathrow Airport. They'd cost a couple of quid and were made of a fake gold with cheap crystals dotted around the band.

Helen stretched and picked it up. It was Jen's ring; identical to the one she'd been shown by Kay.

'Good girl,' she said under her breath.

Jen had been here.

Chapter 48

'Don, are you awake?' Helen asked.

'Obviously, unless I sleep-talk.'

'Funny. I've got some bad news.'

'I didn't think you were calling to wish me Merry Christmas,' he said.

'One of my officers is confirmed as being at the property we searched. I've got a local Cypriot forensic team there now. I'm collating a list of all of the properties registered to the brothers, but I've got a feeling they might have gone north of the border.'

'Where?'

'Theo Charalambous owns a house near Famagusta.'

The seaside resort was once popular with Americans and Europeans before the civil war in 1974. After the invasions, they called it the city of the dogs, because it was deserted and only strays and weeds resided there. In recent years, it had enjoyed a revival, but, regardless of any of that, it was still Turkish territory. Helen felt the case slipping from her grasp. Neither she nor Don could authorise an armed response team to hit a private residence on independent Turkish soil.

'It's up to you, Don, I'm relying on you to get her out,' she said.

'Helen, I'm working round the clock to negotiate something. The High Commissioner is aware.'

'But, Don, that means nothing unless the Russians want to hand her back, you know that. What is this? Why would they take such risks? There's only one reason, and that's that the brothers are acting rashly and unilaterally. That puts her in grave danger, if they are pursued and have nothing to lose. It gives us no leverage.'

'Look, the climate summit is coming up in four months, nobody wants a situation, and Russia wants their pipeline built through Germany.' He referred to a massive gas pipe being built from Russia, under the Baltic Sea, to the European state, but not everybody approved of it, especially the Americans, on security grounds.

'That isn't good enough for my officer right now, Don. The brothers won't give a crap about some gas line being built. All they care about is keeping themselves above the law, and right now, that means helping keep Labib Hassan alive, so he can pursue lucrative arms deals. My officer is trying to sabotage that by jeopardising the free flow of information, at my instruction. She's a target. I'm thinking of going there myself.'

'Don't be an idiot, Helen. You have no jurisdiction, and no back-up. What are you going to do? Drive over there with a British service revolver?'

'I can't sit here doing nothing!'

'Yes you can. That's your only choice, here.'

Helen sighed. 'Can I go public with her photograph?' she asked.

'No. Not yet. An operative off ESBA territory is on her own.'

'Fuck's sake, Don.'

'Do your job, Helen. She should never have followed a subject on her own in the first place.'

Helen couldn't respond to that. He was right. This was her shitstorm, and all she could do now was pursue the case.

His voice became softer. 'I've got some good news, relatively,' he said.

She waited.

'The pictures you sent me. The woman is Katerina Bortkinov, also undeclared on the island. While the practice is completely regular, the last thing any nation state desires is that their undeclared operatives are exposed, especially some-body so senior as Bugov. Believe me, they won't last long in their current jobs; they might have already been removed from post and transferred back to Russia. We're checking flights to Moscow.'

'Which means they'll simply disappear, courtesy of their own government,' she said. 'What I don't understand, Russian operatives aside, is what the Charalambous brothers think they'll achieve by involving British serving personnel.'

'The stranglehold will get narrower, Helen, I can assure you that much. No one wants an international incident, and the death of a member of Special Branch serving abroad is a big deal.'

'Really? A story could easily be made up about her, and why she might find herself north of the border, and fed to her family, you know that, Don.'

'It won't come to that, Helen.'

'What? This time?' she asked.

She sighed and rubbed her eyes. She was back in the office with Kay, who'd listened to the whole conversation. They both felt rotten, but Helen took responsibility. It was her case, and she'd let Jen walk into the face of danger. They'd underestimated the brothers.

'Get some sleep, and if you can't, then read through the case again. The sooner you close it, the better chance we have of getting to the bottom of who ordered Paul Thomas's death, and why. That's leverage we can use, Helen.'

'Goodnight, Don.'

She hung up. Kay waited for her direction.

'It's time we got the colonel in for a formal interview,' Helen said. 'The financial records of the corporals exonerate them on their own; if nothing else, it's confirmation we haven't got the right people. I want that bastard to squirm. It's not a question of what he's up to, but how long he's been doing it. I want it down by the book, so we need ESBA police to bring him here and secure his house for a full search.'

'Warrant?' Kay asked.

'Yep, secured ten minutes ago.'

'That's amazing, Helen. Don't think about this as a failure, anything but. Since you've been on this island, look what you've done. You've got everyone twitching. I've never been on an investigation where that happens. You're so close to getting the answers you want. Jen willingly followed Artemis Charalambous. She wouldn't want it any other way, believe me, I know her very well.'

'It's easy for us to discuss it in the safety of the office,' Helen said. She was weary and depressed.

'Haven't you ever found yourself isolated in enemy territory? Did you blame the mission?' Kay asked.

Helen forced a smile. Kay was right, of course she never blamed the mission. She'd walked into similar situations gladly in her career.

'Tired?' Helen asked.

'Hell, no,' Kay said.

'Right, come on, we've got bank accounts and audits to get through. As soon as Colonel Seaton is located, we'll break.'

'Break him?' Kay asked.

Helen's smile was genuine now.

'What about his wife?' Kay asked.

'Yep, we're bringing her in too. We'll use the ESBA police cells, see how they like it.'

Chapter 49

'Bill! Where have you been?'

Andi still wore her dressing gown; she'd been in the same attire when Major Scott visited the house, and she hadn't bothered changing. She couldn't think of trivia now. She hadn't eaten for worry. For all her husband was aware, she could have only just got ready for bed. He didn't appreciate her mental state.

'Good God, you scared me,' he said. 'What on earth are you doing sat in the dark?'

He shut the door and locked it.

'Why are you locking the door, Bill?' Andi asked.

He ignored the question and peeked through closed blinds.

'What are you looking for, Bill?'

He ignored her again.

'Bill?'

He turned to face her with panic in his eyes, and he smelled of liquor.

'Bill, have you been drinking?'

'Only a few, my love. Celebrating.'

'Celebrating?'

'Our move to Kyrenia!'

'What?'

He walked away and headed to the kitchen. She followed him. He wasn't acting himself. He seemed either drunk or concussed.

'What do you mean? We can't move now!'

'Of course we can, it's all sorted. Things have come along a bit quicker than expected,' he said.

Andi stared at him. 'What do you mean? What about the children? The post? Are they sending someone to replace you?' she asked. She was desperate.

'No, don't worry about all that. We need to leave quickly, they're coming for me, Andi.'

'Who?' She was virtually wailing now, and panic consumed her. Bill, the only one who'd made sense to her, and her life, was rambling about nonsense and it terrified her.

'I just need to phone somebody first,' he said, still not looking at her, pacing around like a madman.

'Bill? What are you talking about? Who do you need to speak to?'

His clothes were unkempt. He looked as though he'd been on an all-day bender with a bunch of subalterns and crawled home to sleep it off.

She went behind him and placed her hands on his arms. 'Bill!'

He spun around, his eyes wide and bloodshot. 'You need to pack a few things, but keep it light. We really don't need that much. My driver will take us to Nicosia tonight.'

'Nicosia? Tonight? No! I won't do it, Bill,' she screamed at him. 'Not without our children.'

Bill stopped striding and Andi watched him nervously. She'd never seen him like this before.

'It's all arranged, they're meeting us there.'

She was lost for words.

'Really?' It was almost a whisper.

'Yes,' was all he said. 'You better go and pack, and, Andi...' He stopped.

She closed her dressing gown around her body.

'You've got ten minutes.'

Andi left the room and her hands shook. She needed a drink and changed her mind about obeying her husband's wishes, for the first time in their whole marriage. Instead of going up to her room, she went to the vast larder behind the kitchen and poured an extra-large glass of wine. She gulped it and breathed. That was better. She filled it quickly and went silently up to her room to decide what she needed for the rest of her life, and what she could part with to leave behind.

Chapter 50

Sergeant Kostas Valentine was tasked with bringing the colonel in. He'd been employed by the ESBA police for fifteen years and in all that time he'd never presided over the arrest of a senior officer on British territory – in fact he'd never arrested a serving Brit, full stop. He was unsure of what was going on, but he'd been given his orders. The Brits manned their ESBA police force with locals, and everybody knew they were hand-picked by the Joint Police Unit, depending upon a range of criteria. Cynics might say that the choice of officers came from a pool of useful locals who were encouraged to apply to be trained by the British for a decent enough wage: contractors, mates and relatives. Officially, they were professional and fully vetted.

All were loyal to their colonel.

Kostas wasn't quite sure how to approach the order, and he took the only other officer who was on duty with him. They were unarmed and inexperienced. Their job consisted of making sure soldiers and their spouses didn't break the speed limits within ESBA land. He was fully aware of the presence of the Special Branch officers, who were investigating the four corrupt corporals – who didn't know about that? But what did the colonel have to do with it?

They agreed to treat it as a routine request to help with enquiries, or at least that's what he'd told his colleague.

'He's not to be cuffed, and he can travel with his own driver,' Kostas told his junior officer, who yawned. It wasn't as if it was a long and arduous journey from the colonel's house to the cells. It was a total journey of under a mile.

'Can it wait until morning?' his colleague asked, in Greek. 'What's the rush? It's not as if he can go anywhere, he'll probably be asleep.'

'Good point,' Kostas agreed. They'd sit outside the house until morning, and then take him to his interview. The cells in Dhekelia Garrison were no place for a colonel.

To their surprise, there were lights on in the colonel's quarters when they pulled up.

'Nice house,' Kostas's companion noted.

'You never been up here?' Kostas replied.

'Not this close,' he whistled. 'Look at that place. I thought the British no longer had an empire!'

They both laughed.

'I won't be long,' Kostas said.

He heaved himself out of the driving seat and walked to the front door of the accommodation. He knocked and waited, expecting a member of the household staff to answer. To his amazement, it was Mrs Seaton herself. He wanted to warn her of their instructions, in case she was worried why an official car was hanging about the property.

'Oh, excuse me, ma'am, I have a message for Colonel Seaton,' Kostas said. The colonel's wife looked understandably distressed. He looked away, averting his eyes from her dressing gown and the dishevelment of her hair. He'd only been up close to her once and thought her a fine woman, but tonight, she looked unwell. 'We can come back, ma'am,' he said.

The colonel's wife looked past him and his colleague waved back at her. Kostas cringed and smiled at her. It must be unsettling to get a call from a marked police car at this hour, and he wanted to reassure her.

'Do you know what this is about?' she demanded.

'Yes, ma'am, Colonel Seaton and yourself, erm, you're to come with us, and await further instruction, ma'am,' he said.

'Come with you now?'

'Only when you're ready, ma'am.'

'Where are we to go?' she asked.

'To an interview room, ma'am.'

'Interview? Am I applying for your job?' she quipped.

Kostas laughed. 'No, ma'am. I can wait until morning if you prefer, I hope I didn't wake you?'

'Well, it is most inconvenient, I can tell you. If it's so important, then leave the details with me and I'll make sure the colonel is driven there first thing.'

'Of course, ma'am,' Kostas said, backing away. 'I'll have to stay outside,' he added.

'Good, God! Go home and get some sleep like the rest of us. Come back at seven,' she said.

'We're good, ma'am, but thank you, we can wait.'

The colonel's wife closed the door and Kostas backed away.

'Are they getting ready?' his colleague asked as Kostas got back in the car.

'Anyone's guess. Looks like we're spending the night here,' he said.

Chapter 51

Theo Charalambous sat at the bar at the Blue Lantern. Music pounded in his ears, but he was used to it. Katerina hadn't answered his calls. A small particle of doubt crept into his mind as to the importance of Secretary Bugov. Perhaps they'd abandoned him for some other set-up along the strip? No; that would never happen, he assured himself. This place was too valuable. Theo's attachment to the secretary was solely through Katerina: perhaps the secretary didn't exist? Maybe Katerina was being replaced. It would be a shame, but Theo understood that people like her outgrew their worth.

The girls were wrapping up the night shift nicely. He looked around and saw that most of the tables were empty now. The music was turned down. The light was still dim and red-tinged, as fitting an establishment of this type, but Theo's eyes were accustomed to the shady hue, and had been for years. There'd been plenty of business tonight and it was time he turned in. Theo didn't need much sleep; he was quite happy to sit on his stool for the best part of the day and night, until the cash flow slowed, and he went to bed happy and at peace.

Somebody entered the club and a shaft of light flashed across the floor. It was daylight. Theo chuckled to himself, it had been a good night for midweek; that was for sure. The winter was quieter and they stayed open throughout the summer months as long as they needed to make as much cash as they could. The heat of the interior was heady and claustrophobic, but Theo was used to it. He'd never been an outdoor kind of man, or boy for that matter. He glanced at the door and wondered why the doorman had left the outer exit open.

He'd spoken to Artemis just a few hours ago, and all was set to use the girl as leverage. Theo had wanted her buried in a hole, deep in the Troodos Mountains straight away, as soon as she'd been found snooping around their mother's place, but Artemis argued that she could be valuable. He'd wittered on about her being a Special Branch officer. Who cared? Jesus, Katerina had taken care of the other one, why not this one?

The whoosh of air stopped and the shard of light receded towards the door as the sunlight was banished from the place.

Theo was about to place his lips to a cold pint of Turkish beer. He had to admit that the stuff was superior to anything brewed south of the border. Then he saw the woman behind the bar dip down. He stopped the glass rising to his mouth, and peered over the bar at her. Her eyes were wide and he turned his head to where she'd been looking just seconds ago, when the exit door had opened, and Theo assumed the doorman had let someone in by mistake. They were all ready for their beds and the girls had performed well. Even they needed a break.

In the time it took him to twist his head, take in the emptiness of the place and assess why that might have happened so quickly, the man was stood in front of him, with a black pistol aimed at his head. Theo dropped his glass and it smashed, spilling beer all over the floor. He felt warm fluid between his legs and knew he'd pissed himself.

The man, who he'd never seen before, looked into his eyes and Theo heard a loud crack. Then everything went black. The only other sounds, except for the three bullets to Theo's brain, which killed him instantly, were the wails of the woman behind the bar and the loud thud as Theo fell off his chair into a heap.

The assassin leant over the wooden top, slimy with alcohol and the night's excitement, and held his finger to his lips, pointing the pistol at the woman.

She nodded. She was terrified.

The three remaining bullets were unloaded into her body one after the other, and she slumped onto the floor.

As the man strode away, a couple of people cowered under tables, and three naked girls huddled in a corner. The assassin strode out, and a swoosh of air enveloped the place once more.

The door banged and the music played. The red lights whirred and one man vomited.

Blood seeped from Theo's head, and his plates of pitta and hummus, now smashed on the floor, mingled with the rusty-looking liquid. The claret puddle grew larger, around his obese mass, and merged into the shadowy ruby background, making it difficult to ascertain where the light began and the blood stopped.

Chapter 52

In a dusty village, to the south of Aleppo, two men met in a café. One of those not obliterated by bombs. They could have been journalists, or doctors, exhausted from a fifteen-hour shift. Or even students. To the east, the city was still held by rebel pockets, but people tried to go about their business. A pause in air strikes brought relief for a while, but food and fuel supplies ran horrifically low and the surrounding infrastructure and health care were non-existent. Trapped, not through choice, enclaves of human beings eked out an existence as best they could.

One of the men held a mobile phone, which was charged during the night, when electricity was supplied to the area for two hours. He expected an imminent call.

The two men were, in fact, best friends. They had to be. The buddy system in the US Special Forces was what held it together when the shit hit the fan. They moved in twos. Always. Undercover, and bearded, dressed in dishevelled jeans and T-shirts, the men sipped their strong sweet coffee. They waited for an incoming call, and spoke Arabic.

People came and went, as if it were any normal street, in any given town, in the middle of a country not torn apart. But they looked different. It was in their eyes. They were the ones who never left. The ones who belligerently defended their homes, and refused to be driven out, even if it meant being targeted by bombs and snipers every single day.

It was difficult to decide which was worse: the summer or the winter. In the hot months, the dust and blood dried, and encrusted everything. Sweat ran into your eyes, and water was scarce. In the winter, rain bashed the muddy piles in the street and broke them down into mushy waves. The cool air brought relief, but only for a few weeks, until the reality of power cuts and darkness hit.

Today, the two men sat in the shade, trying to shelter from the searing heat. Their bodies were salty with sweat, and their skin tanned where rolled-up shirts exposed flesh to the baking sun. Their beards were bushy and the skin around their cheeks was cut deeply with dusty permanent wrinkles. But their eyes were alert.

The call came through silently and it was answered. It was a short conversation, made up of code words and expressions learned and honed after months in the field of operations, getting to know how the local people spoke to one another. It was all right learning Arabic in a classroom, but out here, in the middle of a war, one had to fit in.

They had one mission, and one mission alone: to nail Labib Hassan.

Last time he'd escaped, and at the very last minute. Seven months down the drain for what? They'd never know. But that was what life was like undercover. They had no recourse, nowhere to file a complaint, no classroom to review what went well and what not so well. They weren't rewarded or graded, just either successful or not. This time not. It was a kick to the stomach, but they got on with it. The intelligence about the meeting at the villa, attended by several big players, protected by Russia, was the most significant chance they'd had for years to take out some big players.

But they were used to it. These guys were slippery suckers. If their job was easy, then every lad with a swinging cock and a huge ego would be out here doing what they did. The selection process for the Special Forces was brutal for a very good reason. It took a certain type of psyche to withstand this kind of life, which is why the selection course had a ninety per cent fail rate. But that was a lifetime ago for these men. They'd been entrenched in Syrian life for five years, and had a combined service length of thirty years.

It was difficult not to get personally attached to the brief sometimes, especially when you lived and breathed the life here. They believed what they were doing was not particularly noble, but worthy on many levels. They trusted they saved lives. They didn't stop to talk of the irony of perspective, and what an American life, say, was worth compared to a British life, or an Afghan life, or a life of a baby here in Aleppo.

'Theirs not to reason why... Theirs but to do and die...' was a favourite recited verse of some long-ago poem. Neither knew it was Lord Tennyson, and they didn't much care.

A car drove past and everyone stared at it for two reasons: one, they had petrol; and two, where were they going?

The last couple of weeks had been frustrating but still productive. They'd supplied intelligence, along with other cells deep-rooted in neighbourhoods a stone's throw away, on countless meetings, and general movements, of local notables. It was up to those on high, who sat behind desks for a living, to decide who to take out and who to keep watching. Labib Hassan was a thorn in the side of all the allied powers, especially America. They didn't like baddies getting away and making them look like fools. One only had to consider how much time they'd spent, not to mention how much hard cash, trying to find Bin Laden. But it would have been a career highlight to have been there, of course. The adrenalin, the rush, the buzz, and the moment-to-moment existence was what made these men tick. Another dead man, who negotiated arms for the government forces, backed by Russia, was a mere statistic. But every now and again, one name stuck in your throat, and you couldn't rest until he was bombed to shit.

Labib was their man. They weren't going to fail this time.

They'd tracked three rendezvous points, all set for this week. One of them must be the target. Intelligence sent back home, via a mobile phone that worked sporadically, was all they could do. That, and the odd satellite call, from the privacy of their one-bed flat in downtown Aleppo, when they dared. They moved regularly, but they travelled light. In war zones, it was normal for one's luggage to consist mainly of weapons and ammunition, plus water and a little food. It was amazing how many things became surplus to requirements when one was merely tasked with survival.

Three sets of coordinates were communicated via the phone call. They gave their best informed estimate as to which they thought was the most likely, but they were also aware that, knowing the methods of their superiors in Washington, all three would likely be taken out. None were near residential areas. However, when this was the case, the men couldn't allow themselves to think about those consequences because there lay hell and madness.

The call ended. It was done.

Chapter 53

Helen woke up with her hair and face stuck to her desk.

Kay gently nudged her. 'Someone brought us coffee,' she said.

Helen raised her head and focused her eyes and Eric came into view.

'How the hell did you get in here?' she asked.

'Easy, I'm a fully paid-up member of the Dhekelia golf club, I can come and go as I please,' he said.

'Jesus,' was all she said.

She knew that plenty of civilians came through the ESBA, checked only briefly if they had the correct piece of paper, simply down to privilege or favours, but she'd forgotten about the golf club.

'Do you play?' A creeping feeling settled under her ribcage and she didn't fancy coffee.

'Of course not,' he said.

Helen straightened her body; shafts of dawn light poked through the doors and windows and she rubbed her neck. She took the Styrofoam cup from Eric and stretched. She turned away from him. Nagging doubts played with her mind. Eric buddied Paul up with a stranger speaking in a Slavic accent. He also suggested the dive yesterday morning when they found Anastasia. Now, it seemed, he came and went as he pleased, on and off the ESBA. He was ex-forces and locally entrenched. She swallowed hard.

She turned to Kay and tried to act normal. 'Was Colonel Seaton located?' she asked.

'ESBA police were tasked with waiting outside his residence until he turned up,' Kay informed her.

Helen got up and walked to the door, looking out. 'Eric, can I have a word?' she asked.

'Sure.' He smiled at Kay and went outside, following Helen.

The door banged behind them and she turned to him, hoping he didn't sense her awkwardness.

'Look, I'm dealing with some sensitive shit at the moment, I think you should go home.'

'I thought I was your right-hand man?' he said.

She smiled. Her pulse rate climbed.

'I don't want you getting involved when it gets serious,' she said. 'Please, go to the dive shop and wait for me there. I'll let you know the minute I need you.'

'Are you all right?' He touched her arm and she pulled away. 'What's happened?' he asked.

'Nothing, I've got a lot to do, and I can't guarantee your safety. Thanks for the coffee.' She went back into the office and leant against the door, listening as she heard his footsteps fade away.

'You okay?' Kay asked.

Helen nodded. If Eric was somehow involved in all of this, then she'd been played, and the thought drove her crazy. He'd been with her every step of the way and she couldn't believe she'd been so naive. Here she was chasing a honey trap and she'd potentially fallen for her own.

'Something just came up,' Kay said.

Helen refocused. 'What is it?' she asked Kay.

'Theo Charalambous was taken out in the early hours this morning,' Kay replied.

Helen stared at her.

'Cypriot police are on the scene. It was a professional hit. It's being treated as drugs related.'

'Of course it is,' Helen said. She went to her desk and put a call through to Don Murton.

He sounded groggy. 'You managed to get some sleep?' he asked her.

'My desk is rather comfortable,' she said. 'You?'

'Me too. Thank God for coffee. Helen, we've had intelligence come in from Ayios Nikolaos, and it's different to what was fed to Major Graham by your operative.'

Helen's heart sank at the betrayal, but she felt vindicated too. It was the evidence they needed to apprehend the major for questioning. He was personally and blatantly responsible for changing classified information.

'And how is the original intelligence panning out?' she asked.

'Solid. Operation is set for this afternoon. If this works out, Helen, I'll be recommending you for a service award,' he said.

'Thanks, Don, I'll hang it in my downstairs loo with the others. I need to stop the protests,' she added.

'Protests?' he asked.

'My working theory is that Colonel Seaton hasn't massaged intelligence from the inside, in real time, we always knew that would be impossible. Rather, he's delayed and confused communications by allowing certain activities to go unchecked on the ESBA. This time of year, it's farmers' strikes and lime stickers' activity,' she said.

'Lime stickers?'

She described the method of trapping songbirds to him, adding how it was her opinion that Colonel Seaton could easily use nets getting caught in antennas to shut Ayios Nikolaos down effectively for a couple of hours, allowing targets to go off grid, or turn up at different coordinates.

'Don, I need a small trustworthy squad, armed.'

'I'll communicate it to the CBF immediately. I'll suggest a platoon from the battalion in Dhekelia. They could be ready in a few hours.'

'That might be too late. The protests were heating up yesterday and I saw a whole bunch of bird trappers there. The ESBA police were talking to them like old pals.'

'I hear you. Hold fire. Let me get on it now,' he said.

'Any news on my officer?' she asked.

'Not yet, negotiations are taking place between the British High Commissioner and the Russian Ambassador this afternoon,' Don said.

'I reckon they took out Theo Charalambous in the early hours of this morning. He's dead, it was a professional job, so something has rattled them,' she said.

'Maybe they're ready to negotiate,' Don said. 'The game is up.'

They hung up.

Helen turned to Kay, hoping to avoid direct questions about the whereabouts of her colleague. 'Kay, I'm expecting help from the battalion. I need to head to the Dhekelia Road to sort out these protests properly. Have Major Graham brought in. I'll communicate to JSSU that the station at Ayios Nikolaos is to remain fully operational for the duration of the day, regardless of the protests.'

'Yes, boss,' Kay said.

Helen left the office and looked around, but there was no sign of Eric.

Gem had waited all night and she nudged him gently. He stretched.

'Ma'am,' he said.

'The colonel's house.'

It was streets away, and quiet. But it was a long enough journey to call the chief of the ESBA police and get him out of bed, to inform him that all units should be on duty to apprehend the colonel and his second in command, should they try to leave the base. She knew she'd face resistance. Big fish in little ponds didn't like having water drained away from them. She was treading on his toes.

'With respect, ma'am, I'll need the highest authority to carry out such an order,' he said. She didn't like the way he said *ma'am*. Or *respect*.

'You've got it, now do it, or you might find yourself on a plane back to London tomorrow.' She hung up.

As they rounded the entrance to the cul-de-sac where Colonel Seaton's quarter was – the largest at the end, of course – they could see that a lone squad car sat outside. As they approached, they also saw that the two police constables inside were asleep.

Gem parked alongside and Helen got out of the vehicle, banging on the car door. The two men woke with a start and, at first, were confused as to where they were.

Helen strode up to the house and opened the unlocked door. She banged it on its hinges and went inside. Curtains were open, items were strewn on the floor and lights burned. The bulbs were red hot and she knew they'd been on all night. A quick search of the property confirmed her fear. They were gone.

Back outside, she used the radio in the squad car to trace the colonel's vehicle, which was an old Ford Mondeo, but with flags on to denote his rank. It didn't take long for the information to be fed back to the squad car that the colonel had left the garrison in the early hours of the morning for an important meeting. Yes, his wife was in the car alongside him.

'Didn't you think it odd that he was driving himself?' she bellowed into the radio at the poor sod who was manning the gate. She stopped short of yelling 'fuckwit' when she realised that it wasn't his fault.

Her priority now was issuing an island-wide search for Colonel Seaton and his wife, but she reckoned she knew where they'd be going. If they'd got to him first, as she suspected, she knew he'd take the coward's route and hand himself to them, not us.

He'd be going to Northern Cyprus.

Chapter 54

A tourist wouldn't have any clue that the security forces and local police were in the middle of an island-wide hunt for suspects accused of leaking secret information to Russia. Sunbathing on one of the thousands of white beaches up and down the paradise bays that encircled the gem in the Mediterranean, one could be forgiven for thinking that this was a haven of happiness and serenity. Most visitors had never even heard of the war in 1974, why would they? Who cared? Neither would they understand the nature of the island as a gateway between East and West. Sure, they might have heard that American planes took off from here to bomb the crap out of Saddam Hussein, but that didn't disturb their downing ouzo.

Ledra Palace was the UN crossing point from south to north, in the centre of the capital city of Nicosia, that had been ripped apart during the war. Visitors interested in their history flocked there, to gaze through binoculars at the northern towns that had been abandoned and overgrown with weeds ever since. Passage was relatively easy now, and business was healthy either side of the Green Line. However, the signs of war were still there, if one knew where to look.

The British battalion stationed there received the order to apprehend the colonel at nine-forty in the morning, and a platoon was tasked with the job. Of course, he wouldn't try to cross through Ledra Palace. Rather they'd concentrate their search along the many roads leading from south to north, which led beyond to the heart of the Turkish state.

They might be too late already, given that the road from Dhekelia to the closest crossing point was less than an hour's journey, but there might have been a rendezvous set up just for Colonel Seaton and his wife.

Helen couldn't help feeling shocked that a mother would defect to another country, no matter the seriousness of the suspicion of guilt on her head, without her children. Their schools were easily contacted, because the colonel claimed ninety per cent of their fees from the MOD. The children were all present this morning, in their halls of residence, in the UK.

What were they thinking? The only reasonable explanation was that the colonel had somehow managed to convince Andi to leave with the promise that the children would join them, or already had. Bastard. The colonel's wife had no idea what she was walking into. The bullets through Theo Charalambous's brain were a portent for what lay ahead.

Helen turned her attention to the job at hand, here in Ayios Nikolaos, and assessed her resources. An infantry platoon consisted of thirty men. It was enough to deal with a few protesters. She directed Gem to drive her back to the mess building, leaving the two police constables considering their career choices. To be fair to them, they weren't trained to bring in traitors, or handle the arrest of officers way above their rank. It was unorthodox and daunting. The best she could hope for was that Colonel Seaton and his wife were apprehended before they crossed into Turkish territory.

They arrived at the office. Her eyes darted about, looking for Eric. Where had he gone?

A platoon was lining up outside, and checking equipment. The platoon commander turned to see the car park up.

It was Second Lieutenant Tom Fleet. She nodded to him and he acknowledged her.

She strode across to him. 'Got your orders, Lieutenant?'

'Yes, ma'am.'

'Any chance of a weapon?' she asked.

It had been a few months since she'd had an issued weapon in her hands. Paris was the last time, and she felt naked without one. Left out.

'Nice try, ma'am,' he said.

She walked away. In the office, she found Kay speaking on two phones at once and watching two computer screens.

'Ready?' Kay asked her boss. Not once had she complained about the delay in finding her partner. The officer sent to her by the regiment was not the grumbling type. She knew that the fate of Jen was in the hands of the delicate game of diplomacy now. They had to believe that there was no point in killing another British officer. The first one had caused too much heat. Another would create an international incident and trouble for years to come. However, that didn't take into consideration the fact that Jen was being held, in all probability by a liability: a loose cannon; somebody who, as soon as he found out about his brother, would not think about consequence or compromise.

Helen rested her hand on Kay's shoulder and peered at the screens. Kay passed her one of the phones. Don was on the other end. She looked at her watch. It was almost eleven.

'Don. I'm heading out to the perimeter now, what have you got for me?'

'Some good news. Artemis Charalambous has been located.'

'And the bad news?' She waited for the shit sandwich. 'She's with him?'

'I'm afraid so, yes.'

'And he's using her as a bargaining tool?'

'You got it.'

'So it's not good news, really, is it?' she said.

'Hold your nerve,' he replied.

'I intend on doing nothing else,' she said. 'All set?' she asked. She was referring to the planned hit on Labib Hassan, ignoring the fake coordinates fed to Major Graham and passed to GCHQ.

'Yup.'

284

'Good. I hope you get him.'

She went outside into the sunshine, away from Kay's earshot.

'Don, will you do something for me?' she asked.

'What?'

'Run a check on Eric Dukakis. He's ex-forces and an entrenched local. It's a hunch I want clearing up.'

'Sure.'

She ended the call and went next door to the unisex restroom, where she'd left her uniform hung up, should she need it. Now she did. She changed quickly, tightening her service belt, and buttoning her shirt to the top. The combat trousers felt unusual on her skin, it had been a long time since she'd worn them. The crease down the centre was perfect and she tucked them over strings, perfectly positioned just above her service boots. She straightened her red beret and strode back out into the sunshine.

'Ready, Lieutenant?' she asked Tom Fleet.

He didn't recognise her at first, then he saluted. 'Yes, ma'am.'

She joined the platoon and they filed into khaki-coloured service vehicles, ready to transport them to the Dhekelia Road.

'I want arrests,' she said. She sat next to Tom.

'I've got a present for you,' he said. He passed her some body armour and a service pistol. 'You've got friends in high places.'

'Unfortunate I won't get to use it where I really want to,' she said.

'Meaning?' he asked.

'Long story. When this is all over, I'll tell you over a drink. But not in some dodgy bar along the strip. You need to be more careful where you spend your money,' she added.

'Agreed,' he said.

They occupied seven vehicles in all. The ESBA police already had a squad car watching the farmers.

'We need to keep communications open at all costs, understood?' she said.

Tom nodded. 'The men have been briefed on rules of engagement.'

The integrity of the ESBA was very specific but had never been called into question like this. She could feel the buzz of excitement in the convoy. Soldiers lived to face conflict; it was their bread and butter. No matter the outcome, and standing down was the best for everyone, the fact that they got to do their job was exhilarating.

The vehicles rumbled slowly out of the back gate and towards Ayios Nikolaos. It wasn't long before they heard the ruckus of the protests. They were in full swing, and Helen wasn't surprised. They'd been primed to be so, now she knew, by the very act of ignorance on the colonel's part, which gave them confidence and escalated bravado. They'd been used just as surely as the four corporals under house arrest had been thrown under the bus.

'Look for the nets,' Helen told him.

'They're close to the perimeter, as near to the dishes as they can possibly get,' he said.

'You already know this?'

'We've long suspected that the protests and illegal trapping occurs in some capacity to cause as much disruption to British interests as possible.'

'But, let me guess, the colonel never took the matter in hand? Preferring to shut the station sporadically?'

'It's not our job to police the perimeter,' he said.

'Yeah, that's their job,' she replied, pointing out the lone squad car.

The occupants got out as they approached. One pulled up his trousers. Helen reckoned that the days of attention being turned away from the minor infractions of nepotism and back scratching on this base were drawing to a close. The scandal would throw up major questions for the MOD that they didn't want to face. The irony wasn't lost on Helen. She'd been sent to close this matter quickly and had ended up causing more of a headache than anyone imagined. It made her proud. It caused her to feel jubilant. It reminded her of Grant, who left the forces because, too many times, those on the ground were ignored and overruled by Machiavellian princes, interested only in their higher objectives, at the cost of chaos for those who faced real danger. It was an ancient dance based on an age-old precedent for keeping armies and politicians separate. But she knew she was dreaming. Grant was an idealist; a romantic, who felt that the problems of nations could be solved by listening to the common people. She worked for an organisation that ignored such base considerations. Nationhood was an objective that required elites sat in comfortable offices discussing who they were willing to sacrifice. Soldiers simply did what they were told. But, this time, she'd exposed the abuse of that power, and now, no one could ignore it.

As long as Britain's wider interests were served, Colonel Seaton had been allowed to run free with his tin-pot dictatorship. And another nation state had taken full advantage.

The platoon spread out, at first using calm communication to get across their orders. As expected, the farmers huddled together and showed resistance. The first arrests were made.

The situation deteriorated quicker than Helen expected and Lieutenant Fleet called for back-up. Helen made her way, with a group of eight men, to the edge of the perimeter, where the satellite dishes of Ayios Nikolaos could be seen behind the wire fence. She spotted a group holding a large net, spreading it out, as if preparing to let it go.

She signalled to the corporal to her right and she was aware of Lieutenant Fleet by her side. They approached the group, who stood belligerently facing them, protecting their net.

'Not today, fellas,' Tom said. They stood around the small group, and took the safety catches off their weapons.

'We have journalists here; if you shoot us, it will look bad for you.'

'No one is going to shoot you, my friend,' Tom said. 'We have to move you on. No bird trapping today.'

'We're not bird trapping,' the man, who appeared to be the group spokesperson, said defensively.

'So why the nets?' Tom asked.

'And the lime sticks?' Helen said.

The man jutted his chin towards her. She was the only woman there and the man clearly didn't like being talked to by the fairer sex. She fingered her weapon. It felt good, like an old friend, ready to be of service. Helen was tempted. She'd had enough of the heat, the bullshit, the corrupt nature of the whole fucking garrison.

She took a breath and calmed down. 'Sir, this is your last warning. Should you continue to occupy this area, we'll have no choice but to move you on with force.'

'You will shoot us! They are going to shoot us!' His voice pierced the crowd and they huddled around the small platoon.

Helen raised her weapon and fired into the air. She really had no time for small boys' games right now.

The group ducked.

Tom's platoon assumed a defensive position and cocked their weapons. They were well outnumbered, but Tom was well versed in the restrictive rules of engagement that he was able to employ. They'd have to be attacked first in order to defend themselves. He hoped it didn't come to that.

It wasn't necessary. The ringleader had a quiet word, in Greek, to those closest to him and they nodded, dropping the net.

They turned as more vehicles arrived from the base, and those who'd been arrested were loaded into them. After that, the majority of protesters moved away and miraculously forgot their woes, and agendas, and moved silently off in their vehicles, until the next time. The lime stickers left their sticks in the bushes, and Helen ordered them destroyed. It was heartbreaking to see the birds stuck on them: they had no way of escape, but Helen didn't know how to dispatch them humanely. Some of the soldiers, once the threat of numbers had subsided, and the protest was abandoned, tried to prise them off their sticky deathtraps, but they couldn't do it without causing great harm to the delicate birds.

'That's why it's fucking illegal,' Helen said under her breath. 'Set up a perimeter, here,' she said to Tom, who set about following his brief and doing just that.

Ayios Nikolaos remained fully operational.

Now it was down to Corporal Danny Hewitt to report the whereabouts of Labib Hassan and wait for the news that he'd been taken out successfully, by the bird in the sky that he'd come so used to ignoring, safe in the knowledge that somebody, somewhere, was covering his back.

It made bile rise up in Helen's throat to think that the man responsible for protecting him was a British national, and a decorated colonel. It begged the question if he did it just for the money.

Chapter 55

It didn't take long for Helen's questions about Bill Seaton to get an answer. Back in the small office, she was hot, sweaty and tired from the rush of adrenalin leaving her body. The mission had been a success: no one had been hurt. She sat behind her desk and took off her boots, rubbing her feet.

Kay placed a pile of scanned documents on her desk and waited. 'You might want to take a look at these,' she said.

Helen flicked through them and saw Bill Seaton, in a range of positions suited to the dark web. Everything made sense.

'Where did you get these?' Helen asked.

'Colonel Murton sent them through,' Kay said.

'He was levered out of his moral code,' Helen said sadly. She knew that if it hadn't have been money, it would have been sex. They always went hand in hand. It drove everything. She was reminded of that awful song in the musical *Cabaret* about money making the world go around. It needed a postscript: money makes the world go around, but sex keeps it spinning. 'And he presumably got them from the Russians, after a nice cup of tea at the High Commissioner's house,' Helen added, her voice heavy with cynicism.

'We're all set,' Kay said. 'Should we go?' she asked.

Helen nodded wearily, and put her boots back on. They had another job to do today. An observation room had been set up to use a satellite hub, over at Ayios Nikolaos. From there, they'd been invited to watch activity unfold inside a specific set of coordinates closer to home: Ledra Palace, in Nicosia.

GCHQ had approved it. The negotiations between the British High Commissioner and the Russian Ambassador had been secret but fruitful. A British subject would be dropped off two streets away from the UN crossing point at Ledra Palace at fourteen hundred hours. Helen and Kay would watch it live. They knew it was Jen.

They grabbed their things and went out to get their short ride to the listening station. As Gem drove them along the Dhekelia Road, they passed the remnants of the protests. The road was clear now, as Tom's platoon cleaned up, and the final arrests were processed.

Once there, they were escorted to an ops room, much like the one where Corporal Danny Hewitt fed accurate data to GCHQ, and from there it found its way to an unmanned bomber that flew over Syria. This one, though, contained huge screens, and they joined several operators in uniform, one of whom fed coordinates into a computer. Just as Britannia once ruled the waves, the skies above earth were monopolised by the superpowers of the day.

Images popped up on the super screens. The room was dark and quiet, and Helen and Kay watched, hardly breathing. The view of the street in Nicosia was clear.

'Seat, ma'am?' they were asked.

Both declined.

Kay bit her nails.

Radios crackled with code, and Helen recognised some of the jargon, but it had been many years since she was on the ground. Did she miss it? Yes. She considered in that single moment whether to put a request in to go back to it, after she finished at the MOD. Rank counted for something but so did experience. Watching the operation live made her thirsty for more. Her weapon had been handed back and signed in to the platoon armoury. She missed it already. But then the old dilemma stopped her daydreaming. Who made the most difference? The ones on foot taking orders, or the ones behind

TV screens giving them? Just being in this room gave her the answer.

On screen, a car pulled up on the designated street and a lone woman got out. She walked without aid, and strongly, or so it looked to Helen.

Kay grabbed her arm, but she didn't mind. She put her hand around her fellow officer's waist and squeezed.

The woman walked with purpose and seemed to follow clear instructions as to where to go. She rounded the corner and the satellite picked her up. They could now see the UN checkpoint. They watched as she walked towards it and was greeted by two soldiers. A conversation took place and she disappeared inside a building.

An operative swung around in his chair. 'Job done, ma'am,' he said.

'Thank you,' she said. She grabbed the back of a chair and leant over, breathing a sigh of relief. Solace washed over her. She tapped Kay's arm, and they went outside to the car.

Kay kept her composure until she got into the vehicle and Helen looked at her.

'You all right?' she asked.

'Yes, ma'am.' Her voice was cracked and tired.

Helen's mobile rang and it was Don.

'She's safe and identity confirmed. She's being looked at by a doctor. Well done, Helen,' he said.

'Seaton?' she asked.

'He was picked up with his wife, at the port of Kyrenia, half an hour ago, trying to board a ship bound for Turkey.'

'My, my, what favours did you pull in for that? Wait, don't tell me. I don't want to know.'

'No favours, just a tip-off.'

'In a Russian accent?'

'Maybe.'

Chapter 56

Helen wanted to make the call to Juliana Barnaby herself, woman to woman. She'd read the transcripts of the interviews by military police on the initial arrest of the four corporals, before Juliana had landed on the island. If it wasn't for the young lawyer questioning the case, and thinking outside the box, they might all be facing a very different situation right now. In Captain Thomas's original case notes, the four corporals' assumed guilt played heavy on his mind, and that had been before anyone suspected the colonel's involvement. With that in mind, it was easy to see how that supposition had steered the entire case.

The young lawyer was about to bag her first major win, and, at her age, it was a significant one. Her clients were as good as free to go.

Both Helen and Kay's phones had been checked into the strongbox outside the operations room in Ayios Nikolaos for the duration of the show, as was customary. No one was allowed personal communications access inside the buildings. After getting them back, Helen saw that she'd had several missed calls from the lawyer.

'She can read my mind,' she said to Kay.

Helen listened to the voicemail from Juliana Barnaby, with growing concern.

'That's odd,' Helen said out loud, as they got back to the office.

Kay was smiling from ear to ear and Helen saw that she hadn't heard her.

'That was Juliana Barnaby, the lawyer,' she added.

Kay turned around, after loosening her combat shirt and flopping into a chair.

'She's pursuing a lead in Nicosia this afternoon.'

'What for?' Kay asked.

'Good question.'

'What's her lead?' Kay asked.

Helen summarised the message to her. 'Apparently, an aunt of Lance Corporal Trotter who is a solid alibi for him, on the dates he was down to work in the ops room. An aunt who just so happens to live here in Cyprus and is too elderly to travel.'

Kay's jubilation turned to unease.

'Juliana said she'd never leave the base on her own. What the hell is going on?' Helen said more to herself. 'Why would she be so reckless?'

Kay stared at her.

Helen tried the mobile number for Juliana Barnaby, it went direct to voicemail.

'Shit,' she said. 'How did she get out of camp? She hasn't got an assigned vehicle, unless she arranged an RMP guard?'

'Taxi?' Kay said.

'What?' Helen asked, lifting up her ponytail to get air underneath it. 'Oh, Jesus. It's the same date as one of the protests,' Helen said. She couldn't recall discussing the farmers' protests with the lawyer, but it was possible that the young corporals might use them to argue they couldn't have possibly worked on the days they were accused of mishandling data. But what if Juliana had found some holes in their version of events? She'd want to clear that up, knowing Juliana and how dogged she was and keen to prove her clients' innocence. 'Find out if a taxi picked her up at the guard room, and get a car reg. I'm going to talk to Corporal Trotter.' Helen grabbed her beret, and walked out.

Gem was waiting as always and opened the door for her.

'Corporal Trotter's quarter please, Gem,' she said. He nodded.

They soon pulled up outside the home of Rob and Shannon Trotter and Helen expected a similarly frosty reception to last time. She noticed that the curtains were still closed, but then she reckoned that if she were under house arrest, she wouldn't be getting up every morning bright and breezy either.

The guard stood aside and she rang the bell. No one answered. She rang it again and stood looking at the unanswered door for almost a minute.

'When did you last check on the family?' she asked the guard.

'We changed shift this morning,' the ESBA police constable said.

Helen tried the door, it was, as expected for the houses inside the wire, unlocked. She went in.

'Guard!' she shouted, and he followed her into the small lounge, which was a total mess. Things were strewn all over the floor, toys were thrown aside, and the place was stuffy and dark. She ran to the back kitchen and found cupboards open and empty, then she passed the guard once more and took the stairs two at a time to the bedrooms. Empty. Wardrobes were open and clothes were pulled out, the dressing table next to Shannon's bed was completely cleared out. 'Shit,' Helen said. 'Get your colleagues here now, and alert the local authorities, we have a soldier AWOL,' she barked. 'In fact, no! I'll do it!'

She strode back past the guard and out into the sunshine, first putting a call into the RMP guard room requesting an island-wide search for the corporal and his wife and child, then she demanded two squad cars: one for herself and Kay, and another to follow, to pursue a British citizen who was, in all likelihood, in danger, in the vicinity of Nicosia. Her second call was to Kay.

'Have you got the information from the gate?' she asked.

'Yes. I have a description and a registration number for the driver.'

'Good. We have another problem.' She told Kay about Corporal Trotter.

'What about the guard?' Kay asked.

'That's a conversation for another day. We need to find Trotter, and Juliana Barnaby, I think it's safe to say that Trotter got rid of her so he could jump ship, the slimy sucker.'

'But I thought you said he was innocent,' Kay queried.

'Yes, and I believed it too. Until now. Who picked Juliana up?'

Kay read out the description of the taxi driver.

Helen closed her eyes. 'Who vouched for his company on the paperwork?'

'Corporal Trotter,' Kay said.

Kay had just described a man fitting the description of Artemis Charalambous.

'The cocky bastard,' Helen said.

Chapter 57

The two RMP squad cars joined the local Cypriot police at the front gate of Dhekelia Garrison. A description of Juliana Barnaby was issued to all units, as well as that of Corporal Trotter and his wife and child. The registration plate of the taxi driven by the man suspected of abducting the lawyer was also issued island-wide.

The Cypriot police were armed, and Helen knew they didn't mess around. They followed orders, and Artemis Charalambous was no longer protected from above. His brother was dead and an unholy mess was being mopped up at the Blue Lantern. Artemis was wanted both sides of the line now.

The small convoy sped away and they travelled along the Dhekelia Road. A soldier going AWOL fell under the jurisdiction of his regiment and so a separate unit left Dhekelia Garrison at the same time. Helen's priority was the civilian. They'd catch Rob Trotter eventually. He was small fry and meant nothing to the forces at play in this ever-increasing web of diplomatic lies. If anyone was worth saving, then it might have been Colonel Seaton, but even he was deemed expendable. The young corporal would have been better facing a court martial, if Juliana had ever got to the bottom of the case. Helen couldn't help thinking that without Rob taking this enormous risk, to set Juliana up, he may never have been implicated. His panic had made his position infinitely more dangerous, but, no doubt, he was wooed by the promise of more holidays and favours. She'd personally scrutinised his bank accounts and found nothing to suggest collusion, so she was left with only one possibility: he had others somewhere else, probably in other names.

All this time, she thought to herself as the cars sped towards the road to Nicosia, all this effort, and he was sat there, inside his house, plotting how to sabotage his own defence, so he could run. The young corporal had a lot to learn about the spy game. He thought he meant something. He thought he was valued. Helen knew if they found him in time, then there was a chance he wouldn't be buried in a ditch somewhere, but if they didn't, then she recoiled to think what they might do to him, and the wife and child.

Corporal Trotter obviously trusted whoever his contact was, and it was probably Artemis Charalambous all along.

She tried Juliana's mobile again and was directed to voice-mail. She hung up.

The radio frequency of the RMP squad cars was aligned to the Cypriot police cars and Helen listened to the crackled conversation over the airwaves.

'Vehicle located on the Nicosia Road, three miles outside of the city, heading north.'

'Apprehend.'

Helen waited.

They listened to the pursuit in real time. On the open motorway, now, away from the cloggy roundabouts of the outskirts of Nicosia, the Cypriot police cars ahead threw on their blues, the RMP did the same. Helen held on to the roof strap as the corporal tasked with driving them stepped on his accelerator. Local cars got out of their way and moved aside, making their passage along the two-lane highway easy and smooth.

Helen's phone buzzed and she retrieved it from her pocket with one hand, receiving an email notification from Kay. The guardroom had sent through the CCTV still of the taxi driver who'd registered at the gate to pick up Juliana Barnaby. Helen stared at the photo. It was black and white and grainy, but she was one hundred per cent sure. It was Artemis Charalambous. He looked as confident and innocent as someone making a delivery of milk and eggs.

Her stomach lurched as the car sped up again. Now they had a steady line of spectators on the hard shoulder of the highway, who stopped and stared at the convoy of police in a clear emergency. It was quite a spectacle. They were almost there. Helen thought that if they got there in time, then it would be Juliana Barnaby's own sense of security, and the foresight to contact her office, that might just save her yet. If Artemis Charalambous didn't do anything else stupid. But she also knew that the man had nothing left to lose.

'Up ahead,' the radio crackled again.

Helen saw that two Cypriot blue and white police cars had halted a red Toyota Yaris, lacking the power to outrun the convoy. She asked for the number plate and it came back as the same that had taken Juliana Barnaby out of Dhekelia Garrison. They decelerated from over one hundred and forty KPH to zero in seven seconds and Helen felt her throat being left behind in the ease up of speed.

Officers left their cars and surrounded the vehicle, and she saw that Artemis was still behind the wheel of the Yaris. She undid her belt and got out, making her way towards the vehicle, which was facing the wrong way, towards them. Had it spun? Was Juliana in there? Was she hurt?

Helen stayed in the shadow of an armed officer, and her heart rate threatened to shake her whole body to its core. There was a short exchange in Greek and Artemis placed his hands in the air, behind his head.

'Is he armed?' she asked.

But it was too late, he exited the car and fired off two rounds towards the closest Cypriot police officer. One, directly in front of her, fell down and wailed, holding his leg. Helen ducked and fell on top of him. Instinct took over and she grabbed the revolver out of his hand, rolling on her back and staring into the face of Artemis Charalambous, probably ten feet away. A scream from inside the car reverberated in her ears. Another shot was fired. She looked into his eyes and pulled back the chamber, noting his old Makarov 9 mm steady in his hand, which he must have grabbed from between his legs. It was cocked straight at her. She pulled the trigger and got off a shot which landed between his eyes.

In the split second she closed her own eyes, she heard the rattling old gun get off another round and she hoped she wasn't hit. She heard a thud and wondered if it was the sound of her own life seeping away. She felt nothing.

The revolver shook in her hands and she was reminded of officers in training suffering from the condition known affectionately as gun shy. It happened spontaneously and wasn't conscious at all, it was simply the brain's reaction to holding a lethal weapon. Helen had never experienced it, but now she did, and she dropped the gun. It hit one of her ribs and she cried out in pain, but it meant she was alive. She made a conscious effort to assess her body and she felt with her hands all over her torso, as far as she could reach. She wasn't hit.

Chapter 58

Inside an operations room in Virginia, United States, a machinist tapped in instructions to an unmanned aerial vehicle. The MQ-9 Reaper dipped its left wing and headed to a predestined set of coordinates, signed off and given the green light only moments ago. The bird was on its way.

The twenty-seven-foot sleek grey exterior belied the mission and its deadly arsenal. It could drop Hellfire missiles to within feet of its target, incinerating bodies, rendering them unrecognisable as organic matter. Controlled half a world away, it beamed real-time surveillance imagery back to the office in seconds, and this afternoon, its quarry was two cars going to a pool party on the outskirts of Aleppo.

It wasn't really a pool party, and the operator didn't think so either, but her job wasn't to question the humans she was about to kill by proxy. The sterility of killing from twenty thousand miles away was the concern of the President, not the machinist. She slept soundly at night.

From one-hundred-thousand feet, the operator couldn't see the dust, but Labib Hassan kept the windows of his vehicle firmly shut, because he wore a new suit. He played his favourite music on the stereo – western musicals. And he shelled pistachios. The road was bumpy and jolted him in so far as he could be bounced through the suspension of a Mercedes E-Class.

The first missile hit the car in front and vaporised it.

At first, Labib was stunned into silence, but then he began to laugh because, once again, the Americans had missed.

But then the second missile hit and incinerated his body in under a second. His severed hand was blown out of the wreckage and landed on the side of the road. It was what would identify him: the heavy fourteen-carat sapphire ring he wore to show his wealth and success in life.

It was what would make the evening news in New York, Washington and London: the taking out of a prominent arms dealer, and a friend of Bashar al-Assad. More importantly, a lever of business interests in Russia.

The news would make ripples in the West, when it broke, but, for the main part, the commuters heading home after a day at work in cities across Europe and America would likely skim over the death of yet another foreigner in the desert. War there was old news now.

A dispatch of the hit was received by Don Murton, and his first thought was to communicate it to Helen, to reassure her that her efforts had not been in vain and, on some level, inexplicable to those on the ground; it was a victory.

'You sound breathless,' he said.

'I've been a bit busy, Don.'

'Labib Hassan is dead,' Don told her.

'So is Artemis Charalambous.'

'Really? Who apprehended him?'

'I did. With a bullet to his brain.'

'Fair enough. By the way, Eric Dukakis is clean. Exemplary record, nothing on any international list, or domestic there in Cyprus.'

'Thanks, Don. I need to get cleaned up, it's been a long fucking week.'

Chapter 59

FIVE MONTHS LATER

The snow at the top of Mount Olympus was good, and it was notable because this wasn't always the case. Cyprus's only ski run wasn't high, and dumps of the fluffy white stuff were sporadic. A lone skier pushed off from the top and manoeuvred between the trees. It was a short but interesting run, occasionally used for army competitions by the British Forces Ski Team.

The man was accomplished but wobbled slightly when he turned a corner unexpectedly and faced a barrier that hadn't been there on his last run. He negotiated it badly and ended up hurtling towards it. He knew, in that moment, that he didn't have enough space to avoid whatever was behind the barrier, and he braced his body for impact.

He needn't have bothered, for it was simply air. He shouted out as he left the edge of the cliff and fell towards the snowy trees below. The impact tore off his skis, but not before breaking both legs and twisting his body so that his face cracked against bare rock, splitting his helmet into three pieces.

A terrible accident.

Helen read the article out loud to Eric, who'd anchored the boat off the coast of Larnaca. The weather in December was unpredictable, but today by the coast, it was twenty-five degrees. She looked to the Troodos Mountains in the distance and wondered how it could be skiing weather up there and so gorgeous here by the beach. When she'd been here with Grant, they'd driven from Mount Olympus, after skiing for the day, back to the beach, with a huge lump of ice in a cool box to take a photo. There were few places in the world that offered the unique experience: the SoCal Mountains in California, Mount Taranaki in New Zealand, Morocco and Chile being the most famous. Secretary Bugov had chosen the wrong resort to show off. His death had made page thirteen of *The Guardian* and Don had sent it to her via WhatsApp. Of course, he wasn't named. He was referred to as a Russian politician on holiday. The article was part of the foreign news.

She sat back as Eric leaned over the side. Katerina Bortkinov had disappeared off the island: Helen had no idea what happened to her, and she didn't much care, but it was a fact that the man who was in all likelihood responsible for ordering and engineering the deaths of both Captain Paul Thomas and Anastasia Lebedev had got what he deserved.

She looked across Larnaca Bay towards Dhekelia beach and felt a pang of compassion for the family of Corporal Trotter who'd been apprehended at the Black Knight border crossing behind Ayios Nikolaos Station – he hadn't got far, the bloody idiot. But she didn't dwell on it. His time in the Military Correction facility at Colchester would be long and arduous. Perhaps he and Colonel Seaton, stripped of his title and pension, would be roomies. She spared a thought for Andi Seaton too, who, Helen reckoned, had all her worst nightmares come true, short of incarceration herself: a small soldier's quarter in Bulford, or at least that was the last she had heard.

Major Graham had been exonerated on the grounds that his involvement in the spy ring had been as an unknowing accessory: in other words, he was just following Big Willy's orders. He'd been given a desk job at the MOD main building. Perhaps they'd bump into one another on a lunch break in Whitehall Gardens.

Dhekelia Garrison had a new colonel, and a major shake-up of resource management was underway, and would be for a long time to come.

Helen had returned to the island several times to visit Eric. She'd also made the decision to go back into fieldwork.

But she hadn't shared that with him yet.

This moment was about enjoying her leave. A whole month of rest and recuperation. And well deserved.

She finished the article and Eric handed her a dive jacket and DV apparatus. They were completing their fourth dive on the *Zenobia* in as many days, and she needed to decompress before flying back to London to receive her orders in two days' time. This was their last dive.

The week had been like a pocket of unreal time, spent exploring the island, sharing dinners and getting to know one another. She didn't want to leave.

But part of her also knew that no matter how alluring an escape it was to spend time with this man, other missions were just around the corner, and it didn't matter how many times she imagined herself settling down and living her days beside a man, in the sun, at peace, making love, walking at sunset and taking the boat around to bays like Kyrenia, it would never be enough to pull her away from what she did. What was in her blood.

Helen looked at the ring Grant had given her and she knew that wherever she went in the world, whoever she pursued, whoever she might feel as though she was falling in love with, that was a part of her life that was contained and finite. Beautiful while it lasted. But the real-life source running through her and shining like gems was the chase.

She flipped over the side of the boat and watched as her buddy came alongside her. He gave the okay sign and she reciprocated. She looked beneath her and was amazed anew at the clarity of the water. Her path was carved out as sure as the one below her towards the ship, and she'd never been so sure.

Acknowledgements

There are many memories in this book and I want to acknowledge my military family for inspiring me to write about them in fiction. In particular my sports diving instructors and adventure training guides, who influenced the escapades and challenges faced by Major Helen Scott.

Special thanks go to my friend John Barnes for his expert advice and also John Seaman for his insight and motivation.

Also to my agent, Peter Buckman, whose encouragement, experience and timely judgement, which is always both sound and much appreciated, is indispensable.

Thanks to my editors, Siân and Louise, at Canelo, who steer me to port every time, and whose endless dedication to what they do always produces work I'm incredibly proud of.

Finally, as always, honour to my wonderful family, Mike, Tilly and Freddie, my biggest fans.

Do you love crime fiction and are always on the lookout for brilliant authors?

Canelo Crime is home to some of the most exciting novels around. Thousands of readers are already enjoying our compulsive stories. Are you ready to find your new favourite writer?

Find out more and sign up to our newsletter at canelocrime.com